# Drawing From Life

## Jess Mowry

ANUBIS

## Copyright © 2011 - 2020 by Jess Mowry

PRINT ISBN-10: 0-9985579-0-0
PRINT ISBN-13: 978-0-9985579-0-8

EBOOK ISBN-10: 0-9977379-7-2
EBOOK ISBN-13: 978-0-9977379-7-4

First Anubis Edition 2016

This is a work of fiction. Names, characters, businesses, products, places, events and incidents are either the manifestations of the author's imagination or are used in a fictitious context.

# Other Books By Jess Mowry

Rats In The Trees
Children Of The Night
Way Past Cool
Six Out Seven
Ghost Train
Babylon Boyz
Phat Acceptance
Voodoo Dawgz
Bones Become Flowers
Tyger Tales
When All Goes Bright
Skeleton Key
Knights Crossing
The Bridge
Reaps
Magic Rats
Midnight Sons
Double Acting
The Coyote Valley Railroad
In The Dead Of Night
Ghost Ship
Spencer's Spirit
The Insiders
The Light

## To Ardeth
### For showing me it was possible

# Drawing From Life

**J**erry Mathers stood at the foot of the stairs and wondered why, after all the years of climbing them, he still didn't feel like he'd reached the top. ...And why *should* he still be climbing them? The school had installed an elevator several years ago to comply with new State regulations regarding rights of the handicapped, though there had never been handicapped students in the fifteen years Jerry had taught here.

Unless a kid could be handicapped by being born with too much money.

Most of the kids used the stairs, even the fat and chubby kids, though probably not for exercise; likely it had more to do with the prominent blue-and-white handicapped plaques beside the elevator doors, as if that might associate them with being less than superior. Most of the younger health-conscious staff members also used the stairs, but Jerry was neither especially health-conscious, nor could he call himself young anymore.

He recalled his mother reminiscing about The Jack Benny Show, and the comedian's life-long assertion that he was 39... until he'd died at 80. Jack's explanation had been that there was nothing funny about 40, and these days Jerry could relate. Looking back on 39 years from the bottom of these stairs again, he admitted he'd never been as Bohemian as he'd once imagined he would. Or as artful at dodging time.

Or as successful in life.

Toting his leather portfolio case, a present from his mother in his

1

optimistic days at college, those days when time had been on his side, he started up the stairway to begin yet another, perhaps wasted, year at Morrison Academy. He'd painted all summer as always, even though sadly distracted by his mother's failing health, but had still managed time for daily walks along the shore of Lake Merritt, so it was with some surprise -- and maybe a little foreboding -- when he found himself a bit short of breath upon reaching the upper landing. The words of a Pink Floyd song came to mind, but he told himself to stop being morbid... wasn't 40 now called "The New 30?" And didn't that give him a whole decade to live all over again... and this time with the experienced wisdom not to make the same mistakes?

If only he could be certain of what those mistakes had been.

Pausing for a minute -- to reflect, he told himself, *not* to catch his middle-aged breath -- he remembered once enjoying this job. But that had been back when he'd still believed that he could teach Art. Or maybe that Art *could* be taught... which may have been a major mistake. He was realistic enough -- by this time in life, anyhow -- to know that his class was only offered because proper private schools offered Art... even if not taken seriously. Most of his students took his class either at their parents' insistence because it might look good on their records as being intellectual, and/or in hope of an easy A -- which would also look good on their records -- though Jerry was far from easy with A's. But though many, like most kids, did posses some instinctive talent -- perhaps like rudimentary tails -- few took Art very seriously and none, so far as Jerry knew, had ever gone on to become a success.

At least in the way he still defined it.

Which may have been another mistake.

The logical question, he supposed, was why not get another job? He could certainly teach at a college, maybe Mills or even Berkeley -- he'd had enough minor successes to qualify for such a position -- but this was the first job he'd been offered when fresh out of college himself, a job he'd dutifully taken to pay room and board to his mother until the world recognized his talent in surely no more than a year.

Morrison Academy was housed in a huge Victorian horror three

2

stories tall plus a lofty tower that made no pretense of symmetry, and was perched on the rising slope of a hill, its front doors reached by a grand staircase; and bequeathed for the education of youth by a plump and prim-faced little old lady -- Miss Minerva Morrison -- who did somewhat resemble that queen in the latter years of her life, and whose indifferently-rendered portrait by some obscure artist now also long-dead hung in the shadowy foyer and watched everyone with brooding eyes as if doubting that any who entered were worthy.

Including, possibly, Jerry.

Most of the younger staff members called the house The Haunted Mansion, probably thanks to Disney. Of course there were rumors that Morrison's ghost floated about the hallways at night, and there had been occasional "sightings" by individuals working late – some suggesting a skeletal specter, others a wraithlike manifestation, but all agreeing upon a shroud -- though such reports were discouraged for publicity reasons and were attributed by the Director to immoderate consumption of energy drinks.

Elwood Clay, the custodian, whose father might have seen her alive, having been, it was said, her gardener, had readied the house for opening day and spirits of Pine-Sol haunted the hall as Jerry climbed to the second floor, though reminding him more of boys rooms in underfunded public schools than a place of superior education. Morrison Academy wasn't cheap, but neither was it an overpriced scam: not only did every teacher possess the proper credentials to teach but were *qualified* to teach in their respective fields. And those such as Jerry had also proven that they could actually *do* what they taught... the Writing teacher had three published novels; the Drama teacher two produced plays, and Jerry had sold a few of his paintings.

He was early and the vast house was silent, and all the more spooky for being so, most of the other staff not yet arrived. Elwood, almost a caricature of an early twentieth-century Negro, slender though childishly round of belly, and black as an old-fashioned telephone in clownishly baggy blue coveralls with a huge brass ring of skeleton keys, an archaic-looking leather tool belt bristling with obviously antique tools, a Bull Durham string hanging out of a pocket,

3

and crowned with a battered newsboy cap like a prop from a *Little Rascals* film, was watering a rubber tree -- itself a kind of requisite prop -- that stood near Jerry's office door. Elwood actually tipped his cap, the gesture probably deeply ingrained from all the years it had been expected, though he spoke Standard English and never used "black" expressions.

"Welcome back, Mr. Mathers."

Jerry thought of a seventies TV show. "Good to see you again, Elwood." He really did like the old man, who could fix anything from one of the ancient high-tank toilets to a crashed PC in Computer Lab -- whose teacher had once worked for Dell -- but supposed because of the gulf of race would never actually know him. On his first day here, fifteen years ago, he'd addressed him respectfully as Mr. Clay, but the man had looked disapproving, as if someone should remember their place. Elwood's smile, always warm -- since first putting Jerry in his place -- seemed even more welcoming today, though three months had passed since Jerry had seen it, and smiles in his life had been few in that time.

"All ready for you, Mr. Mathers," said Elwood with a sweep of a hand toward Jerry's door. Then his ebony eyes showed concern. "How's your mother these days?"

Jerry suppressed a sigh. "As well as can be expected, I guess." He caught himself before adding, "at her age," in deference to Elwood's.

It was also rumored, at least by some of the younger staff who, like many twenty-somethings, didn't seem to do math very well, that Elwood had been a young boy helping his father maintain the house during Miss Morrison's time... which of course was impossible since that would have made him well over a hundred; and though Jerry had never presumed to ask, his age, perhaps due to his darkness and unlined alertly amiable face, was really rather ambiguous. Jerry seemed to recall hearing "seventy" mentioned by someone years ago, and supposed he'd simply accepted that, along with the adage "black people age well."

"Hope she's better soon, Mr. Mathers."

"Thank you, Elwood."

The house, appropriately, was academically shrouded with ivy,

4

# Drawing From Life

and leaf-dappled light filtered softly in though the room's pair of tall, narrow windows, which were open admitting a faint Bay breeze that had managed to reach the Oakland foothills despite crossing over the flatlands below with their teeming exhaust-reeking freeways and the subtle but all the more depressing scents of hopelessness and decay -- a kind of second-hand store miasma of discarded dreams and abandoned plans rusting, rotting, falling to dust -- in what it was now politically-correct to call "low-income neighborhoods." Still, there was that ghost of Pine-Sol haunting Jerry with his own lost youth, which, though he'd gone to one of the better -- defined as being mostly white -- public elementary schools, had not been totally halcyon years for a somewhat shy and bespectacled boy who didn't give a damn about sports or competing for a higher place in the juvenile pecking-order.

Gazing out one of the ivy-draped windows, inhaling the hint of oncoming Autumn foretelling the death of another year, seeing the early morning sun reflecting off thousands of windows and windshields in the seemingly desperate -- and in the end, futile -- struggle for life below, he wondered if he'd really risen very far above it all. Few down there would be remembered for contributing anything good to the world, but notwithstanding a few of his works displayed in mid-range galleries, would *he* be remembered for anything?

Releasing the sigh he'd kept from Elwood, he glanced around the high-ceilinged room, its wainscotted walls adorned with his paintings, several seascapes he'd done of the coast between Santa Cruz and Half Moon Bay, though he preferred portraiture -- his class was called Drawing From Life -- including one of his mother painted a decade before, cradling her cat, now long-deceased and buried in her flower garden despite city law forbidding interments of pets as well as people at home. They were there, of course, to impress the parents, as were a few of his students' best works; enough to imply there were many more... even though there weren't.

The chamber had probably once been a bedroom; and Jerry turned to study himself in a slightly de-silvering beveled glass mirror on the door of a former closet now used as storage for stacks of childish, crude, and utterly hopeless art -- to even dignify it as such -- by

5

fifteen years of junior-high cretins... though they were called middle-schoolers these days. Jerry seldom opened that door, except to add more wasted paper and defiled canvas at the end of each quarter, as if many skeletons lurked within.

What he saw in the rose Victorian glass wasn't as grim as he'd almost expected, though the leafy light was kind: he didn't look *quite* middle-aged, though of middle height, about 5' 11", and, by current "health-nazi" standards, a bit more than slightly overweight.

Considering a sedentary childhood of reading or drawing a lot in his room -- he hadn't had his own television -- he might have gotten quite fat as a boy and consequently "obese" by now... not the stereotype of an artist often portrayed as psychotically thin. But though, like most normal kids of his time, he'd regarded McDonalds as the absolute zenith of fine dining out, and still often lunched at the one down the street, he'd never been very much overweight... whatever that weight was supposed to be. He'd never paid any attention to that because the youth of his generation had not been plagued with priests of "health" beating their bibles of BMIs; and "fatties" were only persecuted if they were otherwise uncool.

The few extra pounds he'd had and did carry had always been rolly and soft on his frame, his belly lapping over his jeans and his chubby chest boyishly-breasted: his mother had often called him cherubic, which had made him rather proud of his body, and he'd usually gone shirtless on hot summer days, as had his chubby companion, Trevor, who'd been his best and only real friend since they had met in second grade.

That hadn't changed much in almost four decades -- god, had it really been that long! -- and for that he could probably thank his mother whose meals, though nutritional enough to ward off most of the childhood diseases democratically shared at school, had never been lavish or large. Nor, due to her paltry widow's pension, a pittance from a government that had sent her husband to Vietnam to die for a democratic cause, had she been affluent enough to make McDonalds or other fast-food more than a special-occasion treat or furnish her son with much snacking money.

Jerry turned to her smiling portrait, decidedly done in Victorian style, which befitted her as a woman born many decades after her time. Though from a formerly well-to-do family – *her* mother had known Gertrude Stein, and she often spoke fondly of their "colored maid" -- whose women weren't brought up to work, she'd endured many years as a Woolworth's clerk until that, too, had failed her, victim of another lost war of corporate Capitalism, enabling Jerry to go to college, though partly on a scholarship, and fulfill his dreams of becoming an artist.

At least, so far, sufficient enough to still believe in them.

It wasn't until those college years he'd realized he'd grown up poor despite a nice house in a nice neighborhood -- defined as being mostly white -- and his mother, not knowing how to be poor, had probably worked much harder for less than her old beloved "colored maid." She had known nothing of "poor people's food," how amply available it was -- at least to America's indigents -- would have been ashamed to apply for Assistance, humiliated to use Food Stamps, and would shop at nothing less than Safeway, the reason his meals had always been small, scaled-down versions of those she recalled; and so despite being a physical sloth he'd never progressed beyond chubby.

Though blue-jeaned and T-shirted during his youth, his footwear consisting of black-and-white Keds, these days he usually wore tan Dockers, brown leather sneaks of the type called "deck shoes" by people possessed of ponies and boats, along with pale-blue button-front shirts. Of course the dress code for teachers and staff also required a tie. His mother had bought him a jacket when he'd first begun this job, tweed with leather elbow patches, more suited to an English professor, at least the stereotype of one, though he'd always worn it leaving the house as well as when returning home -- and now when visiting her in a home -- though he kept a brown leather trench coat, his sole attempt at Bohemian flair, in his car for public appearance. He'd met several counterparts over the years who actually affected *berets*, and not only did he think them absurd but suspected their students thought so as well. He'd decided long ago that he would never own a beret, even if he felt he'd earned one.

Which didn't seem likely from where he stood now.

Looking at the man in the glass, blue-eyed of Anglo-Saxon descent with a boyish mop of sandy hair – and all of it still, thank god -- with only a ghost of gray at the sides, reasonably handsome, he supposed, at least by Caucasian standards, his rather archaic steel-framed glasses still looking too old for his yet-unlined face -- one benefit of chubbiness -- he couldn't see any stereotype of either art teacher or artist, though he admitted he probably was in several less visible ways.

Topping the list was being 39, unmarried and living with his mother... at least until halfway through this summer. Each year there were rumors among the students, as well as occasional new staff members, that he was gay or perhaps in the closet, but though at thirteen he'd had what nowadays would be called by self-appointed sages a "gay relationship" with Trevor, he'd always regarded their pubescent pawing, lustfully brutal boyish embraces rolling and writhing naked in bed as if trying to squeeze into each-other's bodies, and kissing with all the *savoir faire* of puppies slobbering babies' faces, along with sometimes slow and gentle though much more often savage and sweaty slick-fisted masturbation sessions, as either purely hormonal or perhaps nature's way of preparing them for future success with the opposite sex and thus survival of the species.

Trevor's parents had moved to Santa Cruz a few months into that phase of their friendship, though probably not because of it -- surely they couldn't have known -- ending what, whether for good or ill, had been Jerry's fondest relationship, and at a time when he'd most needed one. Trevor, now in retrospect, freely confessed to feeling the same but had married a nice intelligent woman during his middle twenties and was now an apparently straight and happy father of three chubby boys.

And more Bohemian than Jerry, since he and his wife owned The Book Of The Dead – double-meaning intentional -- a little book store and coffee house that catered to elderly hippies and youthful UCSC students. He and Jerry still kept in touch, though mostly through email letters these days -- the price of gas being prohibitive to driving down to Santa Cruz and/or for capturing seascapes -- and though neither felt uncomfortable with memories of their final summer, neither had ever expressed a desire to try to resurrect the corpse of something young and innocent that had died with its boots on and rested in peace.

Although in all their adventures together on the youthfully sexual plane they had never done *that* -- or *that*, either -- regarding those things as, frankly, disgusting, Jerry sometimes wondered if would they or could they *have* become gay -- disregarding most current theories -- had Trevor remained in Oakland? Jerry supposed he might have been happy spending his life with the Trevor he'd known sharing his bed in those long-ago days -- and without doing *that* or *that* -- though his mother would never have understood a love that dared not speak its name... if that was the right allusion. But, that was a road not taken, unless, as some physicists proposed – including the school's science teacher -- there were alternate universes and therefore alternate futures. But, Jerry was stuck in *this* universe and maybe digging a grave for his future by slowly immuring the dreams of his past.

Maybe giving up Trevor had been a mistake... though of course he'd had no choice in a time when long-distance calls were expensive and there had been no Internet to keep in constant communication. They had written letters for the first few months – "snail mail" it was called these days -- but adolescent relationships require a physical form to survive.

UCSC, Jerry supposed, was another place of higher learning where his talent -- such as it seemed -- might be put to better use if this year's crop at Morrison again turned out to be nothing but weeds. And soon, according to the doctor, there would be nothing to hold him in Oakland, which might be either the sign he needed to take a few chances while he still had the time.

Or just the opportunity to make more self-defeating mistakes.

As to his own relationships with the opposite sex, and though there had been a few, Jerry had found, and in a very Victorian sense -- perhaps in the way of Sherlock Holmes as well as many artists, writers, philosophers and religious men -- that, though he liked and respected women, the road to romance, apparently, was either closed by a fallen bridge, or maybe he'd missed the turn-off. A few

9

years ago he still might have said that Art was his sustaining love, though today that sounded suspect by modern American standards, which seemed to deny that being a bachelor could in itself be normal; and artists, like male ballet dancers, all had lavender inclinations. Probably better to tolerate the occasional sophomoric student smirk or infantile locker room innuendo that he was gay and/or in a closet than to appear absurd... or possibly in denial.

He'd left the office door ajar, and during these mirrored meditations had been aware that Elwood was still doing something out in the hall. A rubber tree didn't need much sustaining, so it may have been one of the ancient light fixtures, ornate brass scones along the walls like vases for flowers in mausoleums, though these held low-wattage candle-shaped bulbs -- the wiring couldn't sustain any more -- which only seemed to enhance the shadows and were often shorting out, along with the equally aged switches of late 19th-century rotary type. A stipulation of Miss Morrison's will was, apparently, to preserve the old house in all its outdated, inconvenient, energy-wasting, hazardous, and downright spooky former glory, as if she might return some day. To do so much as replace a light switch required the Administrator's approval -- a shockingly aged and skeletal lawyer who could have starred as the Crypt Keeper -- though Elwood kept an ample supply of Period replacements, resurrected from demolition sites, and usually made repairs on his own, which saved the Director a lot of bother, and no doubt money as well. The elevator would have never been sanctioned, but the State was mightier than the estate on the issue of handicapped rights; but even then the Crypt Keeper insisted it must at least look Period with cast-iron grilles and brass-bound features, though the modern signs were still required -- including two more on the boys and girls rooms where Elwood had modified one of their stalls according to more regulations -- which probably angered the old woman's ghost, assuming she still made inspections at night.

In addition to Elwood out in the hall, Jerry heard other staff members arriving, going to the teachers lounge, where Elwood -- though it wasn't his job -- would have made supernatural coffee in the Great Brass Gas-Fired Urn, itself a Victorian Age antique that only

he could operate. It occurred to Jerry that with Elwood's passing --
either in retirement or in the grimly literal sense -- the whole place
might come crashing down like *The House Of Usher.*

He glanced at his watch, a middle-priced Bulova, also a present
from his mother and lovingly engraved as such. The students would
soon be invading, disrupting the albeit gloomy peace, and he found
he rather dreaded confronting another roomful of bestial young
faces; the boys these days fronting ferally thuggish as if they'd all
"come up in the 'hood," the girls looking cynically slutty with carnal
knowledge beyond their years -- even if lacking experience -- except
for the ones who drew horses; and most of those faces would
challenge him, daring him to teach them something they couldn't
find on the Internet and which required an attention span of more
than thirty seconds.

Funny to think he'd once looked forward to accepting that challenge... probably another mistake.

There would, of course, be the Disruptor, distinct from the
Clown, who wasn't malicious, along with the Bully and Alpha Male...
the former kept leashed or allowed to attack depending upon the
latter's beneficence. There would be a Neurotic or two... often emos
these days, and sometimes Cutters as well. Perhaps there would be a
Sociopath using Punk or Goth for cover -- though usually unaware of
it -- and possibly a budding Lolita of either or indeterminate sex who
would try to hone their skills on Jerry; and the rest would be Sheep
who would follow the Judas whose bell of the moment was
sounding.

Sighing again he sat down at his desk, a mammoth mahogany
claw-footed thing with an equally massive mahogany chair which
might have seemed sinfully comfortable to a Charles Dickens era
counting-house clerk. There was a stack of manila folders off to one
side of the fresh green blotter -- were blotters even made anymore,
or had Elwood kept a reserve? -- though records were also computerized. Along with the archaic blotter was an eldritch bottle of
iron gall ink and a steel-nib pen in a heavy brass holder, which he
had never used. There was also an antique bronze ashtray -- a fat
little cherub holding a bowl -- and though Jerry had cut down this

11

summer, it prompted him to search a desk drawer. He found a hard-pack of Marlboro "red" -- once the only type of Marlboro -- he'd left there in June, with three cigarettes. There was also a disposable lighter with still a few drops of fuel. He lit up and sighed out a ghost, then turned his attention to the folders. The Director had probably asked Elwood to bring them in this morning... there must have been a Custodian's Union but Elwood didn't seem to mind.

He switched on his computer, almost the only thing in the room -- besides himself, of course -- that wasn't at least a hundred years old, in case he wanted to make any notes, then took the top folder and opened it, shifting his glasses low on his nose and peering over the frame: he didn't need bifocals... yet.

Official student I.D. photos were taken annually by the school, touted as being for safety in this age of predators, so pictures weren't required for these folders, though Jerry had suggested them... he could usually spot all the typical types, and forewarned was fore-armed. This one included a picture, a standard head-and-shoulders shot, probably from his previous school, of Walter Wadsworth Wain-wright III, whose face, though rather handsome, had that pudgy, pear-shaped look and vacuous open-mouthed expression of kids who stared at screens all day.

Jerry had also suggested that applicants include a few samples of their recent work -- if any were actually serious they would be sub-mitting portfolios to colleges in the future -- and Walter, though having some talent, was being corrupted by anime like so many kids of his generation. Not that anime wasn't Art, but cartooning, like graphic design, was an entirely different field and there was a class for the latter, though students inclined to pursuing the former were usually dumped on Jerry. Walter's intent was serious, but his samples more resembled the 1970s works of Gig and his big-eyed pity pup-pies and kittens.

The next folder, Caroline Holdhurst's -- no photo so probably overweight, spotty complected, or both -- proved My Little Ponies would never die, though Jerry wished he could slaughter them all with an AK-47.

The third folder had a photo and introduced William Malone,

12

who, unless any boy of thirteen could possibly be more handsome, seemed to be this year's Alpha Male. William -- Will, or probably Bill -- might make a very striking model if his body went with his face. His samples, though typically teenage sullen, were actually quite good, though probably hadn't been drawn from life... few young straight males — assuming the straight -- would ask a shirtless peer to pose. There was promise here, though Bill's handsomeness -- presuming his body did go with his face -- would probably be a handicap: he *was* art by American standards so might feel no need to create it.

After fifteen years of culling the herd, Jerry had ceased to expect very much, so as he paged through the folders he wasn't much further depressed. Besides more amateur anime -- intentional or not -- there was also Ed Hardy tattoo art, as well as the usual gothic skulls, enough to populate a graveyard, and obviously none of them drawn from life in either sense of the term. One folder flaunted graffiti designs like those upon walls in the black flatlands -- white imitations, anyway -- and several contained anorexic Barbies... he was seeing more of those every year. Another offered blatant *tracings* of obvious magazine models... also disturbingly anorexic, and all the more scary for being alive.

Or were they *supposed* to be female zombies?

The photos, when included, almost always went with the art -- most of these kids were still too callow to realize what they might be revealing -- though there were a few exceptions: stereotype or not, Jerry expected anime from Kenneth Yamamoto, a cheerful-looking moon-faced boy, but instead found chopper motorcycles... good technical work and he might have a future along those lines. Jerry tapped a note on his keyboard: *Suggest transfer to Graphic Design?*

Then there were more goddammed horses, a *glitter*-sparkled Disney princess, making him think of paintings with lights that passed for "art" in Walmart stores... along with dogs playing poker. And then an appalling, atrocious... *thing!*... combining the absolute worst of both in an anthropomorphic centaur-like creature drawn in a most revolting contortion that more than suggested female self-abuse and which -- if such an abomination *could* exist in a sane universe -- was physically impossible, even for its anatomy, and titled Princess

13

Sparkle-Pony.

Jerry, like several other teachers, kept a bottle in his desk, though his Cutty Sark was mainly for show, academic irony -- also Bohemian, of course -- but Princess Sparkle-Pony almost made him seek its solace. But he only closed the folder, drawing deep on his cigarette and resisting not only the urge for a drink but also his moral obligation to staple the folder securely shut, pound a stake of yew through its heart and bury it very far away.

He was thankful there was no Prince Sparkle-Pony.

If -- good god! -- *Crystal Sterling* wasn't already in therapy, she would and should be very soon if such grotesques populated her skull! Her photo looked normal enough -- though the real certifiables generally did -- and a camera wasn't an artist who could see the soul beneath the face.

The next folders, fortunately, only contained the usual horrors. Only three impending students had tried to render a real human form, and only Bill Malone showed any exceptional promise... handicapped though he probably was. There was one folder left, but Jerry leaned back and sighed more smoke, tempted again to take a drink, though that seemed yet another mistake on a road to eventual ruin. Even if by some miracle his mother did recover, this would not be an easy year... maybe the worst one yet.

Was that the sign he needed?

Elwood still tinkered out in the hall, and students were starting to trickle in, the new ones intimidated by the old house's spookiness as if venturing into a funeral home and therefore quiet, big-eyed and wary, peeping cautiously in as they passed as if fearing to see an open coffin or an embalming in progress.

Jerry opened the final folder, which didn't include a photo: Gabriel Graves. Unusual name and rather archaic, making him think of old New England and Peter Coffin in *Moby Dick*, though neither I'm-upper-class-and-you're-not like Walter Wadsworth Wainwright III, nor working-class risen, take-it-or-leave-it, Norman Rockwellish Bill Malone.

Then he saw the sample drawing, and literally his mouth fell open.

# Drawing From Life

Sitting bolt upright in the chair in a very Victorian way, he abandoned his cigarette to the cherub and cautiously took the paper -- actual quality drawing paper, not printer paper like most kids used -- as if afraid of damaging it, or even leaving a mark upon it, the slightest fingerprint or crease, and stared wide-eyed in wonder.

Just a soft-lead pencil drawing, but full of so much vividness, expressive line and -- *life* -- that it seemed to leap off the page in his face like a stereopticon image.

Recovering from his initial shock, he searched for flaws... there were none. And then he felt...

Was it an actual creep of *fear*? Or maybe the long-expected threat -- even if subconscious -- that a Master might feel when at last confronted by a student's skill that reared up and challenged his own?

Of course he'd never dared to believe -- though of course there was no harm in hoping -- that he'd ever become an equal of one of the truly great Masters.

But, to see this masterful work by a *boy* only the first year into his teens!

Laying the drawing carefully down after making sure, absurdly, the blotter was absolutely clean, he tapped his password, BlueBoy, with fingers that actually trembled to call up Gabriel's file. He had to see this boy! Surely that face would go with this work!

But, again, there was no picture, nor very much else to paint one: in these days of political-correctness asking for race on applications, if not taboo in many cases, was considered, at least, in questionable taste; and this was Morrison Academy where the usual minority was Asian.

But, political-correctness had leached its way into other aspects of physically profiling students, with some of the boxes marked Optional. Birth date, of course, wasn't one of them -- as much as he found that hard to believe when gazing again at the masterful drawing -- and though most of the boxes had been filled: Eye Color, brown, Hair Color, black, Height, only four-feet-three -- small for his age by American standards -- these weren't very helpful in painting a portrait. One picture indeed, in this case, would have been worth a thousand words.

15

The box for Weight, though not left blank, only displayed a question mark; and though many overweight girls, as well as, these days, a few overweight boys, did choose to keep that a secret -- as if not admitting to something on paper could hide anything from reality -- the use of a question mark suggested that Gabriel honestly didn't know... rare as that was in these health-rabid times when kids were forced to obsess about it. Still, he must have been small, possibly even "delicate" in the Victorian sense... though Jerry didn't like to admit it, there had to be something "wrong" with a boy who at so young an age could draw so divinely.

He scrolled the screen with a strange urgency, feeling somehow like a Web predator, while smoke from his forgotten Marlboro ghosted about in the air. ...Private elementary school, though Jerry had expected that: not only did public schools stifle the gifted, they systematically beat them to death. Grades well above average except in P.E., though Jerry could relate. He knew a little about that school, Rutherford Hayes Academy, good but not in Morrison's class, and somewhere at the feet of the foothills. The Graves family seemed to be rising.

Dismissing the otherwise useless file, he carefully took up the drawing again and told himself how absurd it was to in any way feel threatened. Wasn't this what a good Master longed to discover?

And only a failing fraud would fear?

Then, worming its way into his mind, crept a suspicion this might be a fraud... those anorexic models were tracings. But, what would be the point of deception? Gabriel wasn't applying to some prestigious college of Art where acceptance required actual talent, and fraudulence would soon be exposed when the students began to draw from life.

This was real! He was sure of that! The moment he'd always hoped would come but had lost all faith of it coming... most of his faith, anyway.

A sign at last?

# Chapter Two

"Coffee, Mr. Mathers?"

Definitely not one of Elwood's duties, and a first-time honor for Jerry, as Elwood came in with a cup in hand... one of the delicate china survivors bequeathed by the late Miss Morrison and once perhaps touched by her prim wrinkled lips.

"Thank you," said Jerry, carefully accepting the cup, not because of its legacy but to prevent the slightest drop from falling on the drawing. Then, simple custodian or not, Jerry *had* to share this moment with someone. "What do you think of this?"

Elwood seemed to clone Jerry's caution and didn't touch the paper, only leaning in to regard it. A racist joke, and infantile, crossed Jerry's mind and was instantly banished. But, maybe he'd expected too much: Elwood didn't study the picture for long -- and caution for the paper wasn't reverence for the Art -- and simply said, "She looks very peaceful."

"...Well... yes, she does," agreed Jerry. He studied the picture as if, like *The Mezzotint*, it might have changed when he'd looked away, but it was still astounding... an elderly African-American woman, probably someone's beloved grandmother, mainly her face and seemingly napping. "But, so *alive*," he couldn't help adding... or maybe insisting.

"You can see her spirit," said Elwood, and Jerry was satisfied with that: even with all the wisdom of age — whatever that might have been -- and of his patient, long-suffering people, Elwood seldom used metaphors. To make a politically-incorrect pun, he usually called a spade a spade; and one could indeed see the old woman's spirit in the serenity of her face; perhaps all her housework done for

17

the day. ...Or maybe someone else's.

The Graves family's colored maid?

Jerry's mother sometimes looked like that when he found her asleep in the nursing home.

"Welcome back, Jerry."

Elwood tipped his venerable cap and deferentially stepped aside as Crawford Tillinghast, Morrison's Director, steamed majestically into the room like the *Titanic* might have looked had it completed its voyage to New York. Then, offering Jerry another smile, Elwood unobtrusively left with a spectral clinking of skeleton keys.

Tillinghast was "a man of substance," as would have been said in Victorian times, with a prosperous paunch and thick silver hair, attired as always in a suit which, while it was certainly modern, still looked Period somehow... probably due to the gold watch chain adorning the ample silk vest. Though possibly in his early fifties -- which, these days, were called the new forties -- he gave the impression of being much older though very well-preserved.

"Ready for another year?"

A few minutes ago Jerry might have thought, *another year down a high-tank toilet*, but his smile required no fraudulence as he displayed the drawing. "I am after seeing this."

"Thought you might be," said Tillinghast, though only giving the picture a glance. "Of course I'm no judge of art... that's what we pay you for... but it looks pretty good to me."

"It is," said Jerry. "Extremely good." Then a thought flitted through his mind like a bat: *If I could have drawn like him at thirteen...*

Tillinghast offered a big fat cigar, his perennial welcome-back gift to staff despite being Chauvinistic, as well as health-consciously incorrect. "Two firsts for Morrison this year."

Jerry raised a polite eyebrow while laying the drawing carefully down and accepting the plump phallic symbol.

"Our first physically-handicapped student," Tillinghast continued, maybe stressing "physically," though Jerry might have imagined it. "*Finally* a use for that dammed elevator besides a groping booth for kids." Tillinghast's expression soured. "Of either sex these days." He glanced to the hallway door -- Elwood had not presumed to close it -- and lowered his *basso profundo* a bit. "And our first of negro persuasion... if that would be the polite description."

"...Oh," said Jerry, who'd never heard it put that way.

"Of course that wasn't *intentional*." Tillinghast paused as if to consider possible misinterpretations. "Either way," he added.

"...Of course not," said Jerry, working that out.

"Our doors have always been open," Tillinghast seemed to quote, "to any student who meets our standards. ...Though we have acquired a reputation for being a mostly 'white' school. ...Which, it makes me sad to say, has brought us under scrutiny from so-called egalitarians."

Jerry said carefully, "Our standards are high."

"So is our tuition, which also tends to eliminate... less fortunate applicants. Miss Morrison didn't believe in scholarships." He did quote now from the school brochure: "'Anything acquired too easily is seldom valued at its worth.'"

*Including artistic talent*, thought Jerry, glancing again at the drawing and hoping this wasn't a case.

Tillinghast seemed to muse. "Of course she couldn't have foreseen a time when any of... them... would apply to her school. Or perhaps I should say, *could* apply."

The subject seemed to be getting deeper than it may have deserved to be, with explanations -- or justifications -- offered when probably not required; and Jerry offered a chuckle. "Her picture wasn't dripping blood when I came in this morning."

Tillinghast turned to the doorway again as several students, obviously new, crept cautiously past in the shadows... the light fixture must have shorted. "Little pitchers have big ears. ...Or is it pictures?"

"Pitchers," said Jerry. "My mother often said that."

"Well, that's one thing this school doesn't need." Tillinghast lowered his voice again. "People will tolerate diversity... up to a point, anyway... but they won't abide rumors of... those kinds of things."

*A spook in the flesh but not one in spirit.* "I suppose not," said Jerry. He caught himself inspecting the cigar, which had probably cost at least twenty dollars, and quickly placed it beside the ink bottle.

Tillinghast noted the open folder. "I came to tell you that Gabriel Graves is Morrison's first... in both respects."

Jerry felt relieved. "That probably explains his remarkable talent."

Tillinghast cocked his head.

"It's common for handicapped people to excel in other ways."

"Like... what's-his-name... the physicist?"

"Stephen Hawking."

Tillinghast seemed to consider. "It could be said that Gabriel Graves is handicapped in two senses of the word."

Jerry wondered why he felt offended. "Disregarding the latter, though I suppose it's true enough, what's his physical handicap?"

"He's in a wheelchair... but he's got legs so there's nothing distasteful about his appearance. And he does seem rather bright for... his age."

"...Oh," said Jerry, trying to picture a small black boy – perhaps a charming Webster -- partly paralyzed. Maybe in an accident? Nobody got Polio anymore as in his mother's day.

"It's one of those power types," Tillinghast went on. "Of course I know nothing about such things, but it looks extremely expensive... like a Rolls-Royce of those kinds of things. I'm sure you couldn't get one on any sort of Assistance."

Jerry thought of a Silver Ghost, the only Rolls-Royce model he knew of, thanks to a James Bond novel. "Probably not," he said, then looked at the drawing again... maybe Gabriel's grandmother? He'd read that elderly black people often lived with their families instead of being... put in homes. But Jerry hadn't *wanted* to put his mother in a home: she had fallen twice this summer and he couldn't have left her alone all day.

If he'd only been a *better* artist who could have worked at home.

Tillinghast extracted his watch and opened its golden cover, which made his time seem more valuable than someone who simply glanced at their wrist... or these days a phone. "Since your class is his first of the day, would you ask if any of your students might volunteer to be his aide? I don't think he needs *much* help... seemed pretty self-sufficient to me when I met him last week with his guardian... apparently he's adopted... but State guidelines suggest a peer aide for students with special needs. We can offer some extra credit, and it would look good on a student's record."

"Of course," said Jerry.

Tillinghast shut his watch like a bite. "I've instructed Elwood, within reason, to accommodate any other needs a boy thus handicapped might have. ...Wonder if Elwood ever thought he'd live to see this day?"

"Probably not," said Jerry, feeling oddly offended again.

"Is it incorrect to call them boys?"

"I think 'young man' would be safer."

Tillinghast seemed to consider again. "You went to a public school... of course I don't mean that *disparagingly.*"

Jerry's smile required some fraud. "I understand. But in my school it was mostly a case of 'why are all the black kids sitting together in the cafeteria.'"

"I don't know the quote but the meaning seems clear. Of course I wasn't implying..." Tillinghast seemed to weigh choices of words. "That you might be an expert on... them. But you did grow up in lower Oakland, speaking geographically, so you must have had some... contact?"

"I understand," said Jerry.

"And, as you said, the... young man... does seem to posses some talent related to your field, so you'd have that much in..."

"I understand," said Jerry again, a bit more forcefully than intended.

Tillinghast glanced around at the paintings. "Morrison has had many successes... Congressmen, Senators, business leaders... be nice if we could boast of an artist who actually made some money."

"I'm sure it would look good on our record."

Tillinghast smiled. "As well as on yours. The... young man's... guardian inquired about your qualifications." He came about majestically, but paused halfway out the door. "How's your mother?"

Jerry had picked up the drawing again and was regarding the old woman's face... all her work seemingly done for the day and resting in well-deserved peace. He pictured a small black boy, who looked

21

even smaller, fragile perhaps, in a big complicated power chair, quietly drawing from life. His voice caught in his throat for a moment. "I... don't think she'll be coming home."

"Sorry to hear that, Jerry. But none of us are getting younger."

"I know," said Jerry.

"If there's anything I can do..."

"Thanks," said Jerry. People always said that, no doubt with the best of intentions, and usually in situations where nothing *could* be done.

# Chapter Three

The term, "living room," Jerry's mother had said, dated from the late 19th century, originally coined by the middle-class whose smaller and less affluent homes didn't have parlors and sitting rooms. Jerry remembered a novel he'd read, written in the early 1900s, in which "living room" was contained in quotes as if to denote a colloquialism that proper people didn't use. Traditionally, he'd also read, the front parlor in superior homes was used for receiving significant guests, and was also where a family's deceased were laid out before their funerals. For the middle-class the term, "living room," must have caused some consternation when the Reaper came to call.

Nothing so oxymoronic could have occurred in the Morrison Mansion, possessed as it was of seemingly countless front, rear and middle parlors; not to mention sitting rooms, drawing rooms, a sewing room, a music room, a breakfast room, a library and conservatory. And, as evidenced by a photograph in the teacher's lounge -- formerly the smoking room -- the lady indeed had received her last callers in the grandest parlor, which was now Jerry's classroom.

The irony that Drawing From Life was taught in a room where the dead had reposed was offset by its four tall windows -- kept clear of ivy by Elwood -- which, thanks to benign Bay Area winters provided excellent natural light.

Though electric bells had existed in schools during Miss Morrison's time, she had regarded them as vulgar, maintaining that students of proper schools were neither "Pavlovian mongrels nor proletarian factory workers." Consequently, each classroom, hallway, office and staff area had a wood-cased Regulator that tastefully sounded the hours; though keeping each clock synchronized, indeed even operational, must have tried even Elwood's skills. And, since most of the students, no matter what class their former schools, had already been trained to respond to bells, it was common during the first week for some to be a few minutes late.

This being the case, Jerry wasn't surprised, as his Regulator began chiming nine, that three of this year's seventeen students weren't yet in their places with bright shining faces, including Gabriel Graves, the one he most wanted to meet... though that seemed more forgivable being he was handicapped.

In keeping with the late lady's wishes, the desks were also from a time when proper young ladies and gentlemen displayed their good breeding with genteel posture... and probably felt like torture devices to bodies accustomed to boneless slumping at PC screens or sprawling on couches in front of TVs with channel or game controllers in hand.

Jerry usually made his entrance just as his clock struck its final note -- he remembered an old children's book, a bedtime story read by his mother, in which a king had been perplexed as to whether it was something o'clock when a clock began chiming or when it finished -- but today he'd come in early, striking a Bohemian pose by sitting on his desk top, in hope of meeting Gabriel before many other students arrived. The art book in hand was merely a prop to seemingly ponder and thus prove professionalism while glancing up and nodding as each of his pupils came in. ...Also intimidating them by already knowing their names. He easily recognized faces from the folder photographs and, thanks to long experience, was able to guess most of others from the samples of their work.

Bill Malone's body did go with his face, "tightly undone," as a Who song had said, in an underwear shirt of the type called a "singlet" in Morrison's age but termed a "wife-beater" by youth of today. Her ghost was probably very displeased by such blatantly body-baring attire, though fortunately for the students, she couldn't have foreseen a time when children in schools of her class of people would dress in less than collars and corsets so hadn't dictated a dress code. The snowy white cotton looked spray-painted on over high jutting "pecs" like paving stones, and what today's kids called a "six-pack." Bill's biceps bulged like baseballs even though relaxed, and his face was Caucasian perfection -- although technically Celtic -- without so much as a ghost of a zit and framed by a golden shoulder-length mane in 1970s style -- as Jerry had once worn his hair -- though his jeans were currently oversize, giving him a faun-like appearance, and rode low enough so his indigo boxers were partially on display. His big high-top Nikes were worn but spotless, and the I-phone clipped to the top of his jeans was skinned with a skate-boarding animorph that did somewhat resemble a faun.

Though he didn't think he had "gaydar" – nor was sure he believed in it -- fifteen years with young adolescents, and aided perhaps by an artist's eye, had left him with fairly accurate judgment in regard to a student's past, present, and possibly pending orientation; and Bill, to use the proverbial quote, was as perfectly straight as an arrow, neither too male nor afraid to be not... which, now that it came to mind, might have been said of himself and Trevor.

Jerry suppressed a sigh as the faun prince took his proper place at a desk in the very last row -- from which to observe his subjects -- only seeming a little surprised when he found it defied his royal slump. Jerry's stillborn sigh, however, was not because of the boy's perfection but rather because Bill knew he was perfect -- this evidenced by the nonchalant way in which he treated his beautiful body -- and therefore, as Jerry had feared, might feel no need to create anything.

Then came Crystal Sterling, red-haired in black jeans and turtle-neck sweater in sort of a ban-the-bomb beatnik style reminiscent of *Dobie Gillis* reruns, her eyes -- as Jerry had also feared -- revealing a green glow of lunacy and her smile disturbingly toothy, though of course there was nothing wrong with her teeth. Jerry seldom saw braces on Morrison students and sometimes wondered if either there were expensive procedures exclusive to the upper-class to correct orthodontic misfortunes, or whether rich kids with malocclusions were sent to discreet sanatoriums to conceal their durations of grin-ning in tin. She knew that Jerry had seen her... thing... which made him feel like a child-molester meeting an all-too willing victim whose picture he'd seen in cyberspace and who might have a razor blade taped to a finger.

The Bully, Raymond Blakemore, stalked in, deliberately dressed as a working-class lug in jeans, brutish boots, and gray sweatshirt to give a meat-punching Rocky impression, along with a well-practiced goonish expression and pugnacious buzz-cut brown hair, though actually a banker's son, his art of the type one usually saw on muscular forearms unloading ships, his bulk about twenty-five percent fat, which would increase in the coming years because he was an entitled bully rather than one who'd worked for his place... though by the time the ratio reversed his bullying wouldn't require any brawn. Jerry saw him spot the Alpha and take a desk in the next row up where he could prey if the prince would permit.

The others were much as he'd envisioned, goths and emos -- of course just a phase as their parents would say -- horsey girls, sheep; and a male Lolita named Parker Foxworthy with raven hair rippling midway down his back and coyly concealing one winsome brown eye, his marshmallow body girlishly breasted to an Hermaphroditic degree – possibly gynecomastia? -- beneath a tight-clinging Pokemon T-shirt, his belly, although contained by the shirt, softly overlapping his jeans in the twin-scalloped shape of a plump baby's bottom... either another hard-core "gamer" or a boy who lived mostly online; though other students were looking confused, eyes oscillating between those lush breasts and Parker's pretty but boyish face.

No "gaydar" required in his case.

The Disruptor this year was a James Dean type, though it was doubtful he knew it, who'd probably hoped he would be the Alpha, slouching in a minute late, the cigarette in his mouth implied, and probably on purpose.

Mostly a pack of young Republicans still in pubescent denial, synonymous with unteachable cretins... at least in regard to Art.

But maybe this year there was hope of success in the way he still defined it.

Walter Wadsworth Wainwright III, who'd obviously gained a lot of weight since his folder photograph, presently sporting a soft second chin below a now pendulous pear-shaped face, and following a bulbous belly that looked like he'd swallowed a basketball, two of his shirt's lower buttons undone and his navel peeking cartoonishly like a Don Martin drawing for *Mad Magazine* -- though one would have thought a boy so affluent would have purchased a larger shirt -- duck-footed in a few seconds later and properly apologized, which Jerry acknowledged with a nod. Jerry always explained about the clocks after all were present, stressing in proper Morrison style that while position had privileges they came with responsibilities... such as being in class on time without the Pavlovian prompting of bells. He'd also found that breaking the butterfly on the wheel was more effective on opening day than kept in reserve as the ultimate weapon, and would add that, though expulsions were rare, they wouldn't look good on anyone's record.

He doubted if, in flatland schools, that would have been much of a threat, but these kids had been trained from birth — however defiant they thought they were -- to conform to their norm and think of their futures.

But he hadn't given the speech yet because of Gabriel's absence; and the eyes which had animalistically been scanning their peers for weaknesses -- Raymond's lasering "Lolita" with a rage he might never understand -- were beginning to search for the same in him. He didn't need to look at the clock, its archaic mechanical ticking sufficient to prove the passage of time, to know another minute had passed. He suddenly felt a kind of despair -- a Victorian what-will-become-of-me feeling -- as when the doctor had said last week his mother didn't have much time. Had something happened to Gabriel Graves, delicate as he was?

Of course it was ridiculous, unrealistic and downright absurd, but he realized he'd been basing his hope...

Hope of what?

A sign that he hadn't he wasted his life -- at least the best years of it -- pursuing an impossible dream?

All on a single drawing by a crippled black kid he'd never met?

That despair must have shown on his face, because all the animal eyes turned to him... that's what they were and always would be, *beasts* with no conception of beauty who had no higher purpose in

27

life than to grab all the toys they could in their claws and "win" by dying with them.

He almost said it aloud, picturing old Miss Morrison dying alone in her vast silent house: *what will become of me.*

Then, from out in the hall, he heard an electric motor sound, faintly familiar from shopping malls and sometimes on his Lake Merritt walks. He also heard the floorboards creaking rather ominously: Victorian mansions, though built to endure, had not been designed to bear power chairs... at least not those of the handicapped.

But, there was another sound, a sort of muffled, rhythmic padding, perhaps like many marching boots thickly soled in rubber. Absurdly, he pictured a squad of soldiers, then, a bit less improbably, a group of guards accompanying the boy. He considered that for a moment: disregarding the Angloish name, could Gabriel be an Arabian prince, his family wallowing in oil? There had been one of those three years ago who'd actually had a bodyguard, his parents not being popular with the downtrodden peasants they ruled from afar. "Black" would be black to Tillinghast, ambiguously African... though wasn't there oil in Africa? But, surely Tillinghast would have told him if the boy had a troop of bodyguards.

The students' eyes had turned to the door, taking a cue from Jerry that something was out of the ordinary. There hadn't been any conversation since none of them knew each other, only the shuffle of sneaks on the floor and the creaks of the ancient straight-back desks defying young bodies determined to slouch, but now total silence fell in the room except for the tick of the Regulator.

Then Gabriel Graves made his entrance.

Tillinghast had understated the chair: it wasn't simply a "Rolls-Royce of those kinds of things," it was more like something designed by NASA and possibly built by Caterpillar to explore the terrain of alien worlds. It was far too complex to be grasped at a glance, other than being primarily black with glints of silver aluminum or maybe a more exotic metal... magnesium or titanium? Instead of wheels it was fitted with cleated rubber tracks like little bulldozers Jerry had seen at work in streets and construction sites, which explained the rhythmic padding, the cleats passing over the floor, laying down a road ahead and picking it up behind. But it wasn't the chair he'd wanted to see, astonishing as it was, but the boy who had drawn so divinely from life.

One of his mother's earliest teachings was "nice people don't stare," in regard to those with handicaps or physical aberrations, but Jerry found that hard to obey as the boy in command of the mighty machine guided it expertly through the doorway using a single "joystick" control, though there was barely an inch to spare.

To say that Gabriel Graves was "fat" would have been an understatement of gargantuan proportions. The boy must have been, literally, as big around as he was tall. Though Jerry had pictured a small black boy, who looked even smaller, fragile perhaps, in a big complicated power chair, the boy seemed to overwhelm the machine, however massive it was. Jerry had also expected a gaudy "hip-hop" costume or maybe a sinister "gangster lean," but the boy was dressed -- assuming a boy of his bulk *could* be dressed -- in a plain white "beater" and new blue-jeans, both of which had surely come from one of those stores called "big and tall"... though in his case just the former applied. Nevertheless, the shirt, though obviously sized with multiple X's, was stretched as tight as Bill Malone's, seemingly spray-painted over twin orbs that looked like mammoth water-balloons inflated to the verge of explosion, bulging blatantly halfway bare and almost engulfing Gabriel's chins, of which there were seemingly three. Below them his body was basically shapeless, *partly* contained by the arms of the chair, though ebony rolls lolled out underneath, having escaped from his shirt. His gigantic belly was also half bare, cascading over enormous thighs that strained their confines of indigo denim, with a navel like an ironic smile due to overlapping rolls. His calves were proportionally tremendous, and his sneaks – understandably showing no wear -- must have been at least size 13. His upper arms were also huge, pouring out of the sleeves of his shirt and lushly overlapping his elbows, his forearms only a little less so; and his hands, with dimples instead of knuckles, looked like those of "the world's fattest boy" who Jerry had stumbled across on the Web when doing a Google for something.

Gabriel had no visible neck; his chins, as Jerry had already noted, entrapped between the balloons of his breasts, his head engulfed by his blubber-bulked shoulders. His opulent cheeks overwhelmed his nose, which though bridgeless was wide at the tip and only looked small in that full-moon face... a velvet-black moon in this case.

Indeed, and though living in Oakland for every one of his 39 years, Jerry couldn't recall a blacker boy; and though he'd seen a thousand fat kids of every race and color, he'd never seen one of *this* size before... at least of this circumference.

As a boy himself at idle moments lazily lolling upon his bed and fondling his own "boy-breasts" in pre-pubescent self-indulgence, Jerry had imagined fat as something like the clear gelatin always generously included with the canned hams his mother served on holidays and special occasions -- soft, warm, and rather appealing, like a sort of added bonus -- though Gabriel's fat, especially his belly, suggested something even softer, perhaps a viscously liquid substance undulant under ebony skin... he recalled once seeing a picture of a shapeless black rubber fuel container being lifted by a crane.

Regardless of his mother's teaching, Jerry fixed on Gabriel's face, which made him think of an African cherub who had obviously gotten too fat to fly. The mouth, like the nose, might have looked wide -- at least by Caucasian standards -- on a boy of lesser volume, but here it was rather a rosebud, sweet, with full expressive lips, which were probably always open at rest displaying a pair of startling teeth, both for their size and contrasting whiteness in a "Bucky Beaver" way. The eyes below a woolly mane looked as black as the space between stars despite being given as "brown," and even above those spherical cheeks were large and somehow quite charming... though had the boy not been so fat, they might have resembled a pity puppy's.

Jerry's eyes searched for any malaise, fearing to find the brooding self-hatred beat into so many overweight kids, even those who in his generation would have been called only chubby, but instead found alert intelligence regarding him in return; not even a ghost of self-pity haunted those midnight depths, nor any plea for pity from others. No "skinny boy" was trapped in that fat and screaming to be free.

Only a moment or two had passed, the boy navigating into the room on his dauntless Caterpillar tracks. The chair, as Jerry took in more detail, was loaded like an Army jeep equipped for an arduous campaign with black nylon pouches slung here and there, as well as a pair of matching packs, appearing, as Tillinghast had said, very self-sufficient. The boy looked Jerry a question as to where to position himself, and Jerry tried to appear nonchalant, as if seeing incredibly fat black boys was a normal occurrence at Morrison, and nodded toward an empty space between the desks and a row of easels. He carefully modulated his voice so his greeting, "Good morning, Mr. Graves," sounded just as casual as when he'd welcomed the other kids, though his mind was trying to reconcile, to accept the reality of this boy -- this divinely gifted boy -- and abandon the mental sketch he'd made... which certainly hadn't been drawn from life.

Okay, he concluded, the boy was fat; what difference did that make? No more difference than his color. Handicapped as he was — in *three* ways -- it had probably tripled his talent. And, being confined to a wheelchair -- in this case one with bulldozer tracks -- it didn't seem all that unusual for him to have gotten that way. He might have taken easier roads, the roads most boys of his age would take in the same or a similar situation, become a computer or game addict, lost his soul in cyberspace, or simply "zombied-out" on TV; but instead he'd chosen to create, and what he'd created was divine.

The other students, Jerry noted, though still sneaking peeps at the mammoth boy -- Walter most of all, though maybe that was logical with all the weight he'd gained this summer -- seemed, probably due to Jerry's composure, feigned though it was, to accept Gabriel, at least for the moment, as simply a very fat black kid -- or the token at Hogwarts -- who hadn't yet revealed himself as cool, lame, or inconsequential; though Raymond was assessing him for possible victimization. Jerry caught Raymond's eyes flicking to Bill, seeking the sanction he needed, though Bill seemed inclined toward Gabriel and not only ignored Raymond's pleas to pounce but frowned to keep him contained. Then Bill did a very princely thing,

31

proving himself a nobleman possessed of the very rare quality of actually *being* noble: he smiled at Gabriel and pronounced, "Cool ride."

Most of the students giggled or grinned, except for Raymond and the Disruptor... both evidently realizing that if Bill wouldn't let them attack this fat boy they couldn't go after Walter, either. Gabriel smiled at Bill in return, not gratefully but as an equal. Ken Yamamoto seemed intrigued by Gabriel's mighty mechanical steed and -- had Jerry not begun his spiel about the clocks, *noblesse oblige*, and the final solution -- might have started to sketch it. Walter snapped a phone picture, clandestinely from the hip.

Jerry then began his introduction to his class of Drawing From Life, something else he'd once enjoyed, but which for the last few years, had been a mostly mechanical speech like a flight attendant's robotic recital of how to fasten a seat belt and use one's cushion to stay afloat... presumably after hitting the sea at 300 miles-per-hour. But now there seemed to again be a *reason* to introduce these kids to Art, and a hope -- notwithstanding Gabriel's talent -- that one or two might want to pursue it.

This not being a public school where one size was supposed to fit all and square pegs were relentlessly pounded, regardless of splinters and collateral damage, into a plodding assembly line of State-mandated circular holes, Jerry had designed his class to give the less able the basics they needed while allowing the truly talented students -- under his Master's guidance, of course -- to create at their own higher levels. Obviously, those like Bill Malone, possibly Walter and several others whose samples did show promise -- not to mention Gabriel Graves -- would be held back and discouraged if forced to begin by drawing stick figures and learning basic anatomy, while horsey girls had to be convinced that, while horses were beautiful animals, there were few equine paintings in galleries featuring bow ties and derby hats. Skulls and bones were for Halloween posters; while tattoo art belonged on skin rather than quality canvas. Anime was cartooning, a highly competitive field of Art, requiring not only exceptional skills but also more than a few lucky breaks.

## Drawing From Life

Without looking at Ken Yamamoto, who *did* begin to sketch the chair, while Walter snapped another picture, presumably of its occupant, Jerry offered the option of Graphic Design for those more inclined toward objects than people.

That left Crystal's detestable... *thing*... which, like breaking the butterfly, was best gotten over with now. Jerry didn't believe in peer critique -- just as one couldn't learn brain surgery from a fellow first-year medical student, one didn't learn how to draw from life from those who had barely started to live -- but in this case he wanted to see their reactions, if only to confirm his judgment that the girl needed help in a lot more than Art.

Asking Raymond to draw the drapes -- a warning of who would be bullied if any bullying reared its head -- Jerry switched on the projector and took a drawing from a folder, not Crystal Sterling's obscenity -- yet -- but a horse by a girl named Susan Treadwell, who was sunny blonde and perfectly pretty by Anglo-Saxon standards. Her horse, not surprisingly Palomino, was one of the more realistic beasts, though certainly hadn't been drawn from life; and there were careful appreciative murmurs, the kids unsure of whether or not to express what they actually felt.

Jerry followed the horse with one of Ken's choppers, which impressed most of the males; and he noted Gabriel's approval in a slight cock of the head -- all it could manage, engulfed in fat -- which seemed to show he wasn't a snob, at least when it came to other Art forms besides the one he seemed to have mastered.

Jerry reminded himself that he'd only seen one example so far.

To show he wasn't a bully – unless someone provoked him -- Jerry projected Raymond's sample, which also impressed most of the males, though Gabriel might have looked a bit wry... a face that black was hard to read, especially now in the darkened room.

Then, to lighten the atmosphere, Jerry offered one of the My Little Ponies, which delighted most of the girls but got a lot of rolled eyes from the boys; though Gabriel only looked patient, like a connoisseur of serious films sitting through a silly cartoon.

A glance at Crystal Sterling confirmed that she in her loony innocence wanted to see her horror displayed, but instead he projected a

33

Bill Malone drawing -- a shirtless, sullen-looking boy, almost as handsome as Bill himself and pondering fate at a window -- which seemed to impress most of the kids since they could relate without knowing they were. Though he hadn't identified anyone, connecting the art to the artists, he thought he saw Gabriel smile at Bill.

Surely they couldn't have known each other? Not only was there the gulf of race, but the boys were almost antipodes in every other way. Could Gabriel have guessed? ...Or was he as good as Jerry at seeing subjects' souls?

Crystal gave Jerry an expectant look that sent a shiver down his spine. He remembered an ancient TV show from his early childhood -- *You Asked For It* -- then unleashed Princess Sparkle Pony shockingly on the screen.

These were not kids of his generation to whom the apex of deviancy was a *Hustler* found in a garbage can or, as Frank Zappa had said, "a tacky little pamphlet in daddy's bottom drawer;" this was the Internet generation who, despite Parental Controls and Google filtered searches, had probably seen almost every perversion the human mind could devise; but total silence crashed down in the room, and more than one pair of students' eyes expanded to pity puppy proportions.

Raymond finally recovered and attempted a prompting snicker, which fell as flat as a fart at a funeral. Poor Crystal thought she was being flattered by gaping mouths and goggling eyes. Jerry looked for Gabriel's reaction but, maybe due to the darkness compounding the midnight of his face, saw only a thoughtful expression.

It occurred to Jerry that, had this been a public school ruled by religious hypocrites and equally sanctimonious Proles who compounded their own deviations by being abysmally ignorant, intolerant and hateful, he might have been instantly fired, prosecuted, tried and convicted, imprisoned, and forever branded with the new American Scarlet Letter for inflicting this obscenity upon young adolescents... but the same might apply if he'd shown The Creation.

The students' obvious shock, literally rippling through the room like a nuclear EMP, not only confirmed Jerry's earlier judgment but made him feel like the hapless professor in Lionel Trilling's college

34

tale; and this feeling intensified when Crystal Sterling smiled at him as if he'd seen her soul.

He had, and it scared him shitless.

In a way it didn't seem fair, either to her or to Gabriel, perversely a tough act to follow, literally beauty after a beast -- or in this case bestiality -- but he projected Gabriel's drawing.

Again, there was absolute silence, the tick of the clock sounding loud, but this time the silence of awe. Even if only instinctively, the kids recognized the Art they were seeing, and a few of them may have gotten a glimmer of what Art actually was; that even the finest photograph could never have captured that old woman's soul.

Perhaps because of the subject's race, a few eyes turned to Gabriel, though Bill's, Jerry noted, had been the first... *could* they have known each other? An old hippie cliché, which had survived into Jerry's childhood, ghosted through his mind -- *met in a previous life* -- followed by a racist joke: *my great-grandfather owned your great-grandfather*.

He found himself, as he had in his office, feeling like a predator -- or how he imagined one might feel -- wanting to be alone with the boy, though of course with much loftier motives.

Clearing his throat, and wondering why, he instructed Raymond to open the drapes while switching off the projector. Recapturing his Bohemian pose by seating himself on his desk, and also his confidence that he was Master here, his students caught off-guard and cowed by Crystal Sterling's monstrosity and realizing he had the power to shock and awe them if he chose, he reinforced those points by reminding them they were *Morrison* students, expected to be exceptional; not only more intelligent than those of lesser schools, but also more mature. He finished by adding that none of them were compelled to be in his class, and if they didn't feel comfortable here, perhaps they belonged somewhere else. ...They would, he went on, after a moment for that to sink sufficiently in, indeed be drawing from life, and they would be their own peer models.

Comprehension dawned on several faces -- Bill Malone's one of the first -- though Gabriel seemed to already know. Walter cautiously raised his hand. "You mean we'll be drawing each other... naked?"

35

This of course released the tension with various snickers, titters and giggles.

Jerry smiled. "I'm afraid we're not that enlightened, Walter, even here at Morrison, but a decent amount of skin will be shown in the interest of learning anatomy. We're not here to draw clothes for Calvin or Tommy."

This released more laughter: maybe this guy was okay... for his age.

Parker Foxworthy batted his lashes. "How much are we gonna show?"

More laughter, of course, and a feeling of dawning camaraderie filled the air like pheromones: maybe they weren't *quite* the beasts Jerry had condemned them as, though that was before Gabriel Graves had resurrected his hope of salvation.

Or perhaps deliverance.

"No more than on a public beach. Males in boxers if they wish... but no tightey-whities."

Laughter.

"Or swim wear," Jerry continued. "And girls in bathing suits."

"Bikinis?" a boy asked, hopefully.

Laughter.

"What about speedos?" queried a girl, also hopefully.

Jerry smiled. "This isn't kiddie porn 101."

Uproarious laughter now, possibly stirring Miss Morrison's bones, which reputedly lay in a vine-covered crypt beneath somber oaks in the mansion's back yard... one of the last such interments allowed. Maybe this old guy was okay and the kind of teacher worthy of them... intelligent and mature as they were.

Of course there were kids every year, usually the overweight -- or those brainwashed to believe they were -- who didn't want to pose; and of course Jerry thought of Gabriel, though Walter and Parker qualified, too. The others would think of that in a moment, so, without looking at Gabriel, Jerry added that posing was voluntary and no extra credit was given, nor any less for not.

That reminded him of something, though he couldn't bring it to mind.

Peer pressure and/or societal shame would make that decision for some, and though it saddened Jerry, he could do nothing about it; and trying to would just make it worse. Eyes began to evaluate bodies and speculate on what might be concealed, most of the girls' on Bill Malone's, even though much was already revealed. Parker also turned to Bill, though several girls had turned to Parker. Most male eyes studied female forms, and even the cretins of either sex began to see some use for art... or at least an excuse for it.

Jerry let this go on for a minute... for maybe the first time in their lives these kids were trying to see each other as something besides what their clothes claimed to be. Then he announced that their first assignment, evaluating their drawing skills in regard to a human form, would be, for the rest of this period, to sketch a representative model. There was no pressure to finish the sketch; simply to capture as much as they could to the best of their abilities. Today, since the girls were unprepared... unless they had brought bathing suits...

More laughter.

...the model would be a male. So, who would volunteer?

"Can we vote?" asked Susan Treadwell, her passion for horses quelled for the moment by obvious interest in Bill.

"Yes," said Jerry. "But first we need volunteers."

"Can we nominate?" It was Crystal Sterling who, at least for the present, appeared to be just a normal girl also enchanted by Bill.

"Yes," said Jerry. "But this isn't a Chippendale pageant, and real beauty is more than skin deep and what you've been taught by Hollywood."

Again, Bill glanced at Gabriel, who had smiled through most of this, which seemed to show that either he wasn't ashamed of his body, or maybe he simply didn't think that anyone would want to draw him. Of course it was hard to tell what he thought with his lips in perpetual open repose and his big white teeth always visible, but something seemed to be exchanged between himself and Bill; and Bill put up a hand, drawing cheers from several girls. Walter seemed about to say something, but another girl pointed to Parker and said, "I was going to nominate him."

Parker looked surprised, though not at all discomfited despite his androgynous marshmallow shape... and Raymond looked enraged.

"We don't have much time today," said Jerry, glancing at the clock. "And we have the whole year ahead to find the real beauty within each other." He added, though knowing it wasn't true by societal standards, "And everyone here is beautiful, if we will only enlighten ourselves to see the soul within."

That got a few looks of incomprehension, but Jerry turned to Bill and indicated what in Morrison's time had been called a "Japanese screen" -- this one had actually come from Japan -- standing in a corner. All eyes followed Bill as he strode to the screen, casually shedding his shirt on the way -- to various giggles, sighs and cheers -- and disappeared behind it. While Bill was busy disrobing, his shadow intriguing girls and Parker, Jerry asked Raymond -- a final reminder of who was the ultimate Alpha here -- to distribute pads and pencils. Morrison's paper was fine quality, as were the virgin but pre-sharpened pencils, but Gabriel had brought his own and they were the absolute best. His chair was fitted with a retractable surface of black-anodized aluminum that folded over his mammoth middle like a table top, though the orbs of his chest were so enormous that Jerry wondered how he could draw. And it seemed equally hard to believe those fat-padded fingers could wield a pencil with such awesome skill as his sample had shown; but the lingering ghost of a possible fraud was dispelled by Gabriel's confident manner... he would indeed produce another spirit-baring creation.

He'd obviously noted the posing stand over by one of the windows, a four-foot plywood cube, built by Elwood at Jerry's request and draped with sky-blue velvet -- a color that best complimented the usually fair-skinned models -- and maneuvered his chair for a good point of view, gently bulldozing a few empty desks. Jerry told the other kids they were free to chose their own vantage points; then there were cheers, giggles and sighs as Bill emerged in golden glory clad in only his indigo shorts, his muscular legs and large puppy feet as perfect as the rest of him.

Indicating the velvet-draped cube, Jerry suggested that Bill assume a comfortably maintainable pose. Of course he first mounted, stood and flexed in boyishly body-builder style -- though he probably didn't work-out, being blessed with beautiful genes -- which naturally got laughter, but then sat down with a knee drawn up and turned his face to a window in one of his own subjects' brooding poses.

Had he been brave enough, Jerry wondered, or secure enough in himself at thirteen, to have drawn his subjects from life? ...Just as Jerry had often drawn Trevor.

Gabriel had begun to work as soon as Bill composed himself, his pencil sweeping confidently, every stroke, bold or subtle, absolutely sure. And he'd brought out no eraser. Of course Jerry wanted to watch, and of course he would in the future, just he would the other students... but what suggestions could he make to a boy already so masterful?

Again he felt the ghost of a threat, like a specter at his shoulder, as other students dithered, their pencils hesitating as if fearing to commit themselves to anything they might regret, making attempts, hesitating again, then tentatively beginning anew. A few of them, of either sex, were embarrassed to fix their gaze on Bill, as if they felt guilty of something by touching him with their eyes... including Raymond Blakemore. Parker was drawing studiously, no doubt appreciating the subject, long hair almost hiding his face as he leaned close to his paper, the tip of his tongue protruding like a cartoon kid's in concentration; and the others soon lost their shyness as they observed less uncertain peers; and Gabriel's steady gaze at Bill seemed to put them further at ease.

Jerry also usually drew the model, ostensibly to show his students how it should be done -- and probably subconsciously to prove he *was* the Master -- but again he felt a creep of fear... what if Gabriel's Art put his own to shame? He glanced at Gabriel again, noting once more those confident strokes, then sat at his desk and seized a pencil.

# Chapter Four

"**M**r. Graves?"

The last of the other students, Amanda Teabrook -- nefarious tracer of anorexics and evidently suffering herself -- had just left the room after placing her drawing on Jerry's desk atop the other students' works. She timidly followed Bill Malone, who'd emerged still shirtless from behind the screen, to the delight of the girls and Parker, and had only completed his wardrobe while pausing to speak with Gabriel. Jerry hadn't heard the exchange, but it didn't seem like they knew each other, and maybe Bill was just being noble. Walter had also lingered, apparently to meet Gabriel, but, preempted by Bill, had glanced at his Rolex and duck-footed out. After a few words with Gabriel and trading smiles and a handshake, Bill had sauntered into the hall trailed by an obviously wistful Amanda -- who might have hoped he would notice her if she lost what remained of the flesh on her bones -- leaving only Gabriel, who'd been next to last to leave his work and was now Caterpillaring for the door. Gabriel swung his machine around with the grace of a little bulldozer performing a pirouette.

Jerry hadn't looked at Gabriel's drawing, now beneath Amanda's, despite how much he'd wanted to. And now that he was alone with the boy he felt absurdly uneasy again. He resisted the urge to clear his throat, though he probably should have, his voice coming out with the ghost of a quaver. "I was very impressed by your sample drawing."

Gabriel smiled, which was only displaying his teeth a bit more. "Thank you, sir."

Most Morrison kids had been trained to say sir if the situation required, but Gabriel made it sound normal.

"Have you done any others?" asked Jerry, though that seemed obvious with Gabriel's skill.

Gabriel reached into one of his packs and took out his drawing pad. "I did this last night."

It was, as Jerry had almost feared, absolutely perfect... at least he could have done no better. It depicted a black boy of possibly ten -- maybe Gabriel's younger brother -- in face and upper torso view, cherubically chubby and shirtless, reposing with hands folded on chest and apparently asleep; and, as with the old woman's picture, there was serenity in his expression.

"This is very good," said Jerry. He wanted to say a lot more -- words like stunning and masterful -- but somehow he couldn't. ...Because no one had said them to him? He remembered a warning he'd read somewhere that one shouldn't over-praise gifted children. "Er... pardon?"

"I said, thank you, sir."

"Oh." Jerry wanted to ask a million questions, but of course there wasn't time with Gabriel due in another class. Then he remembered what he'd forgotten. "The Director asked me this morning to ask if any of my other students would volunteer to be your aide."

"That's okay, sir, I don't need any help."

He'd said it matter-of-factly, which didn't suggest denial. It was probably normal to wonder how Gabriel answered "nature's call"... as it might have been termed in Victorian times.

Gabriel smiled again as if guessing that progression of thought, but said, "I saw your work in the school brochure, and more in a gallery downtown. You're a great artist, sir. That's why I wanted to learn from you."

"Thank you," said Jerry, feeling almost absurdly flattered. ...Or maybe somehow compensated for fifteen years of darkness without a glimmer of light ahead. He wanted so much to talk with this boy... surely there would be no gulf of age in regard to the subject of Art? In a way it seemed wrong to assume, as if somehow taking advantage, that Gabriel's – condition -- must have segregated him from peers of any color. Although he hadn't spoken in class, concentrating on drawing Bill, he nevertheless seemed more mature than anyone else in his age group; a boy who hadn't wasted his childhood being... well, childish. Maybe he'd never learned to be childish, unable to "run along and play," as would gave been said in Victorian times? Or maybe he'd never been taught?

Jerry thought of meeting with him after school, but he had to see his mother... every day was precious now. Then he had another idea. "I'd like to talk with you about Art... maybe at lunch?" He added depreciatingly, "If you wouldn't mind being seen with a teacher?"

Gabriel smiled again. "That would be cool, but I was going to McDonalds with Bill."

"Oh," said Jerry, hoping he didn't sound disappointed. Bill must have invited Gabriel when he'd stopped to talk with him... and Jerry *couldn't* feel jealous! "No problem," he said with a casualness that was surprisingly forced. "Maybe another day. I often go there myself for a Double Quarter-Pounder with cheese."

"That's my favorite, too," said Gabriel. "But if you want to talk that's cool, I can go with Bill anytime."

This seemed to confirm that Gabriel hadn't learned many juvenile skills: he could be making a career decision and didn't seem to know it. Just as in Victorian times, "no" wasn't a word you said to a prince. It was only the first day of school; there was plenty of time to talk about Art; but Jerry said – though catching himself before saying, "cool," an expression he hadn't used since his teens -- "Great. I'll meet you in the foyer."

"Okay, see you, sir." Gabriel swung his machine around and Caterpillared out the door, the lolling ebony rolls of his sides barely clearing the frame.

Jerry studied the sleeping boy as the padding of tracks and creak of floorboards faded away up the hall, envying the peace in his face and suddenly longing to feel the same... that he was loved and cared for, safe and protected from a world that didn't love or care; and even the boy's chubbiness, despite all the current denial and hate, was proof that he was loved.

Then he took Gabriel's drawing of Bill from under Amanda's childish work -- at best an amateur comic cartoon depicting Bill as a young superhero brooding in his Fortress Of Solitude -- and studied it in the clear morning light streaming through the windows. Just as he'd hoped -- and still maybe feared -- Gabriel's work was perfect. As much as a pencil drawing could show, Bill Malone was real and alive. And, despite his own perfection -- being the handsomest faun in the forest to whom all others would bow down and serve -- there was somehow an aura of good around him.

Jerry held his own work beside it: the skills, he admitted were equal. ...Though didn't that mean improvement was needed? Or at least was possible?

The Regulators began to chime as he sat there comparing the boys... though there was little to compare because Jerry had drawn Gabriel.

# Chapter Five

The school had a lunch room of course, still the mansion's grand dining room, with a *Cordon Bleu* chef who was actually French and a menu defiantly uncorrupted by the current obsession with "eating healthy." The *entrées* were made as in Morrison's time with actual eggs, butter and cream; well-prepared meats were a staple; and while skim milk was available, it had to be requested as if one had a special need or perhaps a pretentious perversion.

The atmosphere with white-clothed tables, Victorian silver and china plates beneath a crystal chandelier was more than a little restrictive to normal teenage behavior, and many students took their meals out to the lush back yard, where wrought-iron tables and chairs were provided for dining amongst the flowers and trees, all carefully tended by Elwood. There were also many sculptures of stone, most of cherubs and chubby young fauns playing or lounging about in the foliage. Jerry had noted over the years that the kids, perhaps instinctively, avoided the ominous vine-covered crypt with its massive riveted iron door, which morbidly stood slightly ajar though secured by a mammoth chain and equally ponderous padlock of obvious antiquity... Jerry assumed Elwood had the key and dusted the tomb on a regular basis. Of course the new kids would venture a peek, though there was nothing inside to see but a single enormous marble box -- far too large for the small skeleton presumably resting within -- upon a granite pedestal in the center of the shadowy space. There must have been a family plot of Morrison generations, but maybe since she had died alone, unmarried, unloved, and the last of her line, she had chosen to remain alone for all eternity.

Many kids went to McDonalds, though the lavish Morrison lunch was included in their lavish tuition, and the last of these were descending the stairs as Jerry stood in the dim-lit foyer by the elevator door across from Miss Morrison's portrait. As he'd joked to Tillinghast -- or tried to, at least -- that morning, the picture wasn't dripping blood in outraged response to Gabriel's presence, though Minerva did seem to look grimmer today.

There was silence after the kids reached the sidewalk and their voices faded away down the street; and Jerry felt a little uneasy beneath the old woman's unwavering gaze, as if she was delving into his mind for skeletons he might have buried... that long-forgotten artist had been better than Jerry had previously thought. Then, and with a little relief, he heard the electric motor sound and the rhythmic padding of rubber treads accompanied by the creak of old floor as Gabriel tractored down the hall. Jerry pushed the elevator button, but there was no answering thrum of cables or hum of responding machinery. He pushed the button again.

"I don't think it works," said Gabriel, rolling up to Jerry. "It wasn't when I got here this morning. That's why I was late for your class."

"That's odd," said Jerry, regarding the ornate iron grille and the blackness of the shaft beyond. Surely Elwood had tested it, especially on opening day? And certainly knowing of Gabriel, since Tillinghast had told him to accommodate the boy.

"But how did you get up the stairs?"

Gabriel patted the chair's joystick the way a steam-age engineer might have patted his locomotive's throttle. "It climbs stairs."

*Of course it does*, thought Jerry.

Still, he felt overprotective, like watching a kid do a dangerous thing -- like Trevor climbing a water tower when they'd been about eight -- as Gabriel launched his machine down the stairs, which creaked and groaned beneath his weight as if the house was crying in pain. Fearful of overloading the structure, Jerry waited until the boy reached the sidewalk. Then, before descending, he glanced at the old woman's portrait again and could have sworn it looked malicious.

"That's quite a machine," said Jerry, quelling his urge to say "cool ride," as they headed down the well-kept street which, unlike many flatland streets in a city named after trees, was actually lined with magnificent oaks.

"My guardian built it for me this summer. It'll go more places than a Jeep. Range, about fifty miles."

"Guardian" sounded rather formal, and Jerry thought of Mr. Jaggers, but maybe the boy had been recently orphaned? Jerry wasn't mechanically-minded -- he'd once tried to tune-up his mother's car, which resulted in having it towed to a shop -- but that seemed impressive for a... handicapped device. "It must have a large battery."

"There's a little diesel generator. It recharges the battery, which is a deep-cycle 8D. And there's a solar charger, too."

Jerry, puffing a bit as Gabriel rolled at a rather brisk pace, refrained from asking the American question, instead inquiring, "You take it... off road?"

"We go camping and fishing a lot."

Jerry remembered fishing with Trevor in the Oakland Estuary, and camping trips with Trevor's parents -- normal boyhood activities -- and wondered why he felt surprised that Gabriel did them, too.

They arrived the corner McDonalds, where Gabriel ordered a brace of Double Quarter-Pounders with cheese, a large Coke, super-size fries, and a strawberry sundae. Jerry had intended to treat despite being bound to a niggardly budget, but Gabriel paid for his deuce Quarter-Pounder, small fries and a medium Coke before Jerry could pull out his wallet. They took their trays outside, where toddlers supervised by their mothers -- or probably nannies in this neighborhood -- were playing on the McDonald Land structures. Jerry saw Bill at a nearby table fawningly being served by Raymond while being admired by Susan and Parker separately from other tables. Bill, who'd obligingly lost his shirt despite the posted regulations, looking again the perfect faun-prince in his oversize jeans and hoove-like sneakers, nodded to Gabriel and smiled.

Gabriel's shirt, though at least triple-X, still couldn't cover all of him. Doubtless larger shirts were made, but maybe he just didn't care? He apparently didn't know what he weighed -- the question mark on his application -- and he obviously wasn't shy about letting it all hang out in public. Or maybe the sun felt good on his skin. Jerry recalled summer days with Trevor roaming shirtless around Lake Merritt, but resisted the urge to roll up his sleeves or even loosen his tie.

Most adults in this neighborhood were proper enough not to stare at the boy; and though many had probably been infected with the anti-obesity virus, glances that would have been razored with hate had Gabriel been a normal fat kid seemed blunted by his handicap. Proof of that was Walter, who'd also lost his shirt, his belly striped like a red-and-white zebra with obviously recent stretch marks, and a lunch of excessive proportions before him, who was getting a lot of hateful looks from people who probably thought themselves "nice."

Jerry chose a table beside the low McDonald Land fence, and Gabriel placed his enormous meal upon his machine's retractable surface. Jerry supposed his first question was normal, though it sounded somewhat crass: "Have you been... handicapped all your life?"

Gabriel smiled while unwrapping a burger. "I'm not handi-capped, I just got too fat to walk very far. To the fridge and the bathroom's about my limit." He patted his vast cascade of belly, making it ripple in ebony waves and his navel undulate like a laugh. "When it hangs down to your knees you have to sort of push it to walk, like getting your own self out of your way, and climbing stairs is a bit strenuous."

"...Oh," said Jerry, surprised not only by that revelation but also by Gabriel's casualness... perhaps like the pressure to be a child he'd also been free of societal pressure to be obsessed with staying thin? He obviously wasn't trying to be what current culture said he should be, either in physical appearance, nor apparently in mind. His voice, though husky like a kid with a cold -- perhaps since his neck was buried in blubber -- didn't sound stereotypically "black." He didn't drop G's at the ends of words or use much current youthful slang -- "cool" seeming the major exception, though "cool" was far from current -- and his sentence structure was somewhat formal, even a bit

47

archaic, which made him seem very mature. Also apparently very astute because he smiled again and said:

"You wonder, sir, had I not been so fat, would I have pursued my Art."

"...Well, yes. ...But how did you know?"

Gabriel chomped a huge crescent of burger. "Logical progression of thought. But I always liked to draw, even when I was little." He laughed and gulped some Coke. "Relatively speaking."

"So, you've been drawing for most of your life?"

Gabriel munched a fistful of fries. "Since I was four... also painting... but of course that was juvenilia. ...You?"

"Most of my life," said Jerry, thinking again, *if I could have drawn like him at thirteen!* "Is that your grandmother in the sample drawing, and a younger brother in the other picture?"

Gabriel masticated more burger... apparently, speaking with one's mouth full had not been discouraged in his family. Or maybe it was a compliment that he treated Jerry as a peer. He would have excelled at Chubby Bunny. "No, just friends. Everyone's a friend in our house."

Jerry supposed it was a "black thing," though it sounded nice. He hadn't touched his own food yet, though watching Gabriel happily eat made him suddenly ravenous. He took a bite of his burger and seemed to be transported back in time: like the old food critic in *Ratatouille* he remembered being Gabriel's age and his mother taking him out to McDonalds for one of those rare culinary treats. It wasn't until his college years he'd realized how dear it had cost her.

The fries were as good as the burger, golden with just the right crispiness, and the Coke just as sweet as he recalled with that peppery nip that teased the tongue and tickled the back of the throat. The palate grew jaded with age, he'd read, demanding more exotic sensations, but kids were happy with simple fare; perhaps why many chose McDonalds over the opulent Morrison meals. Maybe it was ridiculous, but for a moment he forgot he was old: he could have been Gabriel's age again having a burger with Trevor.

Gabriel's smile looked mischievous, as did the "smile" of his cavernous navel, its twin scalloped rolls suggesting plump cheeks. "You

48

wanted to talk about Art, sir?"

# Chapter Six

Lunch with Gabriel seemed to Jerry, in retrospect a few hours later sitting at his office desk and grading the drawings of Bill Malone, to have been as surreal as a Dali painting. One moment he'd been thirteen again, the food as delicious as he recalled, the sun as sensually warm on his skin, with no past regrets or future forebodings as in those long-vanished times with Trevor, and in the next instant, as if he'd been somehow hurtled through time, realizing he was 39 and a teacher lunching with a student. But even when coming back to the future he'd still been amazed by Gabriel.

He told himself now, realistically, setting aside Parker's drawing of Bill, which was actually rather good – which might make for future complications if Jerry had judged him correctly -- it was simply Gabriel's knowledge of Art, the subject to which he'd restricted himself because it would have been improper -- even suspect or abnormal -- to ask the boy many personal questions. It was like the reverse of a predator, who always tried to lure their prey into baring their -- mostly -- innocent souls; though it was jarring to emerge from the past of simple sensations and pure motivations and realize he'd been on the verge of asking something he might have asked Trevor. And maybe because Gabriel was black – not without morals, of course, but maybe a bit less inhibited -- the boy would have answered anything. Jerry had learned how to deal with Lolitas – this year's example possibly Parker -- who could not only topple a teacher's career but also disfigure their own young souls, as well as crazies like Crystal Sterling and the rest of the typical types, but he'd never encountered a Gabriel; a youth who at times seemed an equal.

And yet he *couldn't* just say what he felt in youthful spontaneity,

50

ask the questions he wanted to ask, or metaphorically bare his own soul, because this culture that exploited its children from the moment they first turned on a TV -- that brutally raped their innocent minds, impregnating them with intolerance, xenophobia, narcissism, materialism, hate and greed -- had drawn a line at a calendar year and declared it immoral for him to cross.

In regard to "proper" conversation, and maybe not surprisingly in light of his talent for portraiture, Gabriel's knowledge of Art extended far into the past. He'd even quoted Aristotle: "The aim of Art is to present not the outward appearance of things, but rather their inner significance."

He'd also cited Edward Burne-Jones: "The only expression allowable in great portraiture is the expression of character and moral quality, not anything superficial." Which meant a subject's dress or surroundings... their self-created illusion of self. He might have glanced at Walter -- who seemed to be in food coma from trying to pace Gabriel, his belly looking about to explode, as he sprawled with his virginal Nikes splayed out -- and repeated that phrase: *their self-created illusion of self.*

Jerry had always had similar thoughts, and though it was treading improper turf, he'd asked if, for that reason, Gabriel had ever done any nudes?

"Quite often," the boy had replied, as if that should have been understood, and had added matter-of-factly that all were naked under their clothes, and a good portrait artist could always reveal it. He'd smiled impishly, both above and below, and winked an onyx anime eye. "Sort of like having spiritual vision."

"Baring the soul?" Jerry had asked. "No matter how well, or perhaps desperately, the subject tries to hide it?"

"Exactly," Gabriel had replied, washing down a last spoonful of sundae with a gulp from his bucket of Coke.

Jerry had felt uneasy again, facing both of Gabriel's smiles and the ebony depths of his unguarded eyes and wondering what the boy *could* see, although unlike Miss Morrison's gaze, there seemed to be no deliberate digging.

Still, he'd been almost relieved when Bill had appeared with a strawberry sundae and offered it to Gabriel like a Hobbit's second breakfast. Jerry had excused himself, and Bill had taken his place at the table. As Jerry had walked up the oak-lined street, resisting the urge to loosen his tie -- though he felt like shedding his shirt in the sun and laughing for no particular reason -- he'd wondered what they were talking about.

Of course he knew nothing of Bill, who, despite being physically perfect, might also be very intelligent... despite *that* being oxymoronic in American culture. A boy like Gabriel would not suffer fools; nor after what he'd learned at lunch could Jerry imagine him satisfied with superficial teenage drivel. A thought did ghost across his mind as he'd reached the foot of Morrison's stairs that Gabriel could be "playing" Bill because it would be convenient to have the Alpha on his side in a juvenile environment... though that seemed beneath a boy who was obviously secure in himself.

Jerry had paused at the bottom step. On the other hand, what could Bill see in Gabriel? He could have all the sycophants he wanted and -- barring some tragic disfigurement or lapse of acceptable BMI -- could have them all his life. Bill already knew he was perfect – without any self-created illusion -- so he didn't need a fat black boy to further enhance his perfection by contrast. Could he simply be "good," as Gabriel's drawing seemed to suggest, despite that being a handicap and one he'd surely know by now was only self-imposed? For someone who'd been blessed like Bill, that would indeed be tempting the gods.

Not sure why, Jerry had gone to the elevator and pressed the Period brass button. The cables had thrummed, the machinery hummed, and the cage had smoothly descended for him... though he'd climbed the stairs instead, facing again Miss Morrison's eyes and feeling childishly defiant.

The evening sun through the west-facing windows had taken on a golden glow, giving rich tones to dark old wood and his mother's portrait on the opposite wall, her eyes looking kind as he always remembered, though he'd also captured the fawn-like confusion -- an innocent Bambi expression -- that wonderment of being wounded without any comprehendible cause or justifiable reason. The world was filled with flying arrows shot at random by wounded hunters, themselves only happenstance targets for others likewise handicapped, and she'd never seemed to understand that.

For some reason Jerry pictured those rays slanting in through the foyer doors' glass and illuminating Miss Morrison's face. Would it look less malicious in daylight than he recalled in the shadows?

He glanced at the Regulator as an archaic mechanical whir heralded the striking of five, which echoed through the shadowy halls with a synchronization not quite perfect but surely as fine as Elwood could tune it. Then the house fell silent again except for the creaks of settling timbers as the warmth of the day slowly waned. The students had all departed at three, and most the staff had left by four, Tillinghast steaming in for a moment to ask how things had gone with Gabriel; Jerry replying, "very well," and for some reason reluctant to reveal the elation he felt.

Now he sat listening to silence, which was only enhanced by a creaking joist or the eerie groan of a shifting timber, feeling alone in the vast old house, though Elwood was probably somewhere about. Jerry had seldom stayed this late and had never been in the house after dark, usually doing his grading at home and frequently asking his mother's opinions, which were often more kindly than his.

The truth was, he admitted, leaning back in the stern old chair where Minerva may have penned her epistles with sharp steel nib and iron-gall ink, he didn't really want to go home. Maybe, as Thomas Wolfe had said, he really *couldn't* go home again because time had invaded and ravaged the place and nothing remained there for him.

He'd gone to his mother's "new home" -- her impending final home -- shortly after leaving McDonalds and following a few minutes of counsel with anorexic Amanda Teabrook, who'd explained she couldn't model because she was "morbidly obese." He'd assured her, as he'd done for the class, that she was under no obligation and it wouldn't affect her grade; and she had looked down at her skeletal self and cried, "If I wasn't so *fat!*"

He'd emailed the school psychiatrist -- in residence only a few hours a week, having a self-described private practice "prescribing placebos for rich looney-toons" -- after the poor addled girl had left. She had created her own self-illusion, or in her case a self-fuddled delusion. That made Jerry wonder if Walter stuffing himself at lunch wasn't some opposite sort of malfunction? And he might be sending an email soon for Crystal Sterling's aberration; another tactful variation of, *look, I've found another*, and there was possibly impending Parker... though wasn't he also a little bit mad? He remembered something he'd read somewhere: *If you're successful they'll say you're eccentric; if not they'll call you insane.*

His contract required his presence at school for a minimum of four hours a day, but other than teaching his morning class, being available later to counsel, and attending occasional meetings, his hours were fairly flexible; and Tillinghast probably wouldn't object under the circumstances.

Which, after all, were temporary.

# Chapter Seven

At the home he'd been greeted by Harriet Cole, an enormous nurse as black as her name who could have quelled riots at Bedlam but was remarkably kind and soft-spoken. Of course when he'd gone -- shopping? -- for homes, aware of all the horror stories of elder-abuse and neglect in such places, he'd tried to investigate each thoroughly. But, like finding a funeral home -- he instantly buried that thought -- it was something you only did when you *had* to, a task you were never prepared to perform no matter if you thought you were. And then it had to be quickly done, which left little time to make informed choices.

This, as Harriet Cole had said, simply but as always kindly, was one his mother's "good days," and he'd taken that for a sign... though well-aware he was looking for signs. Though it had ravaged his bank account to the point where he was grateful that Gabriel had bought him lunch, his mother had a private room, cheerfully lighted by leaf-dappled sun though a sliding glass door to a well-tended courtyard of lush green trees and bright flower beds -- Elwood could have done no better -- now open in the warm afternoon to admit the herbal scents of life along with the pleasant play of a fountain... a rather remarkably fat little cherub poised with a vase on a shoulder.

She had chosen three of his paintings "to keep her company," which Harriet had hung on the walls; one a seascape of a beach with a lighthouse he'd done on his last drive down to see Trevor before the price of gas had quadrupled; another a sunny scene of Lake Merritt, where up until midway through this summer they'd gone for daily walks; and the third -- perhaps oddly -- a juvenilia portrait of Trevor in Jerry's room at age thirteen, shirtless and gazing out the

55

window as Bill Malone had posed today... though Trevor had been as chubby as Jerry. He'd wondered why she'd wanted it since she hadn't seen Trevor since that summer, though she often inquired about him, and maybe more these last few years... though that may have been due to the advent of email and Tillinghast generously giving Jerry one of the school's outdated PCs.

She'd been sitting up in the hospital bed atop its cheerful saffron cover, though bolstered by pillows in an old-fashioned way rather than using the bed's mechanisms, dressed in her pink terry robe and slippers, an ashtray on the bedside table, provided by Harriet Cole although against the rules -- no matter if one had smoked all their lives and still survived to a ripe old age, their dying days here would be healthy -- containing a trio of Pall Mall stubs, and re-reading *Great Expectations*, one of her favorite books. The room had a television of course, but she'd never been much of a TV watcher, nor had respected the medium: Jerry's childhood TV shows -- *Sesame Street, Hong Kong Phooey, Fat Albert and the Cosby Kids* -- first seen on a ghost-haunted black-and-white Philco, and the living room furniture not yet arranged to constantly worship this jealous "new" god.

She was a small and delicate woman without looking overly frail; those diminutive meals had been ample for her, and the food here -- Jerry sampled it often -- was well above institutional grade, though she looked smaller to Jerry these days. Her silver hair, thanks to Harriet, was coifed in its usual '50s style, which rather resembled June Cleaver's. Her glasses were steel and simple like Jerry's, not some ghastly "old lady's" grotesques, and she only wore them for reading and driving. She still had a license, the State still unaware of her state, though she hadn't driven for several years "because motorists had become so rude," preferring Jerry to chauffeur her on well-planned weekly shopping safaris -- always armed with a purse full of coupons -- and those ominously ever-increasing visits to her doctor.

Her doctor -- also Jerry's since boyhood -- was probably pushing eighty himself, an "old school" Marcus Welby type who didn't deluge his patients with pills to the point where they needed one medication to counteract the effects of another; and rather than annually

56

ragging Jerry about his childhood chubbiness, had always complimented him for having a healthy appetite. His diagnosis back in July
after Jerry's mother had fallen twice in a grim parody of a TV commercial, and following a series of tests which had gobbled up much
of her health insurance, was simply that she was "getting on," the
natural process of being born and living -- in her case from what he'd
observed -- a long and relatively happy life, and Jerry should prepare
himself for the perfectly natural conclusion. There wasn't, he'd said
in the practical manner of one who had sat beside many death beds,
while tapping the dottle out of a pipe that Jerry recalled first seeing
at five, anything actually "wrong" with her defined as something that
could be "fixed." It was simply her "clock of life winding down."

Jerry had naturally raged against that in what these days was
called denial... which the doctor also said was normal. And of course
he understood if Jerry wanted a second opinion. He'd also added
frankly that with money her time might be extended; "her clock oiled
a bit, so to speak, with rather expensive medications, although its
spring could not be rewound."

His mother, on the other hand, had serenely accepted her doom
as if it was only another bill, each always demanding a little more,
that naturally had to be paid. She had also reminded Jerry, as he'd
driven her home in denial that day demanding she seek a second
opinion, this was the doctor who'd diagnosed a simple case of too
many green apples -- liberated from a neighbor's tree -- when the
"stupid young quacks at the hospital were ready to cut him open."

Besides, she had said, after asking Jerry to stop at Lake Merritt for
a peaceful walk, even if she could afford it -- and she would never
mortgage the house, which was all she had to leave to him -- she had
no wish to cling to life "by grasping at straws of expensive drugs as if
she were some sort of addict," and had quoted a line from *Great
Expectations* about an old woman who had finally conquered the
habit of living into which she had fallen.

The doctor had also described to Jerry what the near future
would bring: if left alone there would be more falls, each of course
risking an injury. There would be lapses -- minutes at first, but
lengthening into hours and days -- in which his mother would "not

57

be there."

In Victorian times they'd been called "black spells."

Today she had been there for him, smiling and setting her book aside as he'd entered in his "professor's jacket," and asking as she'd done each year -- not only the fifteen at Morrison but all the way back to kindergarten -- how his first day of school had been? He'd thought of testing her -- that she *wasn't* asking about kindergarten -- but then she had inquired if he'd found any promising students this year?

The room had a comfortable chair, as if visitors were actually expected, and Jerry had drawn it close to her side, opening his portfolio and offering Gabriel's Art.

"These are beautiful!" she had exclaimed after a long perusal of each; the chubby young black boy asleep, Bill Malone at the window -- a perfect version of less perfect Trevor -- and studying longest the elderly woman. "She looks so peaceful."

"You can see her spirit," Jerry had said, not surprised to be quoting Elwood.

"All her work done and resting in peace."

"That was also my impression."

"This is what you've been hoping for, Jerry; finally a student worthy of you."

Jerry had hesitated a moment, gazing out at the cherub. "The truth is, mom, he scares me a little."

His mother's eyes had followed his to the boy eternally filling the fountain. "It is sometimes scary to get what you wished for, especially if you forgot you were wishing."

Jerry had sighed. "But sometimes you get what you wished for too late. ...Like something you wanted when you were thirteen but can't be of any use to you now."

"You still have your Cub Scout knife, don't you?"

Jerry had patted a pocket. "Yes... but you *do* recall how I got it, since I was never in the Scouts?"

"You traded for it when you were thirteen with a picture you drew of a nice little Cub who came to our door selling cookies... a plump black boy, if I recall."

Jerry had laughed, recalling the boy, whom he hadn't thought of

58

in decades, shiny as polished onyx with sweat from the effort of walking, his unbuttoned blue shirt, several sizes too small though maybe the biggest available, adorned with badges and arrowheads, seeming more a required I.D. to prove he had a legitimate reason for being in the neighborhood, proudly displaying ballooning boy-breasts, his jeans baring more than half of his bottom and apparently only retained by all his belly blubber in front avalanching over his thighs, and smelling very earthy though not in an unpleasant way, with chocolate and crumbs on his pair of chins indicating he'd sampled his wares. "You bought three boxes of cookies from him... which I know now you couldn't afford... invited him in for lunch, and he ate three sandwiches of Skippy, and Welch's jelly on Wonder bread and drank a whole quart of milk while I drew his picture."

"And you made him happy by showing him... well, I might call it his soul." His mother had patted his hand. "The Buddhists say, 'when the student is ready a teacher will appear.' Maybe it works the other way, too. ...Let's go outside, it's a beautiful day."

"Are you sure you feel up to it, mom?"

"I'm going to be lying down a long time, I certainly don't need to practice."

"...Mom."

Jerry had helped her to her feet, keeping an arm around her waist as he'd opened the screen to the courtyard.

"There's a nice bench by the fountain," she'd said. "Harriet sits with me there when she can, but she's run off her feet in this place, poor woman. And her wages are disgraceful! My father paid our maid more than that!"

Jerry had felt guilty, of course, for not coming more often or staying longer, though knowing that wasn't his mother's intent as he'd walked her to a bench beneath trees... hand-carved from marble, he'd noted, like the fat little cherub, not crudely cast of concrete as most "garden art" was made these days.

"Who is this remarkable student?" she'd asked, as Jerry seated her.

"His name is Gabriel Graves. Sounds a little archaic, though the surname might be a slave name."

59

"Slave name?"

"I did some research on-line: originally they were only first names given to slaves by their owners. But, after the Civil War, former slaves either chose family names... which most hadn't had before... and since most were uneducated, they were often simple names, like Wood or Clay... or Graves. Or, family names were given to them by Reconstruction officials, and some were probably jokes, like immigration officials gave to people on Ellis Island."

His mother had looked puzzled, and Jerry had asked, "Will you be all right for a minute? I'll get my portfolio."

"Jerry, it's thirty feet away, I'm not going to decompose while you're gone."

"Mom."

He'd brought out his drawing of Gabriel, and his mother had regarded it for as long as she'd studied the sleeping old woman. She had never derided fat kids, though he expected at least a remark in regard to Gabriel's size, or a question about his handicap -- which was, in a way, self-imposed -- but she said: "He has an artist's eyes. Like yours, he can see a subject's soul."

"Maybe that scares me, too."

"Why in heaven's name would that scare you?"

Jerry had studied the cherub again, who surely must have been carved from life... the details were absolutely perfect, a Shar-Pei boy composed of rolls; and not many artists, especially these days, would have dared to create a boy so fat, his belly concealing his private parts, his breasts already opulent though the model had probably been only five.

"I'm not sure, mom... unless I don't feel worthy of him. ...Like, I'm not a good enough artist for him. ...Like, he has too much of a head start on me, so there's nothing I can teach him now, and..." Jerry had given a helpless shrug. "He's going to realize that soon."

"So you feel like a fraud?"

"...Well... in a way. ...And I've certainly done nothing great."

"You have, Jerry. Beginning with that little Cub Scout. The world just hasn't realized it... 'gotten a clue,' as Harriet says. And you will do much greater things in all the time ahead of you." His mother had laughed. "You don't have one foot in the grave, you know."

"Mom."

His mother's expression turned serious. "You need some new inspiration, Jerry. And a fresh perspective... nine months every year in that old mausoleum trying to teach overprivileged brats who wouldn't know Art if the Mona Lisa posed for them in a pink bunny suit. Then coming home to a creaky old crone."

"Mom!"

His mother had made a dismissive gesture. "Not that it hasn't been good, Jerry... your being there for me... but you've been handicapping yourself. You can't draw from life where no one's alive in any way that matters." She'd pointed to the fountain. "Just look at the life in that little boy, and the beauty the artist saw in him... the beauty and life *you* can see. And your new student can see. He's ready for you and you're ready for him, and you're both in your ways just beginning your lives. So make the most of this year, Jerry, and make the most of him by giving him what you have to give and accepting what he has to give you. Then..."

Jerry had smiled. "Get off my butt and do something great?"

His mother had drawn a pack of Pall Malls from a pocket of her robe and offered one to Jerry, who'd searched his pockets for matches until his mother produced the old Zippo that Jerry had bought for her birthday from a cigarette machine when he'd been thirteen. She had laughed after flicking its flame. "Even after all these years I still feel I'm corrupting you."

Jerry had also laughed while accepting his mother's light. "I corrupted myself a long time ago."

His mother had lighted her cigarette, and asked, "Does Trevor still smoke?"

"As of the last time I saw him."

"That was almost three years ago, if I haven't gone ga-ga."

"Yes, the last time I drove down the coast."

His mother had sighed out a ghost. "Time is fleeting, Jerry. And it fleets faster as you get older until you're too tired to chase it. You should see him again soon." She had paused to gaze at the cherub. "And use the gift you've been given in the way it was meant to be used. ...*Do* instead of trying to teach, and the students who are ready will find you, even if they never meet you, and be inspired to do the same. ...I don't expect you to keep the house. I'm certainly not going to haunt it."

"Mom."

She had studied his drawing of Gabriel again. "May I have this? I'd like it here."

"Of course, mom."

"I'd also like one of these," she'd said, drawing something else from her robe.

Jerry had recoiled in horror... a picture of an old-fashioned coffin!

"Mom!" he'd cried, sounding like Beaver... then, "Where did you get this?"

"Harriet and I Googled her laptop and she printed it for me. Any funeral home can order it, and a decent one won't mark it up much."

"Mark it up?" Jerry had said, still staring horrified at the coffin.

"Most coffins aren't really expensive wholesale, but many greedy funeral homes mark them up hideously. It's called taking advantage of grief. I've been doing some research online... if they'd had the Internet in my day I'd have a lot more to leave to you."

"Mom."

"Stop being silly, Jerry. I know you haven't been doing your homework."

"...What?"

"Like that report on Rosa Parks."

"...What?"

"The one you had to do in sixth grade... you had two months in which to write it, but you dawdled until the night before."

"...I still got a B."

"I'd like an 'A' funeral, Jerry, and at least I have insurance for that."

"You've been researching funeral homes?"

"Not yet, but I will if you dawdle."

"...I'll start checking tomorrow." Jerry forced himself to look at the coffin; a "Victorian Model 97."

"You want this instead of a... casket?"

"A coffin should look like a coffin, not a glorified packing crate to ship someone off to the great beyond."

"...I suppose."

"And the lining looks very comfortable," she'd added mischievously.

"Mom!"

"And, as I said, a *decent* home won't triple the price. Or, you can order it off the Web and have it delivered right to the house."

Jerry didn't care for that picture at all.

"And don't let some undertaker smoke you."

"Smoke me?"

"I borrowed that from Harriet. It means..."

"I know what it means."

"By law they have to use whatever coffin you supply as long it meets State requirements."

"You *have* been doing research."

"I reminded you twice about that report and you still dawdled until the last minute."

"Have you been researching... tombstones, too?"

"Surprise me, Jerry. The plot, as you know, is paid for, up on a hill with a view of the Bay, and includes the price of a moderate stone."

"...Can you give me some idea?"

"Something you'll want to come visit and won't make either of us sad." She had turned to the fountain again. "I've always been partial to cherubs... that plump little Cub would have made a nice one... and that's something I can remember *you* by."

"I wasn't *that* fat."

"But not a sad one, Jerry; no little boy crying alone."

Jerry had taken her hand. "You're not scared, mom?"

"No, Jerry, I'm not. And you shouldn't be, either."

# Chapter Eight

The light in the room was dying, the sun slanting low through shrouds of ivy, and Jerry switched on the Tiffany lamp, its glass shade patterned with dragonflies. He would have preferred a modern desk lamp -- this expensive antique was damnably dim -- but that might have displeased the Crypt Keeper, and maybe the fabled Morrison ghost. And, according to Elwood, a larger bulb would have been unsafe. There were three more drawings to grade with notes of advice to be added to each, and he picked up Raymond Blakemore's.

Not surprisingly, in light of his overly-masculine front, he'd exaggerated Bill's musculature to comic book hero proportions while basically only sketching Bill's face and rendering his pubic region rather fearfully vague. Jerry recalled medieval maps whose borders faded away into mist with legends like Unexplored, or warnings of *Here Be Dragons*. While most of the students had made some attempt to draw Bill's boxers in some detail with folds, creases, and ribs of waistband -- fabric was often hard to depict, even for many experienced artists -- Raymond had only drawn Mickey Mouse shorts, *sans* buttons of course, while enhancing Bill's thigh and leg muscles and further enlarging his big puppy-feet. No doubt the psychiatrist could have explained it, but Jerry figured his own diagnosis was probably close to right-on.

Most of the girls -- and Parker Foxworthy -- had spent a lot of time on Bill's face with widely varying degrees of success; and while none of the students had enhanced Bill's body as much as Raymond Blakemore, most had produced an *Elfquest* look with more prominent chest and narrower waist. Though all had obviously seen Bill in life and had most of an hour in which to explore him, even allowing for untutored skills, all had *interpreted* him in some way, perhaps creating their own illusions.

Except for Gabriel Graves.

Only Gabriel had drawn him from *life*, revealing Bill as he actually was, not only naked beneath his clothes -- such as they were -- but bare inside his body as well as if seen with spiritual vision.

Unless that aura of goodness was Gabriel's illusion?

Jerry picked up his portfolio and took out Gabriel's drawing of Bill, which of course he'd graded A. Though he didn't usually grade on a curve, he hadn't been able to bring himself to depreciate Gabriel's masterful work by giving more than a B to the best of the other drawings... that by Parker Foxworthy. He should have drawn Bill as he normally would have drawn the class model... the Master showing his students how to bare a subject's soul. Would he have seen that goodness, too?

Or simply a very handsome boy who hadn't lost all of his soul yet? A soul for which Satan would offer a lot because Bill was a very alluring Judas.

Though Gabriel's samples had mainly been faces -- the sleeping old woman and slumbering boy -- Bill Malone's body was drawn perfectly, and Gabriel could also do fabric. Then Jerry noticed something else and drew the dim lamp closer, wishing again for more adequate light than Minerva had apparently needed, and studied the drawing intently: the morning sun through the window had rendered Bill's boxers translucent, revealing an erection... at least the ghost of one.

At thirteen that was perfectly normal, and also rather faun-like, though with all those eyes upon him it did seem reckless -- careless at least -- and might have been why he'd chosen to sit with a leg drawn up, and half facing away... though he certainly hadn't been like that when he'd emerged from the screen and first mounted the stand. Had he anticipated it, knowing he couldn't change his pose once he'd chosen one? If one ruled out exhibitionism -- there had been such a student a few years ago who'd been discreetly expelled -- it would have been involuntary. Perhaps he'd been bored and his

65

mind had drifted to fantasies.

Or, arousal by adoration?

He shuffled through the other drawings, damming again the inadequate lamp. The room's other lights, as out in the halls, were low-wattage candle-shaped bulbs in scones from back in a time still accustomed to gas, accepting shadows as part of life, and wouldn't be any more useful. Raymond, assuming he'd noticed, would never have dared to draw Bill that way; and most of the girls would have been too shy... again assuming they'd noticed. Parker probably would have; but, for whatever reasons, none of the other students had rendered that aspect of Bill... though of course it may have been visible only from Gabriel's point of view.

Sitting there in the darkening silence, his desk top a dim yellow island of light amongst a sea of gathering shades, Jerry wondered if, despite all his preaching about the integrity of an artist and obligation to show the truth, *he* would have dared to draw Bill from life at that particular moment in time? ...At least in this environment, which demanded him to deny a truth that all his students knew.

He sighed and slumped back in the chair. Maybe his mother was right and he *had* been handicapping himself? These students, most through no fault of their own, some simply lacking the talent, others the motivation or need, and a few like Amanda Teabrook handicapped by a crippled culture that demanded illusion instead of truth, really weren't ready for him.

Except for Gabriel Graves.

But, was *he* ready for Gabriel?

Of the two remaining drawings, one was Crystal Sterling's, and though he was curious to see how she had interpreted Bill -- pray God not as *Prince* Sparkle Pony! -- he needed a break and a cup of coffee. And a smoke... though he only had two cigarettes left and, with his dwindling finances, should probably hoard them against real need. Tillinghast had once commented, ostensibly in jest, that Jerry's job was easy... what could be hard about looking at pictures?

Since he'd never been here at night, the hallway seemed almost forbidding, its darkness mocking the feeble bulbs spaced widely apart in their wall-mounted scones and barely illuminating themselves. The Period style EXIT sign, glowing blood-red at one end of the hall beside the staircase and elevator, seemed farther away than it should have been, and though it was childish he realized he'd have to traverse that long dark passage, the doors all closed on either side, then descend those shadowy stairs to "escape" Miss Morrison's spooky old house.

Another thought ghosted through his mind... *what if the lights went out*? He told himself that was ridiculous; he would simply feel his way down the hall and likewise down the stairs...

Where Morrison's portrait lurked in the dark.

Then, with some relief, he remembered the LED flashlight on the key ring in his pocket -- a birthday gift from his mother last year -- which made him feel prepared like a Scout, though considering their current stance of discrimination against fat kids, was glad he had never been one.

The only sounds in the ancient house were the ticks of the Regulators... and maybe his own heartbeat. That made him think of *The Telltale Heart*, and he realized he'd only *assumed* Elwood knew he was here, although he hadn't seen Elwood since coming back from the nursing home and reporting the elevator malfunction. ...But, he must have known Jerry was here or the lights would already be off.

He wondered where Elwood might be... still at work on the floor below, or maybe retired to his basement abode? He listened again, holding his breath, but there was only the feasting of clocks relentlessly gnawing away at time like coffin worms eating a corpse. He could hear no cars on the street outside, though that probably wasn't unusual at this time of night in this neighborhood of mostly upper-class residential. He recalled an old photograph in the lounge: the house had once stood alone on this hill with a flight of stone steps leading up to its doors through flowers and trees in a huge front yard where cherubs had played in sparkling fountains and fauns had lounged in leafy nooks... a sort of Victorian McDonald Land of plump stone children and young animorphs. The street had been straightened and widened, and sidewalks added in 1901, devouring the lush front yard, which must have angered Miss Morrison, and the wooden staircase had been built, which, though grand in itself, had not restored the home's former glory. Judging from the present profusion, the fauns and cherubs had been relocated to the mansion's back yard. Then, other houses invaded the hill, expensive but smaller in less lavish styles, which had probably seemed to Miss Morrison -- perhaps looking down from her lofty tower -- as if she was being surrounded by slums.

Had she thought the Victorian equivalent of, "there goes the neighborhood?"

He turned toward the opposite end of the hall, about the same distance as the stairs, though also seeming farther away than it should have been. Like all the others lining the passage, the dining room door was closed, and the kitchen staff wouldn't have left coffee on. The same applied to the teacher's lounge, where Elwood had probably drained the urn and prepared it to light in the morning.

Jerry considered going home, either taking the last two drawings with him or coming back early to grade them tomorrow, but again he felt reluctant: his house seemed so *empty* without his mother.

Emptier somehow than this one.

He looked again to the distant stairs, then crossed his office to one of the windows, still open since the night was warm, and scanned the street forty feet below half obscured by its venerable oaks. The sight of his car at the curb reassured him, though the old-fashioned cast-iron street lamps might have been actually burning gas... but that was the intended illusion. And the golden glow of McDonalds, its arches like an inverted image of the Golden Gate across the Bay, on the corner of a still-busy street lighted by powerful sodium globes and the headlight beams of scurrying cars, were certainly of the present. But again he found himself uneasy at the thought of traversing that long dark hall, then descending those shadowy stairs. And then confronting the old woman's eyes. He realized *he had no choice*, that whether he simply wanted some coffee or decided to go home, *there was no other way out of this house.*

Absurdly, he leaned out the window: as State regulations required, there was an iron fire ladder, one of those old accordion types mostly concealed in the ivy, that could be dropped by pulling a lever.

But that was a ridiculous thought, and he immediately turned on his heel and marched with dignity down the hall, denying that something was "following him." ...And the tingle on the back of his neck was only imaginary. Despite the strange illusion of distance, the hall was no longer than it actually was -- of course it wasn't! -- but he paused at the head of the staircase. There were no lights in the stairwell, nor in the foyer below. Could they have shorted out? Elwood wouldn't have turned them off...

Assuming he knew Jerry was here.

Peering down he could see a faint glow from a street lamp through the front door glass... and pictured it lighting Miss Morrison's face. He almost called for Elwood, but closed his mouth before making a sound. He glanced at the elevator shaft with its modern blue-and-white handicapped plaque beside the Victorian cast-iron grille. Elwood must have fixed it... Jerry recalled the clack of its cables when the last of the staff had left. And, it had worked when he'd come back from lunch. He noted the clock style indicator -- G 1 2 3 -- was pointing to 3. That seemed strange since, so he'd been told -- never having been up there – the third floor had once been servants' rooms, one now used to store old files, but otherwise now deserted. He'd asked Elwood about the tower many years ago, which must have commanded an excellent view of San Francisco Bay surely worthy of painting, but Elwood had only said that "nothing was up there but shadows and dust, and the tower stairway wasn't safe."

He pressed the polished brass button: the elevator would bypass the foyer and let him out on the street.

He felt childish relief when the wood-paneled cage, dimly lit by a milky glass globe, obediently descended for him. Pulling open the grille, he stepped in and pressed the G button. It was somehow anti-climactic to "escape" on the street a minute later after only a glimpse of Miss Morrison's face as the cage sank past the foyer... though he could have sworn it looked mocking.

He hesitated at his car: he could go home instead of...

Tempting a ghost to haunt him?

He gazed down the street at the golden arches and considered the drive-through, but he wasn't too old to walk two blocks!

About thirty minutes later he entered the elevator again, which had waited for him at ground level. Since he hadn't had supper, he'd splurged on a Quarter-Pounder with cheese and fries to go with his coffee, now in a paper bag, their aromas making his stomach growl. He pressed the button for 2, deliberately facing Miss Morrison as the cage ascended through the foyer, though resisting the silly sophomoric urge to flip the now seemingly smirking old bat -- did she think she had scared him? -- a blatantly adolescent bird.

Back in his office and feeling triumphant -- absurdly humming the "Victorious" song from *The Five-Thousand Fingers Of Doctor T* -- he set the bag on his desk and was about to sit down to eat when he noticed one of the drawings lying on the floor. It was Gabriel's rendition of Bill. How had that happened? The windows were open but he'd felt no breeze, either walking to or back from McDonalds.

Then he saw the bottle of ink, which had also fallen, become uncapped, and spilled all over the drawing.

Then the lights went out!

# Chapter Nine

For a second he was too surprised for any reactive emotion -- unless surprise was an emotion -- but then he felt a creep of fear. It was instinctive in human beings to be afraid of the dark; humans couldn't see well in the dark and *anything* might be lurking there. Like many young children, Jerry had been afraid of the dark until around the age of six when, again like many young children, he'd been persuaded by his mother, as well as cajoled by society, that there wasn't anything in the dark that wasn't there in the light.

Though, instinctively, he knew better.

Instinctively he knew better now!

The creep of fear was trying to break into a panicked gallop of terror. He hadn't felt this helpless, this vulnerable, since he'd been five-years-old and awakened from a nightmare. It had been the night after a funeral -- the first and last he'd ever attended -- for one of his mother's elderly friends, a woman who'd lived down his block and who, despite her kindness and tempting abundance of homemade cookies, had always frightened him. Perhaps it was only her shocking old-age and aura of approaching death... which must have also been instinctive for the very young. He remembered waking in his room, his *Star Wars* pajamas drenched in sweat and making him feel as cold as a corpse... his mother had once told him corpses were cold in reply to a childish question. The night had been cold with whispering rain, and his room had been as black as a grave. ...And he'd been *sure* the coffin he'd seen with the withered old woman cold inside was there in the dark beside his bed!

He found he was sweating now, and coldly. And, just like on that

71

long-ago night, he grew more afraid as his eyes adjusted to the glow of street lamps... afraid he *would* see what he knew was there!

He didn't dare look around. Absurdly, and just for an instant, he remembered how angry he'd been at his mother, deep inside and for many years after, that she had taken him to that funeral.

Then a little reason returned, and what came out wasn't quite a scream... like he'd screamed for his mother that night: "Elwood!"

The lights came on.

Dim though they were, his wide-staring eyes were dazzled at first, then focused on what he'd last seen in the light... Gabriel's drawing of Bill on the floor lying in a pool of black.

"Mr. Mathers?"

He had another childish feeling, this of almost tearful relief, as Elwood materialized in the doorway, his dark face seeming the last to appear against the shadows at his back. Though he carried an antique flashlight on his venerable tool belt, he now held a candle in a brass holder... which seemed somehow appropriate.

Jerry's voice wouldn't work for a second, his throat seeming clogged by the not-quite scream as if by spider webs. Then it took another moment to figure out what to say. "...Guess you didn't know I was here?"

Elwood came in with a ghostly rattle of skeleton keys like a steam-punk caricature of a cemetery watchman. "I did, Mr. Mathers. I saw your car was still out front, and I heard the elevator." He paused as if hesitant to offer what might sound like an excuse, then added, "One of the fuses blew. Happens sometimes with my floor-polisher... can't put in more than a twenty amp 'cause the wiring won't take it. I usually warn folks about that if they're staying here at night."

"...Oh," said Jerry. Then his eyes returned to the floor.

Elwood's followed. "What happened, Mr. Mathers?"

Jerry turned to the windows. "Must have been wind," he said, though knowing damn well it wasn't. He knelt to study the mess, and Elwood crouched with the candle. Jerry picked up the drawing, which seemed to be dripping black blood. "This can't be saved." Then he scowled at the ink bottle. "I must have pushed it almost off when I moved the lamp."

That wasn't true either, he knew. "I don't want another one in this room!"

Elwood rose. "Sorry, Mr. Mathers, but it's one of the stipulations of..."

"Then make it an empty bottle!" Jerry snapped. Then he added ridiculously, "That ought to be good enough for a ghost!"

Elwood's face in the candle glow might have looked troubled for a moment, but then he said impassively, "I'll have this cleaned up by morning, sir. Sorry about the picture."

"So am I," said Jerry.

"Best let me see you out, Mr. Mathers, sometimes you can't trust these lights."

"Thank you, Elwood. ...Sorry I raised my voice."

"I understand, Mr. Mathers. Gabriel drew that, didn't he?"

"Yes." That was probably obvious, even to Elwood's untutored eye. Jerry slipped the drawing into a folder, then into his portfolio. Then he added the ungraded drawings and took his trench coat from a hook on the wall. He glanced at the bottle again: there was probably still some ink inside... but of course he'd be fired for throwing it like vitriol in Miss Morrison's face.

If he'd only been a better artist he wouldn't have given a damn.

# Chapter Ten

It was still a nice neighborhood by almost anyone's definition, a median middle-class "Elm Street" of oaks with a mix of small Victorian houses and bungalow styles from the 1920s, lined with mostly centuried trees whose roots roller-coastered the well-worn sidewalks. Burglaries and car thefts were rare; only a few security signs were discreetly displayed on porches or lawns; there weren't any bars on windows or doors; and people still went strolling at night... and presumably unarmed. All the houses' original owners had met the Reaper long ago -- the withered old woman one of the last -- and those who'd moved in during Jerry's childhood were mostly retired late-middle-aged couples, the last of whom were still kicking-off. Jerry's early solitude, at least in regard to his own age-group before he and Trevor had met, had no doubt encouraged his interest in Art, just as his role of surrogate grandson to silver-haired cookie-baking ladies had nourished his childhood chubbiness. After his nightmare about the coffin his mother hadn't taken him to anyone else's funeral, though her older friends and acquaintances seemed to be croaking at least one a month -- leaving him with a neighbor lady, another great artist of cookies and pies, though reassuringly decades younger.

The house was a little Victorian of the kind realtors advertised as "doll houses," though on the verge of needing new paint like an aging spinster turning dowdy. It was two stories tall plus a lofty attic, a basement still having a coal bin -- though the current furnace burned natural gas -- and taller than it was wide. The front yard boasted a well-tended lawn in keeping with a neighborhood where people were judged in inverse proportion to how many dandelions they allowed, mowed once a week and weeded by Jerry since he'd been old enough to know his mother actually needed his help... "manning-up," as they called it today, though fewer boys seemed to be "manning" each year.

The back yard featured a huge weeping willow, which may have been older than the house and rivaled it in size, a dozen rose bushes, a large flower bed, a big though tottering tool shed -- which had naturally been Jerry's secret base for boldly exploring brave new worlds, including his first cigarette with Trevor, soon followed by their first bottle of beer and exuberant hours of masturbation -- and the grave of his mother's cat. The tombstone was simply a brick on which Jerry had chiseled the name. A cross might have brought retribution from the municipality; and assuming there was a feline religion, it probably long predated Christ.

For a few weeks after she'd gone to the home, Jerry had weeded every day -- as if perhaps by killing something Death might be distracted -- but had finally given up in despair and indigenous species were slowly invading.

She had planted her annual garden in May, a ritual born of necessity; potatoes, tomatoes, zucchini, string beans, and a pumpkin patch for Jerry so he would have a jack-o-lantern, which he'd still dutifully carved each year and placed on the front porch for Halloween, but he'd offered this autumn's harvest to neighbors and the pumpkins to the Brown family kids... the only black family, so far, on the block. Their father, Malcolm, who worked at Pixar, had seemed offended at first -- though Jerry couldn't fathom why -- but Jerry had gone on to say that tending the pumpkins, watching them grow, and harvesting them with their own hands might be a learning experience versus simply buying them, and Malcolm had smiled and agreed.

The night had been clear -- *and without any wind* -- when he'd left Miss Morrison's house, ushered out by Elwood, appropriately with candle in hand, but was growing darker with gathering clouds as Jerry pulled into the driveway... merely twin strips of weathered concrete originally meant for buggy wheels, and the little garage for the buggy. ...Or "coach" as proper people had said. Presumably the family horse had been stabled in the back yard shed and hay

75

delivered like coal and ice.

The car's radio was only AM, nowadays mostly religious rants, moronic or hate-spewing talk shows, and fanatically right-wing "news" -- though Jerry remembered AM rock and listening at night to a Monterey station that Trevor had written about -- and the weather forecast was impending rain... though *not*, the announcer went on to rave, caused by fake global warming. Jerry had sold his car last month, a Dodge Neon he'd bought second-hand, to help with the nursing home expenses... which he'd grimly calculated would cover them through October. His mother had told him to sell her car, but a 1976 AMC Gremlin, the only new car she had ever bought -- though with the interest on small monthly payments she had probably paid for it twice -- was worth almost nothing today, even with less than 30,000 miles. It seemed ironic that, unlike the grandfather clock in the song, this reputedly crappy car built by a long-dead company would probably outlive her.

Raindrops freckled the windshield as he stopped and shut off the engine, which had its oil changed and tune-ups performed – disregarding Jerry's attempt -- by ever more youthful mechanics who regarded the car as a joke. Though too polite to laugh when his mother had brought it in, they had openly snickered at Jerry last week as if at some ludicrous perversion... perhaps like wearing women's clothes. Gremlins had been offered in pink, but fortunately his mother had chosen dark metallic blue.

The rain was slowly increasing, but Jerry felt reluctant to enter the empty house... there seemed to be an implied acceptance of what he didn't want to accept. If he went for a walk he'd be soaked, and though he'd never been delicate, this wasn't a time to risk getting sick. There weren't many other options that didn't require money, and all would only be delaying what he eventually had to do. He remembered something he'd read in a book: *you have to get over this sometime, so why not get over it now?*

But, it wasn't over yet.

His own car had always slept in the driveway, so killing the engine had been automatic, but he couldn't leave his mother's car out. Emerging into the pattering rain, the collar of his coat upturned,

# Drawing From Life

he unpadlocked the garage, restarted the car and drove it inside. He told himself that was practical; the vehicle was in good condition, even if worthless to the world, and would serve for this year at Morrison, which might -- and maybe should be -- his last. It would surely make it to Santa Cruz, and possibly many miles beyond down whatever road he chose. He paused before closing the garage doors to study the car's silly emblem... a fat little gremlin.

He locked the padlock again, though only a retard would steal such a ride, then climbed the steps to the high back porch and used his tiny flashlight to guide his key -- still a skeleton type -- into the door's well-worn lock. Although not Period for the house, the kitchen's appliances were antiques; a 1920s long-legged stove, green-and-white porcelain with a high-mounted oven, and a 1940s refrigerator with motor and cooling coils on top. The chrome dinette was early '50s, though he'd gotten his mother a microwave as a Christmas present five years ago after selling one of his seascapes.

He paused after switching on the light, still half expecting to hear his mother's, "Is that you, Jerry?" from the living room... who else would it ever have been? And since it was raining she would have asked if he'd wiped his feet. At thirteen he'd often answered, "duh," though now he wished he hadn't.

He wasn't really hungry, not after what had happened – *whatever had actually happened* -- but he put the burger, fries and coffee into the microwave and tapped the tabs for two minutes. Driving down from the foothills, he'd tried to persuade himself of the only logical explanation: Elwood had come into his office while he'd been at McDonalds, possibly to see Gabriel's work -- and Jerry could understand that -- had accidentally dropped the drawing and somehow spilled the ink.

But, even disregarding the fact that Elwood had too much integrity to lie about such a thing, Jerry *knew* it wasn't true.

Just as he'd expected and feared, he felt the emptiness of the house, magnified now by the drumming of rain and the willow tree's rustle against a window. Even the microwave's rotating plate seemed to be chanting *alone, alone*. He was a single, middle-aged man who'd only had one real friend in his life, without a foreseeable

77

future ahead, microwaving a fast-food meal like a sadly stereotypical joke. The rhythm of rain as it dripped from the eaves seemed to add *what will become of me* to the mocking lay of the oven.

He regarded the old gas oven, which had no modern safety devices: one could simply turn on the gas...

And forget to light it.

He shrugged and said to the silence, "I have to bury my mother. ...Then maybe I'll think about it."

Then he thought of Gabriel... but was he a reason to live? A boy who was his student -- at least until he realized that Jerry wasn't good enough to teach him anything -- but could never be his friend.

The microwave beeped, startling him, but at least interrupting his morbid muse. He took out and unwrapped the burger, which tasted better than he'd expected despite its resurrection, then sat at the table in his usual chair -- when small he had perched on a Sears catalog -- uncapped the coffee and started to eat. Considering the source of the food, it probably wasn't surprising he thought of his lunch with Gabriel. He glanced at the kitchen clock, a 1950s Felix The Cat, who rolled his eyes and waved his tail to mark the relentless march of time... also the name of his mother's cat chiseled out there on a brick in the rain. He'd learned to tell time on that clock, and remembered all those mornings when it had watched him leave for school, preparing himself for a future, but never a present like this. Despite the feeling of lateness -- *it's later than you think* -- it was only a quarter past nine.

What would Gabriel be doing now? A "normal boy" might be watching TV, snacking on something, listening to music, doing his homework, jacking-off, playing a game, surfing the web -- or any combination of them -- and while Gabriel probably did all those things, Jerry pictured him drawing from life as he'd drawn the sleeping boy last night. And envisioning that, and however absurd, Jerry wanted to be there, like he and Trevor in each other's rooms, and long before that final summer when their relationship had... blossomed?

"Budded" would be more accurate; the question being, as he'd thought that morning, would it or *could* it have blossomed? And, if so, would they have been happy? And, since it hadn't had that chance -- one bud uprooted, so to speak -- why hadn't it put out other shoots like ivy searching for something to climb, for either bud in all these years? Or, if they *had* been so inclined, why had they buried those two young cowboys instead of living *Brokeback Mountain?*

Of course there was a "window" theory... another road not taken.

Jerry recalled a story he'd read when he'd been around ten, about a boy who'd run away from a dismal life on a failing farm enslaved by an abusive father. Miles down a lonely moonlit road he'd come to three forks -- three choices to make -- and the story told of three alternate futures depending upon which road he'd chosen. One had led to a wealthy life; he'd worked his way to success in a city, but had died in a fire at age 39.

The second road took the boy back to the farm, but his father died a few weeks later and the boy worked the land to prosperity, living a happy rural life... but he died in a fire at age 39.

The third had led to a modest life as a general store clerk in a village, a sort of Bob Cratchit scenario with a loving wife and family.

And he'd died in a fire at age 39.

Jerry glanced at the oven again... but then to the wall-mounted telephone, which, though it had buttons instead of a dial and was made of plastic rather than Bakelite, was just as black as Gabriel and otherwise looked about the same as its 1940's predecessor. Though they'd exchanged several emails this year, Trevor's always including pictures of his three ever-fattening boys -- one on the eighth-grade honor roll, another playing bass guitar in a pubescent metal band, and the youngest with a passion for drawing, "inherited, LOL, from you" -- Jerry hadn't spoken with Trevor since last year's annual Christmas call. But Trevor would be at The Book Of The Dead and probably busy with customers. The store was open until midnight, and after that it would be too late for a casual call.

And how could it be any other kind? *How's the wife and kids?* What else could Jerry say? Scream for help like he'd screamed for his mother on a dark stormy night at five-years-old?

*Come back and be thirteen with me again!*

It was too late to choose a road not taken... even assuming the ultimate end would always be the same.

He sighed and sipped his coffee, then finished his burger and fries to the patter of rain and the willow tree's rustle. There was a kitchen radio, a wood-cased tube-type Emerson, but his kind of music was called "classic rock," and the sophomoric DJs who played it these days -- while probably waiting for better jobs -- lacked the wit to realize it had *meant* something to youth of the past seeking truth in a world of lies. ...That he and Trevor had cried to *Time For Me To Fly*, danced in savage ecstasy to the ever-mounting *Roll With The Changes*, and listened in uncomprehending respect to the haunting lyrics of *Don't Fear The Reaper*.

The ceramic ashtray on the table, a plump and rosy-cheeked Hummel boy – who'd be hated for being "obese" these days -- a Mother's Day gift from Jerry when he'd been eleven, awakened an urge for a cigarette. His mother, like most of her generation, had smoked since her early teens, and despite all the current paranoia that smoking was responsible for almost all of society's ills -- the rest being blamed on "obesity" -- it hadn't, according to the doctor, contributed to her approaching demise. Like many of Jerry's generation, he'd grown up surrounded by "second-hand smoke," but hadn't met a kid with asthma until he'd been in high school... a girl whose parents *hadn't* smoked.

Despite access to his mother's Pall Malls -- there was always a carton in one of the cupboards -- Jerry hadn't started smoking until Trevor had begun at twelve, and then it had been Marlboros... Pall Malls were "girls' cigarettes."

And, despite being fully aware that his mother's last carton of Pall Malls had gone with her to the home, Jerry got up and went to the cupboard, but of course found only a ghost of tobacco haunting his nose when he opened the door. He considered the three-block walk to a market -- and it would kill a little more time -- but he hadn't owned a raincoat in years and, as he'd thought when arriving, this wasn't a time to risk getting sick. Of course he could take the car, but that seemed yet another admission that time was slowly killing him.

He still had those last two drawings to grade.

And then...?

## Drawing From Life

Below the phone was a small wooden shelf holding the Oakland telephone book, which harkened back to the house's first phone, no doubt a huge wooden-cased thing having a shelf of its own. Maybe, since the ultimate end -- whether inevitable or not -- seemed to be haunting him tonight, he would fight fire with fire, so to speak and start researching funeral homes.

# Chapter Eleven

It had rained all night and was still coming down, a dreary kind of drenching rain that fell with monotonous rhythm, clogging storm drains with leaves and trash; and some of the lowland streets were flooded, Jerry nursing the Gremlin along, pushing a wave that swept the sidewalks, and passing an ironically drowned-out Jeep, its driver looking outraged and astonished. Jerry thought about offering help -- he'd transferred his car's emergency kit, which included a nylon tow strap, to the Gremlin before the sale -- but the twenty-something driver, in urban camouflage hoodie and sporting currently fashionable "scruff," didn't look like he'd accept it from him... or maybe from a Gremlin.

Besides, Jerry told himself as the car climbed into the foothills, the street becoming a winding road that tunneled under surviving redwoods, no doubt he had full insurance.

His mother had carried that, but Jerry had dropped it when he'd transferred the title, saving about fifty dollars. The young insurance agent had raised an eyebrow while scanning her screen and asked if the car was a classic? He could have saved more by saying it was, but classics weren't used for daily commutes and their monthly mileage was limited. Jerry had stripped the car's protection -- and consequently his own -- down to minimum liability and hoped he would never need a tow.

Morrison Academy had health insurance, which, probably thanks to his mother -- not only the well-balanced meals of his youth but also her early insistence on nerdy but waterproof rainwear -- he'd never had to use. But he'd lose it if he quit.

Not only was this no country for old men, but also no land for

82

the uninsured.

He hadn't slept well, which wasn't surprising, waking often from dreams of despair and all too well understanding why the time between midnight and morning was sometimes called the suicide hours; and had left the house in the rainy gray dawn, planning, though he couldn't afford it, to drive-though the foothill McDonald's for coffee and an Egg McMuffin. After grading the drawings last night, and finding Crystal's surprisingly good despite a specter of Sparkle Ponies, he'd taken the brass torpedo flashlight, an artifact worthy of Elwood's tool belt, from the kitchen utility drawer and inspected the spider-webbed attic for leaks as his mother had done whenever it rained. The re-roofing job about nine years ago, his mother dreading "gypsy roofers" -- though the term suggested a colorful picture of bow-topped wagons and men in bandannas -- and doing weeks of research, consulting the Better Business Bureau and every neighbor on the block, though hideously expensive, had been guaranteed for life.

Her life, anyway.

After finding the spiders comfortably dry and regarding, though not opening, a trunk of his boyhood relics, he'd searched the phone book for funeral homes, sitting again at the kitchen table where he'd done most of his youthful homework. He'd been confused, as always, by the book's schizophrenic arrangement, which, unlike the phone books of his youth, seemed designed to deliberately hide whatever you wanted to find. Nor, after he'd found them, were the somberly-worded ads helpful in making an informed decision: all in sadly sepulchral tones were, "most sympathetically dedicated to providing the kindest professional service during your trying time of need." ...Which could also apply to prostitutes.

And all, with copious crocodile tears were, "so sorry for your loss."

None, he'd found on his first perusal, and as his mother had warned, admitted he could furnish a coffin; though he assumed, as she'd also said, they would grudgingly order one... which, though seeming insensibly crass, reminded him of the "mark-up."

Before getting down to serious searching he'd opened his portfolio, taking out the folder with Gabriel's ruined drawing of Bill. He hadn't expected witches ink and it was beyond hope of saving, even if he could afford it, by a professional art restorer. Along with everything else on his mind, he'd wondered what he was going to say when projecting the drawings in class this morning. Accidents, like shit, did happen, but there might be speculation of why had it happened to Gabriel's work, the only black kid in the school. It might be best, he'd decided, to meet with Gabriel prior to class to apologize and prepare him.

Then, he'd re-checked the advertisements for mention of... user-furnished burial items?

He'd already disqualified some of the homes... and why in hell did they call themselves *homes*? At least the old term, funeral parlor, didn't imply a residence. A few seemed like corporate Walmarts of woe, despite "the personal sympathies of every member of our staff," while others were blatantly bargain-basement, several of those obviously black... which was another factor that Jerry had never considered. He supposed it shouldn't matter, but, stereotype or not, he certainly didn't want his mother -- even if only her earthly remains -- lying next to a drive-byed thug.

That raised other questions; would she have to be embalmed? He vaguely knew the process and it wasn't pleasant to picture, no matter what color the hands doing it. She'd said she wanted an "A" funeral, which to him meant an open casket, which probably required embalming. And notifying her still-living friends.

What about Harriet Cole? Was it proper to invite her, though she would have to take off from a job that apparently didn't pay very much. And if she went to every funeral of those who'd departed while under her care, she must have been going to one every month.

He'd have to discuss those things with his mother... surely she'd have more "good days."

He'd wondered if he should invite Trevor? His mother had said he should see Trevor soon, and that would be an excuse. ...Though why did he feel an excuse was needed?

Disregarding the full-page ads, all seeming morbidly opportunistic no matter how, "sorry they were for his loss," and dismissing several others that seemed to be saying, "you cap 'em, we wrap 'em, and dirt-cheap," he came upon a quarter-page ad, its font ornately Victorian, for Serenity Funeral Services... which at least had the decency not to call itself a "home." Nor did it presume to pretend it understood his personal sorrow. But, what first caught his eye, and though he knew he was *looking* for signs, was a picture of a fat little cherub standing upon a pedestal, its face to the sky in a hopeful expression, one arm raised with a chubby hand open, which could have been interpreted as either release or anticipation, perhaps like a little boy playing ball and having just thrown it or waiting to catch it.

There was no question in Jerry's mind that this would be the little boy she'd want up there on the hill with her; and maybe because she had mentioned him while sitting by the fountain, he pictured the fat little Cub Scout – as Gabriel might have looked at eight -- as he'd sat long ago at this very table scarfing sandwiches and guzzling milk while Jerry drew him from life.

Like most of the ads, it listed a website; and Jerry had climbed the staircase to his studio in the house's third bedroom, his latest but oft-interrupted work, a deliberately commercial seascape -- because he was reasonably sure it would sell -- still uncompleted upon the easel, and switched on his Tillinghast-given PC.

The first image was the cherub, though here with much more clarity, a little boy literally robed in rolls like a Shar Pei puppy, his chest a pair of opulent orbs, his belly cascading over plump thighs. Jerry was sure it was carved from life, and noting the masterful detail and style, it probably wasn't unreasonable to assume the same artist had carved the boy eternally filling the nursing home's fountain... maybe another sign?

The gallery page was impressive with many stone cherubs in various poses, though not as remarkably fat as the first, as well as fauns and angelic figures and, disregarding the fact that this Art would grace only graveyards, showed the artist's proficiency and a high degree of devotion. And certainly there was love, transcending professional craft. Jerry had instantly decided that whether or not he chose this place for his mother's funeral, he would certainly commission its artist to carve her cherub tombstone.

He'd wondered how long that would take. Did the artist still have the model? But surely, if not, it could be copied, or another model found.

The business page was businesslike, neither soggy with duplicitous sorrow nor saccharinely claiming the services offered -- as one phone book advertisement had touted -- "would be as forever uplifting to him as the soul of his dearly-departed gently ascending to heaven."

Also honestly businesslike was a page displaying both caskets and coffins -- calling a spade a spade, so to speak -- and explaining the difference. It would have been too much to expect, not a sign but a god-slap, that his mother's choice would be offered -- though there was a similar coffin, and at a not unreasonable price -- but there was a tactfully-worded note that, "personal choices were respected," which to Jerry seemed to confirm that one could order off the menu.

By then it had been almost midnight -- later than he'd thought -- but surely there would be someone on duty since Death worked twenty-four-seven. So, he'd sent an email briefly outlining his impending need and asking about the coffin his mother had specified; also about a cherubic tombstone modeled upon the illustration, stating what her insurance would cover and requesting a quote for services: Harriet had tactfully warned that, unless arrangements had been made, his mother's first stop on the road to her grave would be the city morgue.

After clicking SEND he'd sat there awhile in the rain-pattered silence, the willow brushing the window in a softy-whispering breeze, though of course he hadn't expected to hear an ethereal, "I'm proud of you, Jerry."

Now, out of the last remains of a forest on clean concrete streets with efficient drains, the gutters running vigorously, he drove through McDonalds, bought his breakfast, and parked in front of Miss Morrison's house. He was about an hour early and could have gone up to his office to eat in warm if gloomy surroundings with plenty of time to go back to the street and wait for Gabriel. But he would have to summon Elwood, who probably hadn't unlocked the doors. Of course he'd meet him eventually, but hadn't decided how to deal with last night's "accident."

He switched the ignition to ACC and found the least offensive station on the radio... ironically a talk show about the paranormal. He nibbled his sandwich and sipped his coffee to the steady drumming of rain on the roof while listening to somewhat boring people describe their rather insipid encounters with seemingly equally lifeless ghosts. These days they were called "residual hauntings," like ancient movies replaying themselves with no sentience or conscious intent. Until last night he'd assumed that if anyone staying late in the house *had* actually sighted Miss Morrison, that was probably what it had been. No one had ever reported -- or whispered in deference to Tillinghast's warning about the school's reputation -- any physical manifestations.

Whenever the subject had come up, usually in the teacher's lounge with someone watching for Tillinghast like middle-schoolers smoking in bathrooms, no one ever said they'd been terrified as Jerry had been last night, or felt they were being threatened by any malignant consciousness, or had anything in their offices maliciously destroyed.

Of course, except for occasional jokes about her baleful portrait -- *probably keeps rats out of the house* -- who had ever offended her?

He finished his sandwich and crumpled its wrapper into the plastic litter container nestled between the front seats. Then he wiped steam from the windshield and studied the brooding old house in the rain, its shroud of ivy glistening. Okay, forewarned was forearmed: not only *was* there a ghost in that house, it was sentient as well as malign. And last night's malicious manifestation had been because of Gabriel.

Jerry had probably offended Miss Morrison's Victorian senses, which would have detested Bohemianism -- however silly or slight -- artists who hadn't succeeded, and certainly his methods of teaching where children bared their innocent bodies. But she'd tolerated him for fifteen years without so much as a boo. The elevator had only failed when Gabriel tried to use it... and Jerry had summoned it for him. And only Gabriel's drawing, none of others he'd left on his desk, had been cast to the floor and defiled. In regard to what else he'd experienced, there may have been natural explanations: his distorted perception of the hall could have been fatigue... he was certainly under stress these days. That could also account for his creepy feelings and the portrait's seemingly altered expressions. The lights going out may have been just a fuse...

Or, maybe a warning to Jerry of what she *could* do if further provoked?

He finished his coffee and crumpled the cup. But, why would she be warning *him?* It was Tillinghast who'd allowed Gabriel into her exclusive school; and she must have known how Elwood felt... Gabriel, the first of his race to enter her house as an equal. Why hadn't she warned them of what she could -- possibly -- do to the boy?

But, assuming she still possessed any logic -- he pictured a withered walnut of brain entombed in a grinning yellow skull -- what could she expect him to do? The most he could ever possibly do -- and for whatever incredible reason -- would be to expel Gabriel from his class.

...But Gabriel had chosen this school specifically because of him.

And, granting she *was* still able to reason, she would know that, too.

# Chapter Twelve

Kids had once walked many miles to school through rain, snow and desert heat, braving attacks from mountain lions, bears, wolves and rattlesnakes for the privilege of getting a free education. Other kids had been bussed many miles, braving attacks from hateful humans, to get an equal free education; and Jerry had walked many blocks as a kid, braving attacks from pubescent bullies, to get his own State-granted schooling; but though tuition at Morrison might have bought a bus for every student, transportation was not included.

There was a bus stop in front of McDonalds, but no student to Jerry's knowledge had ever used public transportation. Most rode in luxury SUVs -- BMWs, Mercedes-Benze, Lexuses, Audis and Cadillacs -- either chauffeured by their parents, or often by the real McCoy. During his fifteen years of teaching, Jerry had seen many Rolls-Royces, several Bentleys, an MGTC, and a Reo Flying Cloud. A lot of middle-aged fathers drove various versions of red sports cars, often Jaguars or Alfas, and one had a Lamborghini; though there were occasional Volvos... the "Mom's Taxi" choice of the rich. There were Land Rover "estate wagons," and one student's military father had driven a Hummer H1. Tuna-boat limousines weren't rare, and several of those, including the young Arabian prince's, may have been armor plated.

The *concour d'elegance* had commenced, students disembarking, many without any rainwear, though a few wore designer jackets. But most were merely in T-shirts and jeans as if immune to *common* colds, as Jerry in his leather coat waited beside the grand staircase. Most of the kids who didn't have Art ignored him as they ascended,

89

though several eyed him suspiciously as if he might be a predator... or worse, an indigent begging for money.

Raymond Blakemore snubbed him, though Amanda Teabrook -- who probably hadn't eaten a morsel within the last twenty-four hours -- gave him an embarrassed smile as, clutching a banister like an old woman, she hauled her starving skeleton totteringly up the stairs. Jerry wondered if her discomposure was due to "admitting" yesterday of being "morbidly obese," or having him witness this morning's *Mein Kampf* to get all her "fat" up those steps... though a rather rotund and rosy-cheeked girl propelled herself past without even puffing.

Parker Foxworthy smiled at him as if they were going to be secret lovers -- he was surely impending trouble, and maybe the sooner expelled the better – and Bill Malone, in a rather ragged Lee Storm Rider jacket, granted Jerry a princely nod. William Wadsworth Wainwright III, in outgrown jeans half unzipped, his stretch-mark-striped belly on partial display in an equally outgrown button-down shirt, gave him a cheerful if distant grin as if still half in cyberspace; while Crystal's innocent mad-hatter smile sent another chill down his spine.

There were still about twenty minutes before the Regulators chimed, but Jerry hoped to see Gabriel soon. He still hadn't made a decision of how to explain the "accident," but it might be best to take the blame rather than start any speculation of why it had happened to Gabriel's work.

On impulse he went to the elevator. The indicator pointed to 3, which seemed strange as he'd thought last night, though he'd never paid any attention before and it might have been the default. He pushed the button and instantly there were rattles and hums as the cage descended. It was designed for a wheelchair, of course, but Gabriel's ride would be a tight fit. Jerry opened the grille and leaned in to read the capacity plaque. The load limit was a thousand pounds, and though he assumed an elevator would have a margin for overload, he wondered how much the boy weighed... surely close to five-hundred pounds. And his chair must have weighed at least two. But that was still less than the maximum, even if Jerry rode with him -- assuming he could fit -- and added his own maybe two-fifty pounds. He hadn't weighed himself in years.

Squinting against the rain, he peered up at the ivy-shrouded house, which from his lowly perspective loomed like a Transylvanian castle against the brooding sky. Although reputedly deserted, the third-floor windows were fitted with curtains or they would have stared like empty skull eyes... though the drapes in one of the tower windows seemed to be partially open. That made him think of Mrs. Bates, and then a progression of thought: Miss Morrison seemed to have proven last night that she could manipulate physical things, and if she could spill a bottle of ink, why would it be unreasonable to assume she could also...

He suddenly pictured the elevator, he and Gabriel trapped inside behind that iron grille, being hoisted to the third floor -- four stories above the street -- by machinery that couldn't be stopped, then cables snapping or gears stripping.

Would she, or *could* she, do something like that?

He squinted up at the tower again, and now the curtains were closed. Maybe a breeze past a rotted frame? There wasn't a breath of breeze down here, but the tower was close to a hundred feet high. He thought once more of *Psycho*, then of several Victorian tales of "empty floors" in ancient houses inhabited by deranged descendants... why would a ghost need to open curtains?

He glanced at the elevator, like an oversized wooden casket. Assuming it was Gabriel who'd awakened her slumbering malice, how far would she go to get rid of him? Though childless herself she must have liked children -- perhaps in a wistful grandmotherly way -- or why posthumously found a school? And she had filled her gardens and grounds with charming cherubs and juvenile fauns. Would there be more little "accidents" -- scary but otherwise harmless -- until Jerry bowed to her will?

Or, would she go after Gabriel if Jerry couldn't be cowed?

He remembered last night when the lights had gone out and he'd known *something* was there in the dark... just as he'd known that coffin was there beside his bed on that long-ago night. Granted, he'd only been five... but how brave was he now?

He reached in and pushed the button for 3, the cage ascending into darkness after he closed the grille, then turned to study the staircase. The Victorian age had died with its queen during the year in which it was built; Miss Morrison also passing that year -- her framed, black-bordered obituary on morbid display in the dining room — having truly outlived her time, her grounds devoured by Eminent Domain, her house defaced by scythe-swinging Progress. Nevertheless, the stairs had been built by men who'd taken pride in their craft... though they *were* over a century old; and Jerry recalled the creaks and groans when Gabriel had used them. And the cries of the house's floorboards when he'd Caterpillared the halls. Assuming Miss Morrison did like children and wouldn't harm even a black one, she still might arrange an ominous warning -- those stairs half collapsing or floor timbers cracking -- to demonstrate that Gabriel was simply too fat to be in her school.

With all the current fat-hating frenzy, he wouldn't get any support from the law, which allowed and even encouraged the hate.

Jerry pictured the old woman's portrait smirking in the foyer... that would get Gabriel out of her house without doing him any physical harm. Which might satisfy her conscience... assuming she still possessed one. And Gabriel's Art, his divine potential for creating beauty to help offset in some small way all the ugliness in the world -- assuming Jerry could nourish that -- obviously didn't matter to her simply because of his color. Death, apparently in her case, hadn't brought any enlightenment.

Because she hadn't seen the light... that pure, clear light so often described by human beings who'd gotten a glimpse and lived to tell about it?

Or, maybe she didn't want to see it?

Had she forsaken whatever peace and serenity that might lay ahead, denying the beautiful light of beyond and any divine revelations therein, to entomb herself in that dark old house with earthly hate and ignorance?

Another big black limousine rolled majestically up to the curb, this a classic, either restored or devoutly maintained, an early 1950s Packard, softly round in every contour like a mammothly massive and very fat cat, its gleaming chrome grille like a Cheshire's grin, its rain-glistened paint a midnight mirror, and riding on old-fashioned whitewall tires.

Its black-suited chauffeur was also immense, himself as dark as the vast vehicle, his somber attire perfectly tailored despite an enormous low-hanging belly, and Jerry wasn't much surprised when, with that curious, slow-motion grace often possessed by very fat men, he came around the acre of hood to open the ample rear passenger door and assisted Gabriel onto the sidewalk; a rather ponderous procedure of gathering Gabriel's frontal blubber and sort of pulling him out behind it.

The boy, at least could stand on his feet, though he had to lean drastically backward to balance the pendulous bulk of his belly which, due to his diminutive height cascaded to his knees, its twin-scalloped cavern of navel smiling down at the earth, as the chauffeur unloaded his chair from the vehicle's truck-sized trunk. Despite the grand coach in which he'd arrived, he was wearing an olive-drab Army poncho, which might have been purchased for twenty dollars at the surplus store in Alameda. The style of garment wasn't surprising -- Gabriel needed something that size -- but he certainly could have afforded much finer.

Jerry waited until the gigantic chauffeur had helped Gabriel to mount his machine before rolling off in the gigantic car, its exhaust pipe trailing a specter of steam, then emerged from the staircase shadow. "Good-morning, Mr. Graves."

He'd forgotten how startling the contrast between Gabriel's midnight moon of a face and the dazzling white of his smile.

"Good morning, Mr. Mathers. You can call me Gabe."

The boy's cheerfulness was infectious, but Jerry had serious things to say. Still, he offered a smile of his own and mocked a wary glance at the house. "That's not proper Morrison form."

"I understand, sir," said Gabriel without any teenage sarcasm. "But you can call me that at McDonalds."

"I'm afraid not in front of the other students."

"Well, then when we're alone. Convention is often stifling to one's better nature, don't you agree?"

93

Jerry pictured a sixteenth-century scene of master and apprentice at work... but who would be grinding pigments for whom? "I do, and thank you..." He mimed a stereotypical spy raising a clandestine cloak. "Gabe." Then he glanced at his watch; about fifteen minutes before school began. He could make his confession here, but that didn't seem appropriate. He dithered about the elevator... but surely she wouldn't.

"I'd like to see you before class, in my office if you wouldn't mind. ...It's about your drawing of Bill."

Gabriel looked mischievous. "The assignment *was* to draw him from life."

"It wasn't... that," said Jerry. He decided she wouldn't. ...Or maybe not yet. "The elevator is working today, why don't we use it and save a few minutes?"

Gabriel powered up, his tracks squelching over the puddled sidewalk as Jerry went to push the button. The cage descended flawlessly and Gabriel backed his machine inside. Jerry waited until full-insertion, then followed and closed the grille. As he'd expected there wasn't much room. Then he took a breath and pushed the 2 button. The machinery responded instantly, though it did seem a bit under stress and might have risen a little more slowly than he remembered last night.

As it climbed through the foyer he studied the portrait, dim in the glow of candle-shaped bulbs: Miss Morrison *seemed* her usual self... plump, prim and prudish like the old queen she resembled. Her eyes didn't *seem* to harbor a threat, though they did watch as the cage rose past... but perhaps just the skill of that long-dead artist.

Gabriel's husky voice startled him... he'd been listening to the mechanism, the motor hum, the creaking of cables, alert for any falter. "She must have been very lonely."

"I suppose she was," Jerry granted, though he felt no sympathy... not after what she'd done last night.

Gabriel's scent in the small space was strong, though there *was* a lot of him, but basically young adolescent boy... jeans and sneaks, musky male sweat, a not too surprising whiff of tobacco, and a seminal trace not unlike wet earth, proving that, like most normal

94

boys -- though, and probably naturally, Jerry wondered *how* -- he frequently committed that "sin."

Then, he wondered what would happen if he'd misjudged Miss Morrison's malice. A fall from the first floor might not hurt them -- Gabriel was surely well-padded and had a natural neck brace -- but they had passed the foyer. A fall from two was probably survivable...

He found himself holding his breath, a finger poised on EMER-GENCY STOP, as the polished boards of the second floor hall came into sight at eye-level, along with a lot of expensive footwear and views of students' designer-jeaned legs. He was on the verge of push-ing the button, and half afraid it might not work, when the cage creaked to a gentle stop, its floor and the hall's precisely aligned. Still, Jerry's hand trembled a bit as he quickly unlatched and opened the grille, letting Gabriel tractor out first.

"No offense, Mr. Mathers, but I'll take the stairs from now on."

"You're not... er, claustrophobic?" asked Jerry, feeling relieved on that score anyway.

Gabriel laughed. "Nah, I just like to show off."

Jerry smiled ironically. "You've heard of overcompensation?"

Gabriel laughed again. "For what?"

The students were vanishing into classrooms as Jerry opened his office door, ushering Gabriel inside and switching on the feeble lights. A glance at the floor by his desk revealed no trace of the "accident," though now he wished there was some proof should Gabriel have any doubts.

Gabriel paused to look around as Jerry strode past him to the desk and lay his portfolio, now dripping wet, atop the virginal blotter.

"You're a great artist, sir."

Jerry sat down in the hard wooden chair and turned on the Tiffany lamp. "Obviously not that great or I wouldn't have to be teaching here."

"But, don't you want to share what you know?" Gabriel waved a chubby hand at Jerry's works on the walls. "All your skill and know-ledge, sir."

"I thought that would be on my own terms."

"Man proposes, God disposes."

"I've noticed that," said Jerry, then asked, "Are you religious?"

Gabriel rolled up to the desk. "Not by the definition of most so-called religious people."

"I believe that's called agnostic, as I suppose I am myself."

Gabriel shrugged. "One shouldn't always give names to things; it pretends an understanding of what may yet be out of one's grasp." He noted the ashtray. "Mind if I smoke?"

Jerry regarded the boy, his bushy hair jeweled by raindrops that sparkled like gold in the dim yellow lights, and reminded himself of yesterday's lunch and Gabriel's marvelous knowledge of Art. Though it seemed incredible that in only thirteen years of life he could have amassed so much, why should it be surprising that he might be just as knowledgeable of other things as well? "I hadn't thought about it that way, but I'm inclined to agree. ...And no I don't mind."

Gabriel reached into one of his packs for a box of American Spirit Blue. He offered it to Jerry, who was tempted but declined in light of what he had to say. Gabriel fired a cigarette with an old-fashioned brass-cased Zippo, then, sounding, surprisingly, thirteen, pointed and asked, "Who's that?"

"My mother," said Jerry. "Some years ago."

"She looks very happy, you were a good kid."

"I'm sure I could have been better."

"You were only a kid. That's allowable."

"...Yes... well..." Jerry opened his portfolio and took out the folder with Gabriel's drawing. "I'm afraid there's been an accident... last night while I was grading the work."

He glanced at the inkstand -- the bottle had either been washed out or replaced with an empty one -- then handed the drawing to Gabriel. "I spilled my ink bottle on your work... it was full last night."

Instead of looking devastated, angry or accusing -- how would a young Rembrandt have felt if some cretinish clod had ruined his work? -- Gabriel simply shrugged again. "Shit happens."

"...Well, yes it does," said Jerry. "But your work was extremely good. ...Far beyond extremely good... masterful... and... really cool."

"And you fucked it up."

96

Jerry almost hung his head, then saw Gabriel's impish grin.

"Yes I did, and I am very sorry."

"No problem, and thanks for the praise." Again the boy looked mischievous. "Though one shouldn't overpraise gifted children."

"So I've heard, but I'm sure it won't spoil you."

Placing his cigarette in the ashtray, Gabriel wiggled out of his poncho with many a wobble and quiver of rolls, scattering golden water drops and baring the smile of his navel, his breasts half escaping his 'beater, then opened one of his packs again. Taking out a manila folder, he offered it to Jerry. "I did this last night. Maybe it could substitute for yesterday's assignment drawing?"

Well, Jerry thought, taking the folder, he had been right to picture Gabriel drawing from life last night. He expected another divine creation and wasn't disappointed: this, like Gabriel's other examples, was only a soft-lead pencil work, though just as real and full of life -- just as breathtakingly spirit-baring -- as his rendition of Bill. And just as serene as the sleeping old woman and the chubby slumbering boy.

This black boy was also asleep, but Gabriel had drawn him full-body, a perfect picture-negative of picture-perfect Bill Malone with every young muscle superbly defined, at rest on his back, arms at his sides, on the suggestion of maybe a sheet... though unlike Bill he was all the way naked.

Gabriel took up his cigarette. "I can add a cherub diaper if convention must be served. It'll only take a minute."

Jerry studied the beautiful boy in the golden glow of the lamp. Some would simply call him a thug, just another young black male corrupted by the inner city and maybe passed-out after too many "forties." Others might call him an African prince. ...Was Miss Morrison hovering near and glowering over his shoulder?

Of course he'd shown many nudes to his students, though they were defined as "Classic Art." But he'd never crossed that dangerous line, the American "decency" definition of G-strings and pasties on any body less than at least a few centuries old. Just as he was suspect for simply being who he was, the hypocritical witch-burning warlocks would surely brand him the damming "P-word" for showing kids on

97

paper what most had been seeing for years on screens.

On the other hand, he'd already decided this would be his last year in this place, so why not go out with a bang, so to speak?

Or, in a flash of clear light.

"That won't be necessary, Gabe."

# Chapter Thirteen

"**M**r. Mathers?"

Jerry had left his office door open, something he didn't normally do unless counseling an unstable student, but after last night he'd begun to feel his office wasn't really his. Of course on a literal level it wasn't, but coming in after class this morning he'd felt like a Dashiell Hammett detective whose office rent was long overdue and the landlord was lurking to throw him out.

Assuming he trusted his feelings, those basic survival instincts every child was born with, he'd been sensing a hovering malice like the feeling some people described -- an eerie hollowness in the air and tingling creeps down his spine -- before a lightning strike.

On an adult instinctive level he knew his precaution, not closing the door, was as futile as a five-year-old pulling a blanket over his face... as if that could protect him from anything able to rise from a grave. And if she could spill a bottle of ink, she could slam a door and jam its lock.

Then what? Appear as her moldering skeleton in hope that would scare him to death?

He certainly wasn't an expert on ghosts, having read mostly classic stories in musty old books from second-hand stores during his childhood and teenage years, including those by Henry James, William Hope Hodgson and Perceval Landon, but it seemed to be generally agreed that ghosts didn't have any godlike powers. She might be able to kill him by arranging an "accident," but she couldn't divinely "strike him dead." So, other than a heart-attack caused by some hideous apparition -- appearing as Princess Sparkle-Pony? --

what could she do to him in this room?

In his office after class, the morning's stack of student drawings on the desk before him, he'd thought about that for a while, then raised his eyes to the shadowy ceiling. The house still had its gas lights, and there was a cast-iron triple-globe fixture almost overhead. While it didn't look heavy enough to smash his skull if it somehow fell, Jerry had only assumed all these years that its piping had been disconnected.

And, if she could jam a door, she could jam the windows; and even if he broke the glass, could jam the fire ladder. He might not succumb to the gas itself if that fixture started to leak, but the electric sconces on the walls were notorious for shorting out, and often with a burst of sparks.

Gazing up at the light – kept clear of cobwebs by Elwood -- he'd realized, and with something like shame, that she wouldn't have to do anything if she kept the spectral pressure on, haunting him only with feelings of fear, hollowness and potential doom, which, combined with the hovering dread of both his mother's impending death and the seemingly lightless void of his future, would surely break him soon. He'd read Victorian stories of people haunted by hopelessness until they finally hung themselves -- the fixture looked strong enough for that -- or turned on a stove and "forgot" to light it.

He remembered a Tom Petty song: *The waiting is the hardest part.*

It was now almost noon and the rain had declined to a dreary drizzle, the light still depressingly gray through the windows, the ivy dripping monotonously with that lonely *what will become of me* chant like the haunting lay in *The Beckoning Fair One*; and though the house's radiators, thanks to Elwood's efficiency -- though surely the boiler was fired by gas and he wasn't shoveling coal in the basement -- seemed to be giving off heat, there was still a clammy grave damp in the air.

Or maybe just in this room.

He'd been grading the drawings. The model today had been Susan Treadwell in a two-piece bathing suit, who, in typical teenage American YouTube-watching awareness, was well aware she had something to show; and most of the boys had interpreted her to fit their adolescent illusions -- which were not surprisingly slutty, implying she was "asking for it" -- though Walter Wadsworth Wainwright III had added twenty pounds to her curves. The exceptions were Parker Foxworthy, who'd drawn a revolting young hag with not inconsiderable aptitude, which proved he'd done it deliberately — was he hating on girls, taunting the teacher, or showing off caricature skills? -- and of course Gabriel who'd simply drawn her as she *was*, a young girl sitting at a window dreaming, perhaps, her prince would come... and without any sophomoric pun implied.

Bill Malone had drawn Susan well... was there actually hope that, despite his handicap of perfection, he might want to create?

On the other hand, most of the girls had interpreted Susan as rather plain, minimizing her swells and curves, and therefore not competition. And, as with her drawing of Bill, there were specters of over-sexed Sparkle Ponies in Crystal Sterling's illusion.

In keeping with his resolve that he would make no more compromises during his final year, Jerry, after telling the class what had happened to Gabriel's work -- the version he'd given to Gabriel -- had projected Gabriel's African prince. Though Raymond and the Disruptor had tried to instigate snickers, most of the kids had looked artfully awed, several maybe even inspired... though some of their parents no doubt wouldn't be. And of course there were logical questions that if Gabriel's model had been nude...?

Jerry had answered honestly that Gabriel had drawn at home and, though it *was* hypocritical, the prudish rules of society had to be obeyed in school. However, he'd added -- while thinking, this *will* be my last year -- they were all free to draw at home in any way they wished.

He'd nailed his colors to the mast by offering extra credit.

Several students had snapped phone pictures, and Jerry was sure Tillinghast would be hearing parental outrage tomorrow.

As to Miss Morrison's possible vengeance for showing children a naked child, the waiting *was* the hardest part.

Now, he looked up from Amanda's drawing -- on the back of which he'd been adding advice along the lines of "she's not *that* skinny" -- to see a figure in the doorway. He'd been working in the lamp's pool of light, and the dimness of the room combined with the leaden gloom outside made the shape dark and indistinct like a "shadow man" on a *Ghost Hunters* show. The voice had been a woman's, and Jerry had the obvious thought, which sent a shiver down his spine... maybe wrongly he'd assumed she wouldn't show herself by day.

But the voice had been a younger woman's.

Still, he swallowed to make his voice work as if he *had* been called from the grave. "...Yes?"

"Sorry to disturb you."

*She* certainly wouldn't be sorry, and Jerry's tingle of fear passed away. His eyes adjusted and he saw a black woman, maybe in her middle-thirties. She was dressed boyishly in baggy but not ridiculous jeans, formidable sneaks and a black hoodie, the latter displaying no logo or name, either of team, designer or gang.

His next thought was, Gabriel's Mother? Which was natural in light of her darkness. But, Gabriel had a guardian, which, though perhaps chauvinistic, suggested a male to Jerry's mind.

"Not at all," he said, and rose to his feet. "Please come in."

Her figure in Victorian terms was classically voluptuous, bountifully-breasted and beautifully balanced, her face gently rounded and chubby-cheeked, her nose small-bridged though wide at the tip, with large and long-lashed obsidian eyes and full expressive lips. Her Nikes were as silent as cats, her weight not sufficient to wake the floorboards, as she strode in and offered a hand. "Angela Davis."

The name stirred childhood memories, though Jerry at first didn't recognize them. Then he remembered and took the warm hand. "Any relation?"

He hadn't expected brownie points for knowing that much about black history, then wondered if that was offensive, but Angela smiled.

"Not that I'm aware of, just a common black name in my youth."

Jerry ventured, "Like Malcolm and Huey for boys."

Angela didn't look grateful, and Jerry was grateful for that. "I'm the new Graphic Design teacher. Guess I must have missed you at the faculty introduction."

"I wasn't there this year," said Jerry. He hesitated, then added, "My mother's in a nursing home. She had a black spell that day." He instantly regretted that, but Angela only looked sad.

"I'm sorry."

Jerry forced a shrug. "'The moving finger writes...'"

"'And, having writ, moves on: nor all thy piety nor wit shall lure it back to cancel half a line, nor all thy tears wash out a word of it.'"

"Do you also teach Literature?" asked Jerry.

"Just a lot of eclectic knowledge. Reading wasn't encouraged in my family, it was required... and lots of it... before TV time."

"Wise parents," said Jerry.

"More like monsters when I was ten, though I'm grateful now. ...Sounds like you've read a lot."

"More like bored when I was ten, and cursed with a black-and-white TV. ...I'm sorry... Miss Davis? Please sit down."

"Thanks. It is Miss, despite that not being politically-correct, but 'Miz' makes me think of tight-ass dykes. But, Angela, please. And, if you don't mind..." Angela went to the radiator and held out her palms as if to a fire. "They don't seem to heat this old crypt very well."

"Jerry," said Jerry. "'Mr. Mathers' makes me think of who I never wanted to be."

His classroom had been warm enough for bathing-suited Susan... though some the boys had probably helped. "Might be just this room," he added," though it's been sufficiently heated for the last fifteen years."

"You've been here that long?" said Angela. "I didn't mean that negatively, it's just you don't look old enough."

Jerry smiled. "Thank you. But maybe it's the atmosphere; this house does seem to preserve things." Then he tried to look worldly-wise. "But a common fate for a suffering artist."

"I wouldn't have thought so," said Angela. "I saw your work in the school brochure, also in several galleries." She paused to look around at the paintings. "And these are masterful... obviously I mean your works, though you've certainly inspired your students."

"Thank you," said Jerry again. "But none I know of have ever taken that 'higher road,' most choosing the buying and selling of souls... usually including their own... to leave their mark, or stain, on the world."

"That's an artful way of putting it."

"Thank you again, and I'm still suffering."

"I'm sure your time will come."

"An artist often becomes recognized after he or she is conveniently dead and thus limits the market."

"I'm sure that won't be your fate... that wasn't an artful way to put it."

"I took it how it was meant."

"Is that your mother?"

"Yes, though some years ago."

"She looks very happy; she's proud of you."

"I could have been better."

"Couldn't we all. But we'll never know the road not taken, because we didn't take it."

"Assuming they don't all eventually lead to the same dead end."

Angela shrugged. "If we're trapped in a preordained universe then we might as well sell our souls, because we're going to anyway. That's why I'm not 'traditionally religious.'"

"Neither am I," said Jerry, thinking Angela's mode of dress, though looking quite attractive on her, was testing the traditional limits allowed for Morrison staff. "But I do believe, sometimes anyway, there is 'something else' beyond the grave, and it's not preordained."

Angela nodded. "Preordainment is inherent with most traditional western religions... God knows all, past, present and future; therefore He knew countless æons ago if I would be going to heaven or hell. Which makes that concept of God absurd, because no matter what I do He already knows if I'm dammed or not, so why should I choose to suffer... which really isn't a choice because He knew I was going to make it... by taking any higher road?"

"Unless we're supposed to be so stupid, and/or have so much faith in Him we never question that paradox."

Angela studied the paintings again. "All we suffer in this life should be for something we've earned beyond, because we chose a higher road of our own free will. A road God didn't know we would choose, and therefore didn't force us to choose it. ...Of course that may only be our conceit; we simply think we should be entitled."

"I confess," said Jerry.

"I also plead guilty." Angela shivered, her hands still outstretched, and Jerry asked:

"May I get you a cup of coffee? ...Or would you like a drink?"

"Is the latter permitted in these hallowed halls?"

"No, but it's sometimes required in the interest of maintaining sanity." Jerry took bottle and glasses out of a bottom drawer... no doubt Miss Morrison didn't approve.

Angela went to the door. "Guess I better close it. Those clocks are going to go off in a minute and the kids will be going to lunch."

Jerry glanced up at the gas light, then poured two fingers into each glass. "We're supposed to be setting inspiring examples."

Angela turned the skeleton key. "To kids who probably drink like fish from very well-stocked bars at home, when they're not smoking expensive weed or getting high on designer drugs."

"Or their parents' prescriptions, and fairly often their own," said Jerry, offering Angela a glass as she sat down in the plush velvet chair provided for students and visiting parents. He raised his glass. "Welcome to Morrison Academy, educators of the overprivileged."

Angela lifted hers. "Also the under-suffering. Though I will concede that suffering... at least the perception of suffering... can be relative."

"I'll drink to that... you've already noticed?"

Angela studied the paintings again. "I'm also still a suffering artist trying to earn my earthly reward. I've been doing sculpture since my teens, but Graphic Design is my 'real job.'" She sighed. "And has been for the last thirteen years."

"Really? You don't look old enough."

"Thank you." Angela patted her middle. "Maybe one of the benefits..."

"Probably also in my case."

"I was at Rutherford Hayes. At the feet of these lofty hills."

Jerry ventured, "You're movin' on up."

"Not the heights to which I'd hoped to ascend after I graduated Mills."

Jerry also sighed. "I know that feeling well." Then he had another thought. "Did you know a boy named Gabriel Graves? He attended Rutherford and was in seventh grade last year."

"I only taught eighth and above, but it isn't a very big school so I'm sure I would have seen him. What does he look like?"

It somehow seemed improper to mention Gabriel's color, though that would have been the logical first of any descriptive adjectives had Angela not been black. She apparently hadn't seen Gabriel here, which wasn't at all remarkable considering the mammoth labyrinth of house.

"...Well...he's fat," said Jerry. "Very fat. Rather amazingly fat for his age."

"And black?"

Jerry hoped he sounded clever. "Now that you mention it. But how did you know?"

Angela laughed. "You had that politically-correct look... a lot like constipation. All cats are only gray in the dark." She seemed to notice the cherub ashtray with its stub of Gabriel's cigarette. "Speaking of being politically-correct... or incorrect these days... do you mind if I smoke?"

"Not at all."

Angela reached in her hoodie pouch for a pack of American Spirit Blue -- Jerry wondered if it might be a "black thing" like Kools had been in his youth -- and offered it to Jerry. "Don't mean to tempt you if you're cutting down."

Jerry took a cigarette. "Purely for financial reasons. ...But how did you know?"

Angela pointed. "Despite that butt in the ashtray, there's no prevalent smell of smoke in this room, so you haven't been smoking a lot. You might have had a visitor who smoked, but these days most people who've never smoked wouldn't have allowed it... terrified of 'second-hand smoke.' Likewise, if you were going cold-turkey, because it would have tempted you. And, since there's only one butt

106

and we're halfway through the day, either there was a visitor and you weren't paranoid about it, or you're cutting down."

Jerry laughed. "A deduction worthy of Sherlock Holmes."

"One of my favorite reads." Angela fired a Bic, lighting Jerry's cigarette and another for herself. "'My experience has taught that a man with no vices has dammed few virtues.'"

"Abraham Lincoln," said Jerry.

"Very well-read indeed, sir." Angela thought for a moment. "We had quite a few fat kids at Rutherford despite all the current hate. But there was a black boy who was, as you said, rather amazingly fat for his age, which might have been him in seventh grade. I only saw him in the halls, but I heard he was an excellent student. ...Why do you ask?"

"If he is the same boy, I have him in my class this year, and he's an astonishing artist." Jerry offered Gabriel's drawing of Susan, then the sleeping African prince.

Angela mined her hoodie pouch for a pair of steel-framed glasses and settled them on her nose. "Wow!"

Jerry handed her the serene old woman.

"He is astonishing!"

"I've only seen pencil drawings so far, but he also paints; and I can't even begin to imagine how magnificent those must be." Before he could stop, Jerry added, "If I could have drawn like him at thirteen..."

Leaving her cigarette with the cherub, Angela studied the pictures. The Regulators began to chime, and the hallway flooded with bustling kids who seemed to be overcoming -- or maybe simply ignoring -- any instinctive fears of the house. From the sounds of their footsteps, many more than yesterday, maybe due to the inclement weather and lack of uncool rain gear, were opting for the Morrison lunch. Jerry wondered if Gabriel, well-waterproofed in his Army poncho, was going with blue-jean-jacketed Bill to keep their postponed lunch date at McDonalds.

Angela took up her cigarette. "If I could have created like him at thirteen! ...And he must be the same boy. I heard he put our Art teacher to shame, though she wasn't far off to begin with."

"Your typical 'them who can't do...?'" asked Jerry.

"To the extreme. If I'd been her I would have resigned so they could have hired a real artist and crawled away to a public school." Angela laughed. "Or stuck my head in an oven."

Jerry looked up at the gas light again, hesitated, and finally said, "I admit I feel threatened."

"I do, too. And I'm not even his teacher."

Jerry sipped his scotch. "I suppose that's normal human conceit: don't I deserve something for years of suffering, while you..." He looked up at the ceiling. "Whoever you are... grant a mere boy..."

Then he felt ashamed. "Though I know it wasn't as hard as yours."

"Don't be so sure." Angela took a sip from her glass. "I didn't 'come up in the 'hood.' My family is staidly middle-class, and has been for two generations. My father owns rental properties, and isn't extremely slum-lordish; and a lot of my suffering has been, if I may presume, self-imposed like yours."

"Then, if I may presume, you've also thought about giving up?"

"And sticking my head in an oven."

"Thank you," said Jerry. "But, why Graphic Design? Surely you're qualified to teach Art, and far above Morrison's level."

"I've sold a few of my works through the years, but my parents insisted I major in something that guaranteed a 'real' income. And, to play the race card, it is harder for black artists."

"I'm sure it is... and for most other things as well."

"Thank you." Angela studied the drawings again. "But Gabriel will overcome... though it's good this place has an elevator, I can't imagine him climbing stairs."

Jerry considered mentioning Gabriel's mode of mobility, acquired or required this summer, but that didn't seem necessary.

Angela returned the drawings. "*We* may have some ego to overcome, as in feeling inspired instead of threatened. And, as one artist to another, we both feel like we've suffered enough, so where the hell is our piece of pie?"

Jerry smiled. "Most artfully put."

Angela held out her glass. "But, we're not giving up, are we?"

Jerry clinked his glass to hers. "To future fame and fortune."

"Have you ever used it?"

"...What?"

"The gas light, you keep looking at it."

"...Oh. I don't even know if it works."

"There's one in my office, too." Angela downed the last of her drink. "The lighting sucks in this mausoleum, but I don't think those would enlighten much."

"Probably not," said Jerry, and also finished his scotch. As with Gabriel yesterday, he suddenly felt thirteen again and actually said, "*Um*, Angela?" before, "would you like to go to out to lunch?"

Besides being reckless, if that was the word, it was also completely impractical: between the nursing home expenses, utility bills, gas for the car -- and surely his mother's funeral insurance would not fully cover the cherub tombstone -- even last night's burger and fries, not to mention breakfast this morning, had been a gross extravagance. He'd been planning to live on Morrison lunches until his mother... was gone.

Still, he heard himself saying, "There's a fairly decent cafe nearby. If you wouldn't mind..."

He'd almost said, being seen with a white guy, but finished with: "being seen in a 1976 Gremlin."

Again he felt like a teen, but now in his first school year without Trevor, asking a girl to lunch at McDonalds... and being refused with those soul-smashing words, *You're a nice boy, Jerry, but...*

Angela smiled. "That's your car? It's very cool. Rather Bohemian, actually."

"Most people don't seem to think so."

"Most people in general don't think."

"What do you drive?"

Angela snuffed her cigarette in the cherub's bowl. "I had an old Honda Civic until gas went over four dollars a gallon. This year it's BART to Rockridge, then a bus up here. ...But, as one hungry artist to another, are we going to pass up a free lunch?"

Jerry's face must have fallen as he thought of the stuffy teacher's lounge brimming with Babylonian babble, everyone speaking their

109

own tongue of shop, because Angela added:

"We could eat in my office, it's warmer than this one. And I could show you some of my work."

"I'd like that very much," said Jerry.

# Chapter Fourteen

"**M**r. Mathers?"

He'd opened his office door again, though a rising wind, bringing more rain and moaning far above in the tower, seemed to be causing a draft in the hall, which had made it keep swinging unnervingly shut, its lock clicking ominously, until he'd chocked it with a box of art pencils.

Lunch with Angela Davis had resurrected a part of himself he'd thought he'd buried in high school, and there had been many "Gabriel moments" when, if not actually being thirteen, he'd at least forgotten the present long enough to live in it. Angela's office was similar to his, though its radiator was pleasantly warm, but was located in the rear of the house overlooking the vine-covered crypt. What might have been an obvious thought – "racially responsible?" -- had crossed his mind for a moment, but the former teacher in Angela's field had also been domiciled here next door to the Drama instructor, a fair-haired blue-eyed Teuton and one of Morrison's most successful claims to professional fame.

Angela had remarked, "Cheerful view," as Jerry had gone to the window and peered though its ivy shroud. "That open door is creepy."

The mansion's back yard had been deserted, its fauns and cherubs glistening with rain, except for two boys, one the Disruptor, smoking something under a tree.

"A Victorian custom," Jerry had said. "In case someone was buried alive… they made mistakes in those days... I assume so any screams could be heard emanating from the coffin."

Angela, sitting down at her desk -- which like Jerry's was a claw-footed monster equipped with a blotter, ink bottle and pen, a bronze ashtray of a fat little faun, and a daffodil Tiffany lamp -- had asked, "Do you believe in ghosts?"

The question was unexpected, though probably shouldn't have been in light of the present topic, and Jerry, after considering whether or not to commit himself, had finally answered, "Yes."

Which had naturally prompted, "Do you?"

Today's *entrée* was poached salmon, its white wine sauce aromatically tempting, with golden *pommes frites* on the side as a nod to juvenile appetites; and being starving artists, both had loaded their china plates, which Angela had arranged on her desk with proper cloth napkins, genuine silver, glasses of milk and cups of coffee.

"I suppose I do, though I've never seen one." Angela indicated the chair, another wine-red velvet antique provided for students and visitors, which Jerry drew up to the desk. She'd added as he'd seated himself, "I presume this house is haunted?"

"You've heard the rumors?"

"No, but Tillinghast warned me I might, and to pay no attention to them. 'Nor to further propagate them.'" Angela had laughed. "But a house like this *should* be haunted; it certainly looks like spook central." She'd picked up her fork. "Don't be so gentlemanly... eat. I'm sure you're as hungry as I am... and this food is delicious. Are doggie-bags are available?"

"I've never asked," Jerry had said, starting on his salmon and resisting the urge to shovel. "Though there must be leftovers since a lot of the kids go to McDonalds."

"Must be nice to have money."

"I take it you don't live at home?"

"Logical progression of thought. I have the requisite leaky old loft. At least until gentrification raises the rent much higher. ...You?"

"I have my mother's house... now. There... isn't much chance she'll be coming home."

"I'm sorry."

Jerry had feigned a gallant shrug. "No one gets out of this life alive." Then he'd looked up at the gas light, a twin to the one in his office.

Angela had followed his eyes. "Something I should know?"

"...Well... assuming you think I'm halfway sane, I'd say this house is definitely haunted."

Despite her admitted belief in ghosts, he'd almost expected her to laugh, but instead she had only looked thoughtful. "Neither of us is sane by this society's definition, but you don't seem like a hatter. Is it... he or she... somehow connected to those lights? 'The gaslight ghost' sounds Victorian."

"She," Jerry had said

"Miss Morrison, I presume? Her bones are in that crypt, I've been told, and judging from her portrait she ought to be able to haunt a whole graveyard."

"I also presume," Jerry had said. "Though I've never met her in sheet-shrouded person." He'd glanced up again. "But, as for the lights, I'm not sure they're connected... I mean to pipes or something."

He'd lain down his fork and considered: as he'd thought that morning, assuming he trusted his instincts, he knew *something* here was malicious -- or, perhaps more accurately, a malice had been awakened because of Gabriel -- but, except for the ink bottle spilling, how many of the other "attacks" -- the elevator failing, the lights going out in his office – could have been merely coincidence in an ancient house with antique wiring? And, how many of his ominous feelings were simply due to fatigue and stress?

He'd read that "manifestations" required a lot of ghostly power -- ectoplasm or something -- and a ghost had to gather it somehow -- charge their battery, so to speak -- before doing anything physical. Maybe she didn't have much power? A spectral touch on a sheet of paper? ...And maybe he *had* moved the bottle and made it easy for her? So maybe she *could* only haunt him with fear... unless he made it easy for her?

He'd finally said he had no material proof of anything immaterial, and Angela had looked thoughtful again.

"You'd warn me of anything really scary."

"Of course."

She had smiled. "That wasn't a question."

113

"...Oh. Thank you."

"But I assume it's more than what's called a residual haunting? I might expect a little more fright than simply sighting her shrouded bones while making my way through her ill-lighted halls?"

Jerry had wanted to say she probably wouldn't be bothered as long as she...

Stayed in her place... remained a mere servant like Elwood.

Or until she befriended Gabriel... which of course she would.

But that would have brought up the color issue and he wasn't comfortable with that.

Instead he'd only repeated that he didn't have any actual proof and, due to his present state of mind, his testimony might be suspect. Angela seemed to understand, and they'd finished their delicious lunch discussing, naturally, Art. She had only brought a few small examples to decorate her office... parents being more impressed by sellable skills she could teach their young. She was really quite accomplished in drawing from life in stone, so to speak -- or, as Michelangelo had said, freeing the souls within -- and Jerry had thought of the cherub carver. Indeed, she had done a boy and girl, both cherubically chubby, in a classic pose of an innocent kiss. Her subjects were mostly African, which she admitted matter-of-factly, made them harder to sell.

The wind had risen as they'd talked, the ivy writhing against the windows as raindrops rattled the glass, and Jerry had heard himself offering -- so she wouldn't have to walk in the rain -- perhaps a ride home after school?

Angela had hesitated, and at first he'd thought he'd gone too far, though his intentions were honorable. Then she had smiled and thanked him but said her loft was in West Oakland, a considerable drive from his part of town, and with the price of gas today she couldn't impose on him.

It didn't sound like a put-off -- though he wasn't sure of what -- and he really couldn't afford the fuel despite the Gremlin's small appetite, but he'd offered a ride to the Rockridge BART so she could be spared the wait for a bus, which she had accepted, and which had raised his spirit in a boyish way.

114

However, after they'd parted -- she remaining in her office to grade her students' work -- a call to the nursing home had brought him depressingly down. His mother, according to Harriet, "had not been at her best today," and she had suggested an evening visit, "when her spirit might be stronger," so Jerry had returned to his office to finish grading the drawings.

Strangely, or maybe not, combined with the eerily closing door -- at least until he'd chocked it -- the old gas light distracted him like something hovering over his head. *Was* it still connected? He could have asked Elwood, of course, though he hadn't seen him all day... probably tending the boiler.

It was now near the end of last period approaching three o'clock, the light an even gloomier gray beyond the rain-rippled windows, the ivy rustling like things wanting in; and Parker Foxworthy stood in the doorway. For a moment Jerry thought of *Psycho* and Norman appearing in the fruit cellar dressed as his mother with knife in hand.

Of course he'd known this time would come, but Parker had started weaving his web sooner than any previous peer. Though he'd been draped in a hoodie this morning, he'd lost it revealing a white T-shirt way too small like a little kid's, its sleeves riding almost up to his shoulders, its fabric straining across his breasts, that couldn't cover the rolls of his waist above suggestively low-slipping jeans, the soft shapeless spill of his twin-scalloped belly lolling loosely over in front. He didn't seem to be wearing shorts, the top of his bottom blatantly bare; and doubtless he'd purposely planned to come when it didn't seem likely he'd be interrupted.

Despite all his years of experience, every encounter was a first, and Jerry kept his voice neutral: "Yes, Mr. Foxworthy?"

"I need to see you, sir."

*Of course you do*, thought Jerry. "Come in..."

He was going to add, "Don't close the door," but Parker out-maneuvered him, spotting the box of pencils, clearing it with the toe of a sneak, and shutting the door behind him, the click of its lock sounding dramatic above the drumming rattle of rain and moaning wind in the tower. Jerry could have commanded it open, but that might interpret as fear and give the boy an illusion of power... which

115

might not be illusionary if Jerry wasn't careful.

Parker advanced with sway-backed posture, his belly like Jell-O contained within skin jiggling and jouncing with every step, a shamefully out of shape marshmallow boy by currently dictated health-nazi hype, but dangerous as a Gestapo thug. "I wanted to see you in private, sir." He showed his big teeth innocently like a tiger trying for harmlessly charming, his long hair coquettishly hiding an eye. "I'm a little shy."

*A little something, anyway.* "Please sit down, Mr. Foxworthy."

"You can call me Parker."

"That's not proper Morrison form." Jerry indicated the chair before the boy got any closer... like raising a cross to a stalking vampire. He could have turned on his computer cam to record whatever might be afoot, but that could be a double-edged sword. And he knew enough about computers to suspect that nothing on Morrison's web was actually deletable. The 21st century memory hole.

Parker theatrically yawned and stretched, which made his jeans slip even lower so part of his pudgy pudendum peeked below his belly scallops like an impending Kilroy Was Here, and he flicked a glance to the mirror to see how he was doing. "Sorry, Mr. Mathers. Didn't sleep very good last night."

*We have that much in common.* Jerry made a smile. "Only a few minutes left, then you can go home and take a nap."

Parker subsided onto velvet, his baby-chub arms draped over the chair's and dangling limply down, his legs splayed indolently wide displaying the soles of moon-boot sneaks which hadn't seen much wear. "I was thinking about your class... like I said, I'm a little shy."

*One would never imagine.* "I assume you mean about modeling?" Jerry said in a casual tone. "But, as I told the class yesterday, no one is compelled to model."

"But I want to, sir." Parker spread his arms. "I just don't think I'm very good-looking." Then he said in a little-boy voice. "Maybe I need reassurance from somebody older like you."

No doubt he'd rehearsed this in front of his mirror, on his feet and shirtless in seconds, revealing his softly androgynous self all peaches-and-cream in the Tiffany light, his breasts bursting almost

116

explosively free as he tugged the T-shirt over his head, and all the more opulent bobbling out bare, their "innie" nipples so pale a pink as to be almost indiscernible, which gave him a somehow unfinished appearance as if an uncompleted creation whose artist was still undecided. It occurred to Jerry as Parker's hair tumbled back down to smother his shoulders that Parker might be an hermaphrodite in the actual physical sense instead of just an indolent boy with overly prosperous pectoral pudge. He also found himself wondering -- and not without a hint of humor despite the serious situation -- if, that being the case, which of Parker's pair of aspects – disregarding the obvious pun -- Parker had hoped would be most alluring. Or maybe he thought he had both bases covered. But it wasn't his sex -- whatever that was -- that made him a plutonium peril.

And this was the most perilous moment, not only for Jerry but also for Parker... who was, after all, just a fragile young boy who Jerry might irreparably damage with only some ill-chosen words. And Jerry had fucked this up before with vulnerable youth of either sex, saving himself like a coward by throwing them, wounded, to the wolves.

Instead of snapping to put his shirt on, Jerry honestly looked at the boy the way he'd appraise any subject... a model, perhaps, for a young Dionysus decadent and dissolute. It came to him that, at thirteen himself, he *would* have found Parker alluring if maybe just in a physical sense, perhaps like Hermine in *Steppenwolf*... and probably very confusing.

And, to be confused at thirteen was also being threatened.

Parker, of course, was holding his breath, even if not literally. Although he'd surely rehearsed his show, he was clueless to what might happen next, and certainly a little scared: no doubt he'd watched many versions of this on a computer screen – "cute young twink with old professor" -- and Jerry felt a terrible power of knowing he *could* damage this boy. ...Just as he could have damaged Amanda by calling her a neurotic nut whose suffering was all in her mind -- and just as he might damage Crystal -- if he didn't see their souls and metaphorically draw them from life.

After a moment of looking at Parker, who stood in an unconvincing pose *enfant sauvage* defiance, and letting him know he was

117

being seen, Jerry said, "You're a very handsome young man, and any artist worthy of name would be honored to have you model."

Parker looked childishly confused -- genuinely this time -- and looked down at himself. "You really think so?"

"Yes, Mr. Foxworthy."

"You don't think I'm too fat?"

*Oh please not you, too!* This culture so horribly fucked-up its kids! "Everyone is beautiful in their own shape, color or size, if one has the empathy to see it." Jerry indicated the mirror. "And that includes seeing yourself."

Parker faced himself in the mirror, and Jerry added, "You have been nominated to model."

"...Yeah, but by a girl."

"Which I would take as a compliment, since she probably knows she hasn't a hope of seeing this much of you anywhere else."

Parker considered that while considering himself. "Um... think Bill would like to draw me?"

"I'm sure he would. And he seems to have a perceptive eye."

"Yeah, he's a pretty good drawer. ...Um, what about Gabriel?"

"I'm sure he'll see your soul." *And probably already has.*

Parker turned back to face Jerry. "Sometimes I don't think I'm a very good person... like, the soul part, I mean."

"We all have room for improvement," said Jerry, "especially the soul part. Which, trust me, Mr. Foxworthy, is much easier at your age."

"...I think I know what you're sayin'. ...I coulda drawn Susan better today."

"You have considerable skill; and I'm sure you will in the future. And all your other subjects as well... if you will look for the soul inside and see it through the eyes of your own."

Parker seemed to come back from somewhere, though as Jerry had hoped, didn't seem shamed or embarrassed while crossing his arms over his chest and shivering a little. "Kinda cold in here."

"Yes it is," said Jerry. He glanced at the radiator. "It doesn't seem to be working."

Parker put his shirt back on. "Thanks, Mr. Mathers."

Jerry smiled. "Thank you for your modeling preview. See you tomorrow morning."

"Who's gonna be the model?"

"A male, since we alternate. And I'm sure everyone will be very pleased if you volunteer." *Except Raymond Blakemore, because you scare the shit out of him.* "And remember, boxers or swim wear."

"Yeah, I was in a hurry this morning." Parker hoisted his jeans and went to the door... which easily opened. "See you, Mr. Mathers."

"Have a good evening, Mr. Foxworthy. And I hope you sleep well tonight."

"Thanks. Want me to leave the door open?"

"Please."

# Chapter Fifteen

Well, Jerry thought, as Parker's footsteps padded away, one less threat to worry about; and maybe he'd even helped save a soul. Or at least shown one a better road. He raised his eyes to the gas light again and challenged as if he'd been thirteen: "Shove that up your shriveled old cunt!"

So, what was next on his avatar list -- besides protecting Gabriel -- convincing Amanda she wasn't "obese?" Exorcising Sparkle Ponies from Crystal Sterling's batty brain? Ridding Raymond of his demons? A lot to ask of a teacher of Art who may have been on the wrong road himself.

*That fucking light! He had to know!*

The tap, he'd noticed years ago, was on the wall beside the door just above the wainscot, an ornate brass knob in a plaster rosette. He got up and crossed the room, and found it couldn't be turned... at least not with his fingers. In his desk was a pair of pliers, part of a set his mother had bought him when he'd been thirteen, "because men should have tools."

At first the knob only seemed to bend when he applied the pliers, but then it finally turned. Looking up at the light, he listened for a hissing sound... but that would have been hard to hear with the rattling rain and moaning wind. Of course, if the piping was still connected, he would smell gas eventually, but maybe it wasn't safe to wait.

He dithered for a moment, almost turning off the tap, then pocketed the pliers and climbed atop his desk. This put him eye-level to the fixture's globes... and, yes, there was a hissing and the rotten smell of gas.

120

At thirteen he would have leaped, flying halfway across the room, but he got rather clumsily down, yanked out the pliers and ran to the tap... but the knob snapped off when he tried to turn it!

Then there was a gust of wind... and the door slammed shut!

He stood paralyzed for a second, another icy skeleton finger running down his spine, then with a nightmarish shudder, grabbed the doorknob... which came off in his hand!

"This is not happening!" he yelled stupidly. For a moment he almost screamed for help -- the house was still full of living people -- but maybe it was a "man thing," simply not wanting to look like a fool. Or a scared little boy.

"Don't panic," he said. "Not yet, anyway."

His Cub Scout knife had a screwdriver blade so he could put the doorknob back on, but he could smell gas at floor level now, though it probably wasn't dangerous yet... as when his mother had scolded him for forgetting to turn off a stove tap and had opened the windows to air out the kitchen.

Dropping the doorknob, he ran to a window... but it wouldn't open!

*The rain, idiot! The frame is swollen!*

He almost grabbed the desk chair to hurl it through the glass, but again he fought down panic. *Light the fucking light, fool!*

But, he hadn't carried matches since he'd stopped buying cigarettes!

Again he almost screamed for help, but then remembered his lighter. Yanking open a drawer, he grabbed it and scrambled back on the desk.

The lighter was empty! He tried to spark it to light the gas, but the wheel broke off and flew away!

"Mr. Mathers?"

Elwood stood in the now open doorway.

"The tap's broken! I can't shut it off!"

Far from looking alarmed, Elwood said in a fatherly tone, "Best get down from there, Mr. Mathers, before you fall and hurt yourself."

"...But...!"

Elwood calmly went to the closet and took out what looked like a walking stick, about four feet long with a heavy brass tip. Pulling a wooden match from a pocket, he struck it on his coveralls leg and lit what appeared to be a wick in the tip of the shaft. He smiled a little, raising the "cane" and lighting each of the three glass globes, which flared with pale-blossomed whuffs. "That's the way it was done, Mr. Mathers, we didn't climb on the furniture."

# Chapter Sixteen

Raymond scowled. "Do I gotta draw *him?*"

Jerry glanced up from his classroom desk as Parker Fox-worthy in silver silk boxers mounted the blue velvet modeling cube to lazily lounge uniquely himself, one eye coyly concealed by his hair, in the kind of immaculate light that often followed a rain. Most of the students seemed intrigued by Parker's softly androgynous shape, males and females regarding his breasts with expressions ranging from interest to envy, a couple of boys maybe aroused -- and whether or not they wanted to be -- at the sight of something seen on screens but otherwise probably only in dreams requiring the changing of sheets in the morning, but now lolling lushly in fully-fleshed life and apparently free to appreciate without any shame or secretiveness.

Several gave Raymond curious looks as if wondering why he'd want to pass up this Art-sanctioned opportunity; Bill Malone looked princely displeased by Raymond's uncouthness; and Jerry said, "No, Mr. Blakemore," while thinking, *you're giving yourself away*, "you're not compelled to draw anyone." He broke another butterfly, drawing snickers and giggles. "You're not even compelled to be in this class."

Then Parker brought the house down by grinning Raymond a tigerish, "Grrr."

Raymond's cheeks flushed, but seeing that the Disruptor wasn't going to take his back -- and might be a little suspicious -- grudgingly took up his pencil. Bill moved to a desk closer to Parker, demonstrating there was nothing to fear; other students began to draw; and Gabriel tractored, the floorboards creaking, to find his own perspective.

123

Jerry also took up a pencil while wondering, as he had yesterday, what would be the consequences should Gabriel prove too much for the floor... assuming Miss Morrison wanted to prove it.

He still hadn't formulated a plan of how he was going protect Gabriel from any possible "accidents," or even how to warn him without seeming mad as a March Hare... though didn't black people in general tend to believe in ghosts? He obviously couldn't be with the boy during his other five classes, or when he was out in the halls; though Bill Malone, enigmatically, seemed to have become his aide, or maybe simply his friend. There had been jokes in the teacher's lounge of "the white boy making restitution." Walter Wadsworth Wainwright III had also befriended Gabriel, and both had been waiting for him this morning at the foot of the staircase... assuming they could be any protection from possible malice beyond the grave.

That reminded him of the gas light adventure. Had it been another warning? Or simply a few coincidences, all perfectly normal in such an old house? Plastic lighters did often break; and he'd been the one who'd turned on the tap... and it seemed paranoiac to wonder if Miss Morrison had somehow made him do it.

Elwood hadn't seemed upset, though Jerry's "curiosity" had meant extra work for him... Jerry had found a new antique valve had been installed this morning. Elwood had even seemed pleased that Jerry was interested in such things -- though of course Jerry hadn't said why -- and had boasted that all the gas lights worked, and had been very useful after the earthquake of 1989.

Jerry had only been fifteen then, his second year of life without Trevor, their communications having dwindled to short and very infrequent letters, sophomorically smutty birthday cards, and their annual Christmas call. Trevor, of course, had made new friends though was tactful enough to not give many details and always say he really missed Jerry.

It had been a year later when Trevor had lost his virginity, which had rated a letter... assuming they both hadn't lost it with each other at age thirteen. It had taken three months of boyish bumbles and childish conniving, several humiliating rejections and an almost broken heart for Jerry to even the score; though by his twenties he'd realized there had been no need to match Trevor then... or "now" by marrying anyone. Their paths had divulged in a wood, so to speak, and their roads to the future were not parallel.

Elwood had instructed him in the use of the "igniter" -- a kerosene wick on the tip of the "cane" -- of which most rooms in the house were equipped, though were discreetly concealed, being only common things, and suggested that Jerry keep matches on hand.

Jerry had expected a scolding -- proper though it would have been -- and had felt relieved by Elwood's indulgence as well as emboldened enough to ask why the elevator was sometimes on the third floor. Elwood had only said, "Maybe a relay sticking." Then he'd repeated what he'd told Jerry many years before, that "nothing was up there but shadows and dust." He'd added that the only reason the elevator went that high was during the time it had been installed the Administrator, thinking of profit -- or possibly how to offset the expense -- had considered enlarging the school. However, the cost of refurbishing the house's empty upper floor and complying with State regulations, which would have required a sprinkler system, besides "disturbing the peace up there," would have been too expensive.

The Regulators had sounded during their conversation and the house had quickly emptied of students and more than a few of the staff. Then there had been a creaking of boards and the rhythmic padding of rubber tracks as Gabriel rumbled up the hall. Jerry had mentioned his concerns about the ancient timbers and possibly the staircase, but Elwood said Gabriel was safe.

Gabriel had appeared in the doorway with Angela behind him, and Elwood had smiled -- maybe as one black person to others in a white environment -- then, handing the "ignitor" to Jerry, had bid a polite farewell to all. Angela had sought Gabriel out -- he *had* been the boy at Rutherford -- and Gabriel, being Gabriel, had invited them both to McDonalds for an after-school snack as if they were peers.

And, Jerry conceded, on an artistic level they were.

Still, it had seemed a little surreal to ride in Gabriel's huge black car chauffeured by the enormous black man -- who may have been his guardian because Gabriel introduced him as James, and without

125

any irony -- then to be treated to burgers and fries, Cokes and strawberry sundaes, which they had accepted graciously despite their ample lunch. James had remained in the car, its original tube-type radio tuned to an oldies AM station like a ghost from Jerry's past, playing, somehow appropriately, *Don't Fear The Reaper* by Blue Oyster Cult, though Gabriel tractored him out a tray of Double Quarter-Pounders with cheese. Jerry had the impression he'd met James before, though couldn't remember where or when.

Of course the topic of conversation over the meal had been Art, and Jerry had been amazed again despite his previous encounter; while Angela seemed astounded and had said, sounding only partly in jest, after being chauffeured to Jerry's Gremlin -- a long step down from the old limousine -- she did feel a little threatened.

To which he'd replied, only partly in jest, while waiting for the car to warm up and wiping steam from the windshield with his mother's trusty "anti-fog" cloth ("not sold in stores") that, at least so far as he knew, Gabriel didn't do sculpture.

Then he'd looked up at the looming old house and noticed the tower window curtains were slightly parted again.

Driving down from the foothills, the rain thrumming loud on the Gremlin's roof, the wipers streaking the windshield a little – probably needed new blades, though he dreaded having to ask for them at an auto-parts store and admitting what kind of car they were for -- he'd ventured a cautious preamble about Miss Morrison's possible ghost and – assuming it might exist -- its evident malice toward Gabriel, the first black youth to enroll in her school.

"And," Angela had added, "to enter her house as an equal."

Aside from the issue of race, which made Jerry uncomfortable, there was the added discomfiture of speaking of ghosts on the assumption that one -- Miss Morrison, he presumed -- could do any physical harm. Even if his gas light encounter *had* been a series of accidents, there was the elevator malfunction occurring on Gabriel's first day of school and which, though quite excusable, had made him late for class; and, if not for his mighty machine, would have shown him dependent upon the lift... which, although required by law, might have become unreliable, and which, if needing frequent re-

126

pairs, would make him a liability. Tillinghast might have been able to say the school was complying with regulations but Gabriel was too obese for the lift. Was the school expected to bear his weight, both legally and physically, by making expensive accommodations above and beyond the letter of law?

Which might have brought up other questions; such as if a boy so fat could use the fire escapes? Which might have created a legal question, if Gabriel simply being fat entitled him to equal rights... including attending Morrison?

Angela had asked if most people wouldn't simply assume that Gabriel had gotten that fat because of being immobile, not the opposite, so to speak, and therefore *was* entitled to all his rights under the law?

Jerry replied he'd thought so, too, until enlightened at lunch the first day; but Gabriel didn't keep it a secret he'd gotten too fat to walk – at least, as he'd said, very far -- he'd likely told Bill, and possibly Walter. And he'd surely made friends in other classes, so word would eventually reach Tillinghast. However, that point seemed presently moot since Gabriel wouldn't use the lift, which had thwarted – assuming there had been -- any paranormal plan to prove him dependent upon it. And Elwood apparently seemed to think the house, at least physically, would bear him.

And, granting that a coincidence, Jerry had said while rounding a curve through a grove of rain-glistened redwoods, what about the ink bottle and only Gabriel's drawing destroyed?

He'd explained that occurrence in detail, stressing the absence of breeze that night and the fact that the bottle had been unopened for possibly a hundred years.

Angela had asked: could there have been someone else in the house... somebody with their skin still on?

To which Jerry admitted, excepting Elwood, he didn't know. The last living person he'd seen before going to McDonalds was Tillinghast leaving around four o'clock.

Angela had said, "*Presumably* leaving."

...Well... Jerry couldn't be *sure* he'd left.

Angela had said that he probably snooped in offices: someone certainly snooped in hers.

Jerry had never considered that when finding things in his office disturbed, attributing it to Elwood's cleaning, and agreed point-by-point with Angela that Tillinghast might not have left, may have come in while he'd been out, could have dropped Gabriel's drawing, and possibly upset the ink. ...But that bottle had been securely capped.

But, Angela had returned, did he really know that? Had he ever tried to open it?

...Well... no. ...But, if it hadn't been tightly capped, surely the ink would have dried up.

Angela had steepled her fingers, inclining her head in thought and touching the tip of her nose. But, was it the *same* bottle of ink that had been on his desk all those years? Miss Morrison's will, apparently, required the house to be preserved as a functional relic, so maybe the bottles were replaced every year? Who would know, since nobody used them? Or maybe Elwood revived them by adding a little water? So, the cap may have been loose.

Possibly, Jerry admitted, as they'd tunneled under a last grove of trees.

Then Angela had asked why Elwood seemed beyond Jerry's suspicion? Simply because he was black?

That made Jerry squirm a bit; but Angela didn't know of Elwood's family history, so he'd told her what he'd heard.

She had considered that for a time, thoughtfully wiping steam from the windshield and clearing a defroster duct of one of Jerry's pencils, then had said:

"Math wasn't one of my shining subjects, but it seems a lot more probable that it was Elwood's *grandfather* who did Miss Morrison's gardening, and his *father* may have been a boy then. Even granting that Elwood could have been born in ... say 1900 to keep it simple math... while Minerva was still alive, that would make him a hundred-and-thirteen today. Possible, but improbable. And he doesn't look much over seventy."

Jerry had asked, "But, don't black people age well?"

Angela had laughed. "'Black don't crack?' I find myself hoping so these days." Then her face had turned serious. "And sometimes if we're lucky... you heard about that boy last week? Only thirteen, shot and killed by a BART cop who claimed the boy went for a gun, but all he had was a phone."

Jerry had shaken his head. "I haven't been listening to news very much... too many other things on my mind. ...I suppose the cop will get away with it. I remember a few years ago a BART cop claimed that he'd 'accidentally' pulled his gun instead of his Taser and killed a black man."

"Probably." Angela had looked resigned. "But aging *that* well, I don't think so. If we accepted the story and defined a 'boy' as at least being five... old enough to do useful work like helping his father garden... that would make him a hundred-and-eighteen today. Still possible, but improbable to very highly unlikely degree." She had laughed again. "No matter how well that house 'preserves things.'"

Then she'd looked thoughtful once more. "But I understand what you're saying about him serving the house. He probably feels like a part of it now. But, assuming he isn't an Uncle Tom..."

She had paused, and Jerry had nodded.

"He would be proud of Gabriel for crossing Morrison's color line. Also very protective, though probably in subtle ways that most white folks wouldn't notice. ...No offense."

Jerry had stopped for a red light. "None taken, and I understand."

"But we still can't eliminate Elwood as a living spiller. ...Have you read the *Borrower* books?"

"All of them, and I know the allusion."

"So, suppose he spilled the ink? He'd feel like a black man on Rosa Parks' bus who'd spilled a box of tacks on her seat."

"I guess he would," Jerry had said.

"And, despite his integrity, that would be hard to admit. ...And you didn't *ask* if he did it, afraid of affronting his dignity. ...'The terrible protective dignity of the negro.'"

"John Steinbeck, *Of Mice And Men*." Jerry had nodded. "I understand."

"You seem more disturbed that he might have done it and not admitted it to you, than Tillinghast did it and won't man-up."

129

"Tillinghast wouldn't feel obligated... *his* school, *his* office, even his ink. ...Of course he wouldn't have done it on *purpose.*"

Angela had looked wry. "That might have been too obvious. Tampering with elevator so Gabriel couldn't use it would be more his style. ...How much do you want to see, Jerry?"

An ancient rock song had come to his mind... *Doctor, My Eyes.* "Enough to know that whatever is there in the dark is also there in the light."

Angela had smiled. "To quote Sherlock Holmes, 'you've been looking but you haven't been seeing.' And, 'after one eliminates the impossible, whatever remains, however improbable, must be the truth.'"

"Meaning, in this case," Jerry had said, "we must first eliminate a living suspect... which, as you have pointed out, has not been proven impossible... before accepting improbable ghosts."

"Elementary," she had replied as they descended the rain-swept streets, the gutters running less vigorously and flooded places here and there as they reached more level terrain. Then she'd quoted a James Bond novel: "Once is happenstance; twice is coincidence; but the third time is enemy action."

Jerry had stopped for another red light, this time in an oily lake, though the Gremlin didn't seem to mind and forged ahead as the light turned green, pushing a gunmetal wave. "In this case it might be the fourth. A case of too many coincidences, as Mr. Holmes might have said... though he didn't seem to believe in ghosts. He denied them in *The Devil's Foot* and also *The Hound Of The Baskervilles.*"

"Arthur Conan Doyle didn't believe in ghosts at the time." Angela had offered an American Spirit, lighting two in her own lips and passing one to Jerry... as Jerry and Trevor had done for each other. "Your mother smoked," she'd stated. "And I won't insult your intelligence by explaining how I deduced that."

"Still does," Jerry had said; and of course the Gremlin's interior was haunted by ghosts of Pall Malls past.

Angela had looked thoughtful again. "Assuming we accept that someone... the *probable* explanation, with Tillinghast being the prime suspect... or even, improbably, some *thing*, ostensibly Miss

130

Morrison's ghost... doesn't want Gabriel in that house, there are going to be more 'accidents.' And since I'm now on Gabriel's side, I'd think a few would happen to me."

"And if any more do, we have to warn him," Jerry had said.

"The game is afoot." Angela had offered a hand and they'd shaken like conspirators.

Jerry had another thought. "If Elwood is on Gabriel's side... which would make him a traitor to both Tillinghast and Miss Morrison's ghost... why hasn't anything happened to him? He doesn't seem anxious or fearful, even that night when I said the G-word."

Angela had considered that while tapping ashes into the tray. "Since he's lived in that house all his life, even if only seventy years and not a hundred-and-eighteen, one would assume he would know if it's haunted. And if there is a ghost, he's obviously learned to live with it. Like a wise old slave who knows his master and what he can get away with. Which also works on an earthly level; who else could Tillinghast find these days to maintain an old relic like that? And, Elwood would know every skeleton stashed in Tillinghast's closet. You can't run a private school, or even a public one, without burying a few dark things you wouldn't want seen in the light."

"That makes sense," Jerry had said as they'd reached the BART station, "I guess, in regard to Tillinghast, I've looked, as you said, for fifteen years, but I didn't see."

"Because it was never blatant or personally offensive."

"...Yes... But, it brings up a logical question..."

"Why did he hire me?"

"Logical progression of thought."

Angela had smiled again. "No doubt because, despite my race, I was best qualified for the job at the price he wanted to pay. The most impressive resume to put on display in the school brochure. ...Or, the best mammy, so to speak, to suckle the masters' young."

Jerry had winced but nodded. "I'm surprised he's kept me this long."

"I think you know the answer to that."

"Successful enough to look good on his record for the elective of Art at the price he wants to pay."

Angela had pressed his hand before getting out of the car. "Stop dawdling, Jerry, and you won't need this job."

# Chapter Seventeen

Jerry had gone to the nursing home but had found his mother "not there" for him. *She* had warned him about dawdling, but had obviously meant his sixth-grade report. She had also gazed out at the rain-glistened cherub and said she knew he'd been "ditching" his raincoat, no doubt because Trevor didn't wear one, and "both silly boys would catch their deaths."

Still, he had stayed for an hour, holding her hand while she spoke to him as if he was still between three and thirteen, always loving, sometimes chiding, reminding him to stay out of drafts, keep his feet dry and not play in puddles, and how nice he had been to draw that cute Cub, while tears at times ran down his cheeks and the fat little cherub smiled in the rain.

Returning to his empty house, he'd regretted already grading the drawings, which left him with nothing to do... strange with time seeming so short he desperately needed something to kill it. Likewise, thanks to Gabriel's treat, there was no excuse to go out for dinner -- even if he could afford to -- and dawdle some time away over that. He'd glanced at the old gas oven and shivered, but then recalled something his mother had said while he'd been holding her hand: *The best way to kill time is work it to death*. He'd thought of his unfinished painting, his only hope of additional income to get him through whatever lay ahead.

He'd climbed the stairs to the second floor and paused at his bedroom doorway. He hadn't intentionally preserved it, but except for disposing of childish things, mostly to the trunk in the attic, it didn't look much different today than when Trevor had spent his last night, which had seemed like the end of all life as they knew it, and

133

they'd cried in each other's arms.

His feet were wet, so he'd put on fresh socks and donned old sneaks, recalling, as he'd sat on his bed, that he hadn't changed the sheets for weeks after Trevor had left, preserving, at least, the ghost of his scent; and his mother, fastidious though she was, had allowed him that adolescent mourning.

Then he'd gone to his studio. His seascape looked commercial in the clear light of the halogen lamp, perhaps not a blatant sell-out, but something only created to sell; in sure and certain hope of selling; to please the eye but not to inspire.

To inspire was to make someone *think*, to open their eyes to other perspectives and alternate conceptions of beauty... a different arrangement of prosaic things, to paraphrase Edgar Alan Poe in *The Fall Of The House Of Usher.*

Perhaps he'd done that for the fat little Cub, even not knowing what he was doing? As he hoped he'd done for Parker.

Then he'd told himself to get on with the job; that he didn't have the luxury of trying to inspire anyone with this work but had to do what he had to do like any responsible man. He'd picked up his palette and a brush, but his strokes were mechanically skillful, a robotic hand on a robotic arm programmed to produce something pretty to others but not satisfying *his* soul. He might as well have been painting a house. One could paint a house very well, take pride in the work and be properly paid, but he hadn't suffered for most of his life to be a successful painter of houses.

Then he'd pictured Gabriel as he'd imagined the night before, drawing from life, revealing souls... possibly even freeing them. Souls that had somehow risen above -- even if only in fleeting sleep -- all their earthly suffering. Laying his tools aside, he'd opened his portfolio and regarded the peacefully slumbering boy, the perfect picture negative of picture-perfect Bill Malone, though he'd probably suffered much more at his age than Bill would suffer in all his life.

He'd suddenly wanted to paint Gabriel. He had an extra canvas, but of course not the model to draw from life. He could paint from memory sketches -- Gabriel drawing Bill in class -- but that wasn't the way he *wanted* to paint him.

That made him remember his email to Serenity Funeral Services. He'd switched on the PC and accessed his box. There was a reply: it had been sent the night before shortly after his midnight query, though that might have been automatic, as in, *thank you for you inquiry and we will respond as soon as we can.* Businesslike, but rather cold considering the emotional state of those who made such inquires.

But, no, it was a personal answer from someone who must have been "on duty." ...Which painted a grim and lonely picture, if hazy and lacking specific details. Trying to bring it into focus was like trying to resurrect scenes from a dream with images from horror movies and macabre descriptions from ghost story books.

The writer was clearly educated; the wording was thoughtful and formally kind, using the editorial "we," and more than a little archaic; but neither pretending, as Jerry had feared, to understand his personal sorrow, nor treating the making of funeral arrangements as if he was ordering pizza.

As stated on their website, they would gladly order the coffin he wished, adding only the cost of shipping... in this case by railroad, that in itself seeming archaic. He'd pictured a glass-sided "motor-hearse" from the early twentieth-century backing up to a wooden boxcar drawn by a steam locomotive.

Plus a small additional charge for "preparation and handling," which he granted reasonable.

It was a good choice in their opinion, "constructed of the finest materials by a firm established in 1880," though, because it was "built upon order," delivery usually took two weeks; "a period one should allow for when making final arrangements; and there would be no charge for storage."

At least the writer hadn't said, "If ordered prematurely."

In regard to funeral services, they would gladly accept his mother's insurance as payment in full, "for respectful transport..."

Presumably a "motor-hearse" instead of a delivery van.

"...for pre-funeral preparation..."

Presumably embalming -- which he didn't want to picture -- and would have to discuss with his mother when she was "there" for him again.

"...and either a quiet parlor viewing to pay last respects and bid farewells, or a mosque or chapel service -- all beliefs respected -- for up to twenty persons."

No problem there.

Also included was, "transportation for six friends or family to and from the cemetery. And of course the hearse."

They actually called a spade a spade.

Jerry had imagined himself riding alone in a modern version of Gabriel's mammoth limousine. Or, would Harriet want to come? ...And maybe Trevor?

As to his query about a headstone, "such a figure indeed could be carved -- they did quite a lot of cherubs -- though of course he would meet with the artist for a consultation."

The approximated cost wasn't impossibly far beyond what his mother's insurance would cover... though, unless he sold that seascape, he'd be begging for Morrison doggie-bags for the rest of his final year.

"Until actual size and specifics were set, they could only give him an estimate of around thirty days to complete such a work, though of course it could be installed any time after interment."

Jerry already knew the latter, but he wanted the cherub to be there when his mother... arrived. Of course if she could "see" it then, she could "see" it anytime... for all eternity. But, maybe to prove he hadn't dawdled, he wanted it waiting up there for her. ...And surely she had another month?

He'd glanced at the seascape again: he could finish it in a week at most; it would, hopefully, sell within a month and pay for a life-size cherub. For a moment he'd felt as if doing this was somehow sealing his mother's fate, like buying her a one-way ticket on a certain ferry-boat, but he took out his bank card and keyed its data to make the suggested deposit, then set an appointment for tomorrow.

Which was now today.

# Chapter Eighteen

Jerry was grading the morning's art as the Regulators were chiming eleven, the hallway beginning to fill with kids on their way to their final class before lunch. The day had remained clear and sunny, and Elwood, gently using a crowbar -- obviously another antique of probably hand-forged gunmetal steel -- had opened the office windows infusing the room's atmosphere with new life.

Parker had been a challenging subject for many of Jerry's students to draw: while Bill was masculine angles and planes, and Susan graceful feminine curves, Parker's softly androgynous body and handsomely boyish yet pretty face had been difficult for most to render, though Gabriel captured him perfectly. And Bill Malone's skill was developing fast.

Walter Wadsworth Wainwright III had also drawn Parker well, though as he'd done with Susan, had added twenty phantom pounds to Parker's baby-bottom belly and lavishly ballooned his breasts, creating, of course, his own illusion of the perfect Parker. Raymond, not surprisingly, hadn't wanted to look at Parker, as if the boy had a loathsome disease which might be transmitted optically, and had basically only sketched him with a muddled mix of savage slashes, almost tearing the paper at times, and frightened-looking softer strokes -- or maybe "hesitation marks" -- that faded into The Unexplored.

Crystal Sterling's illusion was pure adolescent depravity and ferally Dionysian with shades of Aleister Crowley; a universe, apparently, where it was always afternoon in a golden land of over-abundance, and indolent anthropomorphic beings -- Parker a perfect

137

model of same -- lived by the law of do-what-thy-will. Though with only subtle shades of animalistic attributes, she had seen a randy faun on the verge of jacking-off... what had been a listless hand idly resting on his thigh she had interpreted *very* well as more than suggestively reaching for something beneath the soft spill of his belly -- something so obviously over-indulged that only a squeeze would set off a surge – while what had been a shift of the other to momentarily scratch an itch, she had portrayed as fondling a breast, making Parker sort of an Ouroboros sexually self-satisfying circle.

Was it sad that she had real talent... though most "normal" people would find it revolting? And more so because she was showing the *truth*; that young adolescents *were* bestial creatures fallen from childhood purity into slimy seminal mud that steamed and seethed like a volcanic swamp; and if left to themselves with no higher guidance would only indulge their insatiable lust for any pleasure of the moment.

This seemed to leave Jerry with the question of whether, as a custodian of a society's self-professed morals -- and whether or not he believed in them -- he should try to coax Crystal out of it, dissuade her from a path of peril; or as the artist he claimed to be, should affirm and encourage her on the hazardous road she seemed to have chosen.

Jerry's own portrait of Parker, though faithful to his physical form – he *was* a challenging subject, and even Jerry's professional pencil had sometimes struggled to segregate fat from femininity -- had maybe been shaded by older impressions previous to his office encounter and seemed to suggest – at least to his eye – a plumply-pampered tiger cub coyly concealing teeth and claws. He wondered which of the three portrayals – his of a charmingly dangerous boy, Gabriel's lazy Artful Dodger, or Crystal's oversexed dissolute Puck -- Parker might recognize as himself?

"Jerry."

Jerry lay Crystal's drawing aside, resisting the urge to turn it face-down, though assuming Miss Morrison had already seen it -- possibly glowering over his shoulder -- as Tillinghast steamed into the room.

Although it seemed inconsistent, considering his "Victorian vest," gold watch chain, and the implication, at least, of spats, Tillinghast drew out the latest smart phone after pointedly closing the door and dramatically turning the key.

"I've received several calls from parents this morning," he foghorned with somber gravity while navigating across the floor. "One or two I would simply ignore after smoothing a few ruffled feathers, but there have been *three*... so far." He came to ALL STOP, his paunch encroaching upon Jerry's desk like the bow of a liner over a dock, and thrust out his phone like a bowsprit. "Concerning *this.*"

As Jerry had expected, it was Gabriel's sleeping African prince, obviously caught by a student's phone when Jerry had projected it. He had a fairly good idea which of his students had tattled... a pair of somewhat prudish girls, one of whom wore a huge crucifix that probably wasn't to ward off vampires, and also Raymond Blakemore in revenge for the anguish of drawing Parker. "It's very beautiful work."

Tillinghast frowned. "It's certainly anatomically-correct." He cleared his throat with a rumble and added, "Not being, I think, a cretin, I'm well aware that on *some* occasions, and after appropriate introduction, *classical*... nudes... of either sex probably have to be shown. But *this*..." He regarded his phone distastefully as if he'd fished it out of a toilet. "...is obviously contemporary and perhaps too advanced for your students' age-group. May I see the original?"

With a strange reluctance -- though of course Tillinghast wouldn't tear it up -- Jerry surrendered the drawing. Tillinghast studied it for a time with an expression of prudish dislike.

"The *skill*, as you've said, does seem quite good. I assume Gabriel Graves, for the obvious reason?"

Jerry felt a prod from the Imp Of The Perverse. "I'd think that *would* be obvious, though for a different reason."

Tillinghast dropped it on Jerry's blotter as if discarding a used Kleenex. "He certainly didn't draw this in class."

Jerry watched Tillinghast's face. "No, but I accepted it in lieu of his classroom assignment... which was, unfortunately, destroyed."

Tillinghast looked surprised. "Destroyed?"

Again watching Tillinghast's face, Jerry explained the "accident" with the version he'd given his students; and Tillinghast glanced at the empty ink bottle without an apparent change of expression. "I'm sure that drawing was also quite good... and at least partially clothed. I'll have Elwood replace that."

"He already has."

Tillinghast frowned again. "I'm afraid that won't do." He regarded Jerry like a captain who had yet to encounter an iceberg... at least one of any consequence. "While I realize that for *some* staff members it may be annoying or inconvenient, the stipulations of Miss Morrison's will must be obeyed to the letter."

Jerry threw caution to the wind. "In case she wants to write one?"

Several expressions crossed Tillinghast's face, including a shade of suspicion and possibly a phantom of fear, but he quickly battened his hatches. "Come now, Jerry, you've been with us for fifteen years: you're not going to tell me you've had a 'sighting?'"

"Would there be any reason for me to have one?"

"Come now, Jerry," Tillinghast echoed, back on course at FULL SPEED AHEAD. "Even for an artistic type you've always seemed fairly down-to-earth. ...Though I do understand you've been under stress because of your mother's unfortunate illness."

*Are there fortunate forms of illness?* Jerry considered options: it seemed unlikely that, barring something actually perverse – engaging a Sparkle Pony to pose? -- Tillinghast would fire him. But, didn't he have enough problems already without digging up any more? He conceded with, "That's unfortunately true."

"Completely understandable, Jerry, and of course I'll make every allowance until you're though your troubles."

*Until my mother is dead.*

Tillinghast added generously, "You're going to be with us a long time."

It wasn't toned as a question, but of course it wouldn't be... Tillinghast assuming that Jerry's course was set for life. Then, off-the-wall, Jerry asked, "Have you ever been up in the tower?"

Tillinghast might have looked startled. And again a flux of expressions flickered across his face. Finally he said, "With the exception of Elwood, I doubt anyone has been up in the tower for probably many decades." The question may have sounded too casual: "I assume you've never been?"

"No, but the view must be superb."

Tillinghast might have looked relieved. "One can get a much better view by driving up Harwood's Road."

"Harwood's Road?"

"These days it's called Telegraph Road." Tillinghast pumped a chuckle from somewhere in his bilges. "I keep forgetting you're just a youngster. ...But the tower stairway is dangerously dark; electric lights were never installed. And the stairs aren't safe... riddled with dry rot, according to Elwood."

He laughed and patted his bulbous bow. "I certainly wouldn't dare them. And you're no pennyweight yourself. I'd imagine even Elwood is cautious when going up there to check for leaks."

That might have explained, Jerry thought, why the tower's curtains had parted twice during yesterday's rain.

Tillinghast's face turned serious. "And the entire third floor is off-limits... to *staff* as well as students. And Elwood has the only key to the door at the top of the main staircase."

"What about the elevator? Kids being kids, you know?"

Tillinghast's face seemed to cloud. "I was against that installation going up that far. As I told the Administrator, refurbishing the third floor would not be cost-effective. Being mostly servants' quarters and a labyrinth of mean little rooms, walls would have to be taken out. And, like the tower, that floor isn't wired. But as far as any students sneaking up there for god knows what... smoking 'weed' or petting each other... including pairs of *boys* these days... the elevator grille is locked and Elwood has the only key."

"I heard old school files were stored up there?"

"Yes, in one room but not for much longer... too much weight, according to Elwood. I've planned to have them computerized." Tillinghast noticed Crystal's drawing. "Is *that* one of your students?"

"Parker Foxworthy, as interpreted by Crystal Sterling."

"Both from old and respected families... too many *nouveau riche* these days. Mongrels flaunting diamond collars. ...The boy didn't actually pose like that?"

"Crystal interpreted him, as I said. In her own way she's very

141

talented."

Tillinghast gingerly picked up the drawing as if it might ejaculate. "I find her 'talent' disturbing."

"As I said, that's how she saw him."

"She shouldn't be 'seeing' a boy this way."

*Too bad you missed Princess Sparkle Pony.* Passing over his own, Jerry selected Gabriel's work and held it up for display. "This is Parker as he is."

This may have also "disturbed" Tillinghast, but he only said, "Good-looking boy. ...A bit pudgy perhaps, but he'll never have to do physical labor... father's in Investments."

"The buying and selling of others' labor."

"A gentlemanly occupation. ...The boy should have his hair cut; he's far past the age in Miss Morrison's time when boys were often dressed as girls." Tillinghast dropped Crystal's work and seemed to resist wiping his fingers. "Have your other students seen this?"

"Not yet."

"You're not going to show it to them?" Tillinghast pointed to the sleeping boy. "Not after *that* yesterday?"

Jerry unfurled his Jolly Roger. "Of course I am, it's their Art. And, being young, it's still mostly honest... or at least they still draw what they think they see."

Tillinghast regarded Jerry like something new on the horizon. "You're aware I could forbid it?"

Jerry caught himself before firing a duh. Instead he only nodded.

Tillinghast re-studied Parker-as-faun. "Is Crystal your only student who 'interpreted' him this way?"

"Yes."

"Wouldn't it embarrass her to have this shown in class?"

*Quite the contrary, sir.* "My students are aware their work will be shown for discussion."

Tillinghast looked like *we are not pleased*, but seemed to make a course correction. "Can you give me a sound explanation to use *when* I get more parental complaints?"

"Besides the fact that it's real Art created by a teenage soul?"

"I'm afraid I need something practical... besides my usual ultimatum that Morrison is a private school and if parents don't like our curriculum they are perfectly free to withdraw their children and, if without an acceptable reason… which is up to me to judge… forfeit a year's tuition."

Jerry picked up the sleeping boy. "How about we acknowledge actual Art to the supposedly vastly superior young of our alleged elite, not proletarian prudery consisting of G-strings and pasties and the pretense the Emperor always wears clothes because he's our model for morals? Revelation of beauty in *all* its forms as seen through yet uncorrupted eyes, not though the constipated distortion of sanctimonious hypocrites, their own shit dribbling down their chins as they spew their supposedly spotless belief in a nasty, cruel and vindictive god who bellows out virtuous commandments while blatantly breaking them all."

Jerry paused, surprised at himself. "And if that's not practical enough, tell them to check their innocent darlings' browsing history."

Tillinghast seemed to back-water a moment, but then again corrected his course. "You realize, Jerry, that some may question *your* morals?"

Jerry pictured Parker, innocently vulnerable as many young teens had been in this room, until Jerry had learned to see his own soul, to know he wasn't being tested because there was never a question. "The normal occupational hazard of trying to show kids beauty and truth in an ugly culture based upon lies."

Tillinghast possibly pondered, then said, "While I may admire your integrity, I must say that's a dangerous road to take." He glanced at Crystal's raunchy faun. "I'll allow this… with misgivings. But carefully, Jerry, carefully. As I've said, we want you here."

Again, Jerry surprised himself: "You didn't want Gabriel here, did you?"

Tillinghast hesitated on the verge of looking indignant, but glanced to the door instead -- the hall beyond now silent again, the students back in classrooms -- and said in a matter-of-fact tone of voice, "This will not leave this room… and frankly, no. The opening of doors to *them* invariably lowers the bar, so to speak."

He navigated to the windows and seemed to regard an ice-choked sea. "It *begins* with their gifted, of course; and that being the case with Gabriel Graves, there were no defensible grounds... legally speaking, anyway... upon which I could have refused him. Not since that dammed elevator... which I've heard he doesn't need."

*And, that being the case, will probably function perfectly.* Jerry turned in Miss Morrison's chair to smile at Tillinghast. "You did say he seemed self-sufficient. Just as you also said, 'our doors have always been open to any student who meets our standards.' ...Which were set by the grand old lady... whom, as you also said, could never have foreseen a time when any of 'them' would apply to her school." His laugh came naturally. "I'd imagine she's spinning out there in her grave."

Tillinghast seemed to start for a second as if he'd pictured that; a yellowed collection of bones in a shroud -- and probably at high RPM -- but only shrugged and said, "People *knew* during her time, and honestly acknowledged the *fact*, that some races are superior, while others... *perhaps* through no fault of their own... could never rise to their level. And, as in breeding animals, Jerry, while mixing superior and inferior genes *may* produce better median stock, it only *benefits* the inferior, while dragging down those of higher order."

"It seems more logical," Jerry replied, "or perhaps biological, that with a higher median, the superior... no matter what color... would not only rise, but would rise even higher."

Tillinghast made a dismissive gesture. "Politically-correct thinking, Jerry, the primary curse of the present... privileged Pollyannas ignoring what they know to be true so they can feel good about themselves for being so 'enlightened.'" Tillinghast pointed to Crystal's drawing. "Such as seeing 'truth and beauty' in that."

Jerry picked up the sleeping boy. "And this?"

Tillinghast shrugged again. "All I see there is a *physical* Gabriel, if you take my meaning, whose superiority in that respect... say for example to Parker Foxworthy... would not get him into this school. ...Going back to the herd analogy, while superior traits of any group *may* eventually benefit all, higher evolution has been delayed... forced to take a time-wasting detour."

"Assuming the 'superior race' was on the right road to begin with."

"One has to trust their superiors, Jerry."

"Unless one is a lemming." Then Jerry had another thought. "Was she a Darwinist?"

"That was the term in her day."

"So, she didn't expect to see any light."

"...I'm afraid I don't follow you, Jerry."

"One doesn't look for anything they don't expect to see. ...But back to the present topic..." Jerry sifted through the drawings, holding them up one-by-one. "I have in my class... from 'old, respected,' and by your definition 'superior stock'... one anorexic starving to death; several budding neurotics; a bully concealing his own self-hatred for being the very thing he hates; a directionless rebel without a cause, who, if not being rich and white, would probably be in prison already; a manipulative male Lolita... though, hopefully, he's seen the light; a boy who, for reasons I can't comprehend, seems to be forcing himself to get fat.. which has to be some kind of aberration in a culture obsessed with the opposite... and a girl who by most definitions is mad... at least in this society."

He segregated a pair of works. "On the other hand, I have two 'lower-class-risen' boys... one of whom happens to be black... who seem to embody the very best of all the higher human traits by most professed definitions of same. ...Who then, I ask, is dragging down whom?"

Tillinghast only shrugged again. "As I said, it begins with their gifted, but always degenerates from there. ...William Malone, I assume, is your other 'lower-class-risen boy.'" Tillinghast's nose wrinkled slightly. "His father owns a garbage truck fleet."

*Rather makes him a prince of stench.* Jerry realized that "lower-class-risen" was something Gabriel and Bill had in common beyond their ages and artistic talent. But had they known that, or somehow sensed it?

Tillinghast extracted his watch. "I have a parental conference pending, though not concerning you. ...At least so far not today." He crossed the room and unlocked the door. "I say again, Jerry, we hope you'll be with us a long time, so choose your future road with care."

*I think I finally have,* Jerry thought.

# Chapter Nineteen

"Mr. Mathers?"

The Regulators had chimed twelve o'clock and students had flooded the grand staircase -- so why worry about Gabriel's weight? -- forsaking their lavish "free lunch" for McDonalds, or perhaps just the freedom to act like kids without adults saying they shouldn't. Someone, probably one of the staff, had used the elevator, which of course would be functioning flawlessly.

Jerry had finished grading the art, slipping the drawings into a folder, then into his portfolio. He would have left them on his desk but though the ink bottle was empty he didn't trust leaving them out, especially Crystal's and Gabriel's. Maybe Tillinghast wouldn't have touched them -- probably too obvious -- but a ghost wouldn't have such concerns.

And on an earthly level, there was a gentle breeze off the Bay, the window frames were still swollen tight and he'd found he couldn't close them.

He'd made his appointment for four o'clock at Serenity Funeral Services, and called Harriet at the nursing home to confirm his mother was "there" today... there was still the embalming question, which probably wouldn't upset his mother but which he dreaded having to ask.

Now he looked up to see Gabriel and Bill, Gabriel filling the doorway – at least on the horizontal plane -- like a mammoth young centaur on bulldozer tracks, Bill at his back like a perfect boy-faun. Gabriel, as on his first day here, was clad as much as possible in jeans, sneaks and a beater, while Bill wore "saggers" and beater."

"Come in," said Jerry. He had a date with Angela for another Mor-

147

rison lunch -- Pasta Alfredo today -- which they'd planned to eat in the sunny backyard, but of course he could spare time for Gabriel, who rumbled in followed by Bill. He was going to offer a few words of praise about their morning's work, but Bill spoke first:

"You said you'd give extra credit for stuff we did at home?"

"That I did," said Jerry.

"We drew these last night," said Gabriel, offering a folder.

It was almost a shock to Jerry -- though he wondered why -- to find the boys had drawn each other. Then he felt an absurd jealousy because Bill had rendered Gabriel as Jerry had pictured him two nights ago, shirtless and drawing from life in his chair, though Gabriel's model wasn't shown and the details around him were indistinct... one form of classic portraiture.

Within his expanding limitations Bill had done remarkable work, and though Gabriel's shirts concealed very little, his body of multiple ebony rolls, the inflated-to-bursting balloons of his breasts and the vast cascade of his belly blubber were all the more astonishing bare even if only in pencil on paper.

Again Jerry felt an absurd jealousy that Bill had usurped his...

Privilege?

...of drawing Gabriel from life.

Accepting that as absurdity, Jerry could only console himself that it wasn't how he'd wanted to paint him.

He then studied Gabriel's portrait of Bill -- also shirtless and also drawing, his subject also invisible -- though with much more detailed surroundings in what was obviously Bill's room. Of course it was no surprise that Bill was drawn as masterfully as in Gabriel's classroom assignment, though here in jeans instead of boxers; and though, as they had discussed over lunch, surroundings were not considered important in many schools of portraiture, there were shelves behind Bill's back, on one of which was a stereo system of 1970s vintage that included an eight-track player... almost eerily similar to the relic in Jerry's room at home. Another shelf held models and toys, all of which were garbage trucks.

Had Jerry himself been privileged to draw such an intimate sitting of Bill, he couldn't have done any better, and there followed a progression of thought... who had been in whose room for these sittings?

"We did 'em on cam," said Bill, as if guessing Jerry's unspoken question. "I guess that's still drawing from life?"

Again Jerry felt absurd jealousy, but it quickly transfigured into regret; and the kind of regret that was probably normal for someone too old to be friends with the young... at least in a culture that called it abnormal. "Of course, and you both deserve an A."

But, Bill asked as if to a peer, "Wanna have lunch with us at 'Dees?"

"That's very kind of you..." said Jerry.

"Hi."

Angela appeared in the doorway, dressed today in carpenter's jeans and a workman's blue chambray shirt, which certainly challenged the dress code for staff, as well as Tillinghast's tolerance. ...Was she deliberately baiting him?

Jerry finished, "...but I have a pervious engagement."

The boys exchanged benevolent glances, forgiving adults for acting like kids, then bid farewell and departed, Angela smiling and stepping aside as Gabriel cleared the doorway with maybe an inch to spare.

"Sorry I'm late," said Jerry, rising as Angela entered and offering the drawings. "They did some extra-credit work."

Angela took out her glasses, the lenses of which, Jerry noted, bore evidence of flying stone chips. "These are well worth waiting for. An Irish princeling and..."

"An African godlet?" Jerry suggested.

"I'd put them on equal footing in regard to earned nobility. Do moments like this make teaching worthwhile?"

"They would if there were more of them. Do you have the same moments?"

"Only on a commercial level when I was at Rutherford; a new design for airline seats being considered by Boeing, an adjustable toilet-paper holder, patent currently pending. And, on a more artistic plane, a computer-animated cartoon in development at Pixar."

"Wish I could boast the equivalent."

"I'm sure you've planted many seeds that just haven't germinated yet."

"Or were buried by cretin grave-diggers."

Angela raised an admonishing finger. "None of that now." She went to a window and took off her glasses. "It's a beautiful day and full of life. No ghoulies and ghosties and long-legged beasties."

Jerry glanced at the ink bottle. "Or things that go bump in the night."

"Your windows have a cheerful view, though even her crypt looks less creepy today from my rearward perspective. ...Have you ever been up in the tower? That vista must be magnificent."

"No," said Jerry. "As Tillinghast just reminded me, the entire third floor is off-limits to staff as well as students."

Angela cocked her head. "Why would he have to remind you?"

"I asked him about the tower... we had an impromptu meeting this morning." Jerry opened his portfolio. "About these."

Donning her glasses again, Angela sat in the velvet chair to study the drawings of Crystal Sterling's randy adolescent faun and Gabriel's sleeping African prince, then indicated the latter. "Obviously Gabriel's work, and as amazing as all I've seen. ...I think I've seen his subject somewhere." She smiled. "At least his face." Then she regarded Crystal's picture. "A portrait of Parker Foxworthy... or rather, I'd say, an interpretation."

"You know him?" asked Jerry.

"Met him in the hall this morning after second period; he'd gotten lost in the back of the house looking for Mrs. Fokker's office... he's in her Drama class... so I took him there. Seems like a very nice boy."

"A natural for Drama," said Jerry.

Angela smiled at the drawing. "And very well endowed for a boy; almost makes me envious."

Jerry caught himself before saying she had no reason to be, and presented Gabriel's Parker.

"Still abundantly blessed for a boy," said Angela after perusing, "though I'd guess more realistically... he was wearing a hoodie when I met him, but Gabriel saw all."

"Including his soul?" asked Jerry.

"I'd agree with that."

Jerry hesitated a moment, then presented his portrait of Parker; and Angela's eyebrows arched. "Another of your students' works? You seem to be artfully blessed."

"...A student," Jerry hedged, actually holding his breath as Angela regarded his drawing side-by-side with Gabriel's.

"The same boy," she finally said, "but from different perspectives."

Jerry decided to leave it at that; and Angela took up Crystal's work. "Parker didn't pose like this?"

"He did in Crystal's universe."

"She has considerable talent."

Jerry sighed. "Of the sort that often drives artists mad. And/or gets them stoned to death by a mob of pitchfork and torch waving goons. ...Speaking of intolerance, Tillinghast is more than an armchair racist; I'd say there was a sheet in his closet along with all the skeletons."

Angela handed back the drawings. "You did say you wanted to see."

"He finally revealed himself in the light... though I admit I was never looking for what was also there in the dark."

Angela took out her cigarettes and offered one to Jerry. "Better late than never. But not very late in your case."

Heeding Elwood's advice after the gas light adventure, Jerry had bought a new Bic lighter, and fired their American Spirits. "Which makes him our most probable suspect should there be any more 'accidents.'"

Angela exhaled a ghost. "Though a difficult one to thwart, being he has free reign of this house. And a dangerous one to accuse... assuming we want to keep our jobs."

Jerry sighed smoke. "Which I must. At least until my mother is... gone."

Angela nodded. "I'm not well-off myself at the moment, and of course I lost all my benefits from thirteen years at Rutherford."

"Why did you take this job?" asked Jerry.

"The usual plight of an artist of needing money to keep on creating, and Tillinghast made a better offer, though benefits are pending until after ninety days. As I mentioned yesterday, gentrification is creeping in, the rent is going up on my loft, and I need breathing space to finish a project; one which I hope will make my name."

Jerry thought of his unfinished seascape, the sale of which would help his finances and pay for his mother's cherub tombstone but wouldn't make any name he wanted. He remembered his feelings last night, that crystal flash of inspiration to cast aside what he should be doing and paint a portrait of Gabriel. ...Which was completely absurd because he could never ask -- not in the present time and place -- Gabriel to pose for him. It was, he supposed, ironic, that he being basically "pure of heart," as might have been said in Victorian times -- not only artfully dodging the webs of those such as Parker Foxworthy, but trying to disentangle the weavers -- could not create what he'd suffered for in fear of facing accusations that *he* was a predatory spider.

He suddenly felt very tired of life and all its hateful hypocrisies. He glanced around the gloomy room, its brooding shadows somehow resisting the clear light of day through the windows, and could almost feel the *weight* of the house, that floor above with its shadows and dust, its windows like the tower's blind to all the sunlit life outside. He turned to Angela. "Maybe someday, perhaps after school, you'd like to drive up Harwood's Road? For the view."

Angela smiled. "You know your Oakland history; it hasn't been called Harwood's Road since the early 1900s."

"Apparently so does Tillinghast... though I suppose that's natural, being connected with this house and all the 'old and respected families.'"

"How long has he been Director?"

"I got the impression he'd been here for many years before I came, though he doesn't look much over fifty."

Angela tapped her ashes into the cherub's bowl. "There must have been a previous Director; this school was founded in 1902."

Jerry discarded his own ash. "One would think several in that length of time." Then he laughed. "But, as you said about Elwood, this house can't preserve anything *that* well."

"It's done a good job on you."

"You should see my portrait in my attic."

Angela laughed. "I'm up for that drive any time you are."

Jerry sighed again. "I wish it could be today, but I have an appointment this afternoon... funeral arrangements for my mother. And meeting a tombstone carver. She wants a cheerful cherub."

Angela crushed out her cigarette. "This might not be the right thing to say, but she seems to be taking it well."

"A lot better than I am." Then Jerry smiled and snuffed his smoke. "But, as you said, it's a day full of life, at least without these gloomy walls."

Angela smiled, too. "And that food smells delicious. I wouldn't mind being full of that."

# Chapter Twenty

"**C**ool ride, Mr. Mathers."

Jerry was leaning against the Gremlin. He'd been gazing up at the tower, but despite the gentle afternoon breeze rustling the oaks along the street, the curtains were closed and hadn't moved; though several third-floor windows were open – presumably raised by Elwood to dispel any dampness from yesterday's rain -- their pale curtains stirring with wraith-like ripples.

During their lunch in the mansion's back yard, after finding a vine-laced cast-iron table in the leaf-dappled light of an ivy-draped bower not too uncomfortably close to the crypt but apart from the strident chatter of kids at other tables out on the lawn, and observed by a fat-tummied juvenile faun with a span of stony pipes to his lips, Jerry had offered Angela another ride to the Rockridge BART. Smiling, she had reminded him the price of gas had gone up again, but he'd said the funeral parlor wasn't far from that part of town, at the feet of the North Oakland hills and logically near a cemetery -- the one where his mother had purchased her plot -- and Angela accepted. Then he'd remarked while regarding the faun, who seemed to smile in approval:

"He could have been modeled from one of my students... from the waist up, anyway."

Angela had turned to the sculpture, whose elbows rested upon his belly, which bulged between his furry legs as he sat silently playing his pipes. "Walter Wadsworth Wainwright III."

"How did you know?"

"He's also one of my students." Angela had laughed. "Probably keeping his lifeboats on board, no doubt at his parents' insistence,

154

by learning something saleable. And our young friend serenading us with ethereal music beyond our perception does share his impressive tumescence." She had laughed again. "I seem to have waxed Victorian... probably the atmosphere, or maybe time got warped in this place from mixing too much old with new."

Jerry had looked through leaves to the lawn, but the kids weren't dressed in collars and corsets. Several boys had lost their shirts, including Walter Wainwright, who, with a heaping plate before him, seemed to be trying to stuff himself into insensibility. Then Jerry had patted the faun's bulging belly. "He's had a hundred years or more of sitting there on his furry butt, while Walter, judging from all his stripes, seems to have ballooned this summer and obviously strives for greater expansion."

Angela sipped from her glass of milk. "I take it you haven't heard of gainers?"

"Some new kind of neurosis? Like anorexia in reverse?"

"Usually no. They don't see skeletons in their mirrors in reverse of anorexics who think they see obesity. They're more like bodybuilders, either male or female, who want to achieve a physical shape which they and their peers find attractive. It's a growing counterculture... no pun intended... especially among adolescents, and probably the natural result of mainstream obsession with losing weight and paranoically staying skinny."

"Paranoically, as in 'fat is out to get you?'"

Angela had laughed again and wound tasty pasta onto her fork. "As well as any kind of food that actually tastes good. If it does, you've committed a sin and weighty retribution will follow."

Jerry had also indulged his fork. "I suppose it's a modern manifestation of normal teenage rebellion."

"I suppose for some it is, with all the current health-nazi fanatics goose-stepping to the supreme command of 'you *vill* be skinny'... society trying to control your body, dictating a physical standard for all while implanting xenophobic hate of anyone who won't conform. ...But, that's hardly surprising in a culture mostly controlled by fear: fear of foreign terrorists, fear of immigrants taking jobs... while sending those jobs overseas... fear of becoming bald or gray, or of having

155

body odor, or teeth any less than unnaturally white. And fear of getting fat, of course, and..." Angela had smiled, "of becoming old."

"Do you think Gabriel is a 'gainer?'"

"I'd say he just doesn't believe that souls are judged by BMI or how much one denies one's self all the good things while here on earth in hope of heavenly reward and/or societal approval." Angela had smiled again. "An artist's personality, though also shared by most of the people who've made the world a little better; though I'm sure he's inspired Walter, even if unintentionally, to expand his own horizons in what he considers beautiful."

"As has, apparently, Parker," Jerry had said as Parker appeared descending the mansion's rear staircase bearing a well-loaded lunch tray and clad less alluringly today than yesterday's début for Jerry in a somewhat bulky black hoodie above his usual jeans and sneaks. Walter may have been hoping for him, often glancing back at the house while steadily stuffing down food, and now eagerly invited him over, even rising to seat him. Jerry couldn't hear what was said, but Walter seemed to make a request, and Parker smiled and shed his shirt while Walter looked ready to Rapture.

Angela had remarked, "An idol for Walter's adoration almost as grand as Gabriel, at least in two attributes, though I would imagine Gabriel's glory far surpasses Parker's."

Jerry had replied, "Another of my students, a talented boy named Bill Malone, drew Gabriel from life last night *sans chemise* on computer cam, though I doubt he was worshipping Gabriel's weight." He'd regarded Walter again. "At least that's one mystery solved."

Some of the other kids had initially stared at Parker, their mix of expressions mirroring the students in Jerry's class when Parker had disrobed to pose. A few boys seemed to inspect him to assure themselves he *w*as a boy and therefore shouldn't interest them -- at least not while in company with other hetero males -- while a couple of girls looked resentful that boys could go bare up there while they couldn't, as if they'd committed a carnal sin by simply being born female and had to live their lives atoning by always staying covered. Then Jerry had noticed Raymond Blakemore sitting alone at another table mostly concealed in the shade of a tree and glowering at Walter and Parker... or possibly only at Parker... his expression a very scary mix of murderous hate and lonely longing, which had brought to Jerry's mind a recent newspaper photograph of a middle-school massacre shooter. He'd been about to mention that when Angela had said:

Parker is an intriguing model... maybe the son of Anubis and Isis if I were going to portray him... but what of his own artistic skills?"

"He has talent," Jerry had said, "which, as with most kids, could be developed if he was passionate about it, but I would guess, like most Morrison kids, he feels no need to create anything since his future is secure and probably already planned by his parents... 'father's in investments,' according to Tillinghast."

Angela had laughed. "Most of these kids are just going through phases and trying out different identities, but I can't picture Parker a corporate clone in a suit and voting Republican. As you said, he does have a talent for drama, which Mrs. Fokker also mentioned... he's going to be starring in Hamlet next month."

Jerry had glanced again at Parker, who seemed to be simply being a boy, now sharing Walkman headphones with Walter... or rather I-something earbuds. "I could be cretinishly crude and ask if he's playing Ophelia."

"Actually the leading role."

"That should be worth seeing," Jerry had said. "Mrs. Fokker's productions always are... her being sufficiently successful in the way this culture defines it... and far above the ludicrous level of the middle-school messes I recall."

Angela had asked, "Were you in any of the latter?"

"Hamlet, as a matter of fact. I played The First Gravedigger: 'What is he that builds stronger than either the mason, the shipwright, or the carpenter? ...It is the gravedigger, for his houses will last until Doomsday.' My best friend played The Second Gravedigger; we had fun throwing bones and skulls around."

"Speaking of which," Angela had said, "Mrs. Fokker dropped her Yorick this morning; asked if I could glue it together, but it's as hopeless as Humpty-Dumpty." She'd laughed and indicated the crypt. "Suppose we could borrow Miss Morrison's?"

Jerry had said, only half joking, "That's really taunting a haunting."

He was now waiting for Angela as the stream of students flooding the staircase like a rowdy waterfall was being absorbed by vehicles, while another substantial diversion was flowing down the street to McDonalds. He turned to see Gabriel and Bill, the former again like a mammoth young centaur on bulldozer tracks -- at least in regard to circumference -- the latter a muscular stripling faun, actually admiring the car.

Jerry asked, "You really think so?"

"Certainly, sir," said Gabriel. "Did you restore it?"

"No, it was my mother's." ...Though it seemed wrong to say it that way, as if she was already gone.

"My dad's got a '38 Corbitt," said Bill.

"A car?" asked Jerry, who'd never heard of that make.

"Nah, it's a garbage truck. One of the very first packers in Oakland, mechanical instead of hydraulic."

"...Oh," said Jerry, resisting the urge to add "cool." Apparently, like Gabriel, Bill wasn't the least uncomfortable being seen naked under his clothes.

Gabriel offered, "We're going to McDonalds, and you're welcome, sir."

"I'm buyin'," added Bill.

Jerry smiled. "Thank you, gentlemen, but..."

Gabriel laughed. "You have a previous engagement."

The boys traded smiles and perceptive glances as Angela descended the stairs. Jerry reached to open the Gremlin's door... when something black -- his first thought was a bat -- plummeted past the edge of his vision.

There followed a loud metallic CLANG as the object hit the sidewalk. A chip of concrete struck Jerry's cheek, and Gabriel muttered, "Shit!"

Bill's ejaculation was, "FUCK!"

There followed lesser clatters as the object bounced and came to rest by the car's front tire... a small crowbar of gunmetal steel.

"Damn!" cried Angela.

# Drawing From Life

Everyone looked up at the house, but its windows stared down indifferently, no face or form in any of them.

Then Jerry scanned around: the last of the students, none in his class, were getting into cars. The group on their way to McDonalds was halfway down the block, and no one else seemed to have seen.

Then Bill shouted, "Gabe!"

Gabriel held one huge upper arm with the other's dimpled hand. There was a trickle of crimson, stark against his midnight skin. Nevertheless, his smile looked wry as he faced the towering house. "Missed me... well almost."

"Fuck!" yelled Bill again, springing close. "Let's see, man!"

"Let me look," said Angela, nudging Bill aside.

Jerry hadn't run anywhere since casually plodding the track in high school to earn his quarterly D in P.E., but he dashed to the house and raced up the stairs as if trying for a belated A. He thought he saw the ghost of a smirk as, panting, he charged through the foyer past Miss Morrison's portrait and continued on up to the second floor. Arriving almost out of breath, he scanned the hall but saw no one, the doors all closed on either side.

Sweat now sheening his face, and puffing like a steam locomotive, he peered up into the stairwell shadows. The treads to the third floor, though dusted by Elwood, were naturally far less worn, and the candle-shaped bulbs in their sconces weren't on. Still puffing hard, his underarms wet, he climbed to the dim upper landing. Though, because of the warm sunny day, many second floor windows were open, he was sure the crowbar -- Elwood's crowbar -- had fallen -- or been thrown -- from the third.

The door at the top of the stairs, a massive mahogany portal, was locked. But Elwood had the key, and who else would have opened a third-floor window. And he would have needed his crowbar to overcome the rain-swollen frame.

Jerry pounded the door with a fist. "Elwood!"

Silence.

He crouched and peered through the keyhole, but could only see, dimly, across a hall, a wainscotted wall with cracked plaster yellowed like unburied bones.

159

He pounded again and roared Elwood's name, but again only silence replied.

He yanked his tie loose to get more air, then puffed back down to the second floor. The lift's indicator pointed to 3. He stabbed the button and the cage descended. He hesitated a moment -- that vision of falling haunting his mind -- then opened the grille, stepped inside and pushed the button for 3. He kept a finger on EMERGENCY STOP -- for whatever good that might do -- but the cage ascended smoothly and creaked to rest in gloomy half-light.

As Tillinghast had told him, the third floor grille was locked... a modern padlock and chain. Jerry peered out like a prisoner, seeing a long empty hall. The doors lining it were closer together than on the two lower floors, indicating smaller rooms. A few of these were haphazardly open and, except for the elevator's bulb, the only light came from the doorways of those at the front of the house... presumably the westering sun through their pale-curtained windows.

No sound seemed to penetrate this place, and the silence was eerily hollow. The hall's floorboards were deep in dust as if gray snow had fallen, except for a narrow trail down the middle, probably worn from Elwood's inspections.

*Shadows and dust.*

Also as Tillinghast had said, there were no electric scones on the walls, only spider-webbed iron gas fixtures, and these with only single globes... this must have indeed been servant's quarters. At one end of the hall -- which seemed farther away than it should have been -- he saw a steep spiral staircase rising into darkness, which must have led to the tower.

Again, like a prisoner, gripping the grille, Jerry shouted Elwood's name.

"Mr. Mathers?"

Elwood's voice had come from below, echoing up the shaft.

Then came Angela's: "Jerry?"

He pressed the 2 button and moments later emerged to find Angela and Elwood. Elwood held the crowbar, looking troubled... and possibly scared.

But Jerry's first word was, "Gabriel?"

160

"He's fine," said Angela. "It was only a scratch. He and Bill went to McDonalds."

Elwood added, "Born under a lucky star!" He glanced at the crowbar. "Could have gone right through his skull!"

"But, how did it... fall?" asked Jerry.

"For the life of me I don't know, Mr. Mathers. I used it to prop open one of the windows."

"On the third floor?"

Elwood nodded. "Most of those sash cords rotted away, and Administration won't pay to replace 'em. Air gets damp up there, causes rot. ...But those window frames are heavy." He clasped the crowbar vertically between his flattened palms. "Can't figure how it could have slipped out."

Jerry's room window at home had to be kept open that way, though with a light piece of broomstick that wasn't potentially deadly. He turned to Angela. "Gabriel is okay?"

"Doesn't seem bothered, though I sure am."

Jerry turned back to Elwood. "Is Tillinghast still here?"

"I don't know, Mr. Mathers. I was coming up from the basement when Miss Davis told me what happened." He looked at the crowbar again and repeated, "Could have gone right through his skull!"

"When did you open the window?" asked Jerry.

"Right after lunch, Mr. Mathers. Haven't been up there since."

"Did you use the elevator?"

"Never do, Mr. Mathers." Elwood puffed his chest a bit. "I'm not too old to climb a few stairs."

Jerry turned again to Angela. "Of course I can't speak for Gabriel, but since he wasn't seriously hurt I see no reason to tell Tillinghast."

He wasn't sure if Elwood looked relieved or not, but Angela seemed to search Elwood's eyes, perhaps seeing more than Jerry could, then met Jerry's again. "Accidents, like shit, will happen."

# Chapter Twenty-one

"You don't think Elwood was..." Jerry hesitated.

Angela smiled. "Call a spade a spade, Jerry. Being politically-correct just substitutes one slur for another if people don't want to be enlightened. 'Mentally challenged' still means retarded; 'physically challenged' still means handicapped... and even an 'African-American' can still be a lying house nigger."

Seeing Jerry wince, she patted his hand on the steering wheel as the Gremlin descended a winding road through the last remains of a forest. "Let's say I'm inclined to believe him, and, I admit, for racial reasons."

"You don't think he's a... lying house nigger."

Angela smiled again. "Tell it like it is."

"Should I have said it with an 'A?'"

"That would make you sound retarded."

"A lot of black people say it that way."

"Which sounds even more retarded. But I don't have African Voodoo sight, so I can't see into Elwood's soul. And the best way to lie is tell part of the truth."

"I did get the feeling he knew more than he told us." Jerry rounded another curve. "But, regarding our probable suspect, it seems *improbable* to me that Tillinghast would go *that* far. That bar *could* have gone through Gabriel's skull!"

Angela drew out her American Spirits, offering one to Jerry, who said, "Thanks, I can use it."

"Me too. I'm not used to near-death experiences."

"Nor I," said Jerry. "Though when I ran up the stairs..." He laughed. "I didn't know I *could* still run. But I was more pissed-off than scared. Just adrenalin, I guess."

Angela lit two cigarettes and passed one to Jerry. "I didn't nigger-lip it."

Jerry laughed. "Stop that shit." Then he considered. "Gabriel didn't seem scared at all. If anything, he seemed... I'd say defiant."

"I noticed that, too," said Angela. "Of course the young are more resilient than us feeble elderly folk." She exhaled a ghost. "We assume that bar was meant for him... but maybe just as a scare?"

"As opposed to attempted murder?" said Jerry. "I imagine we've all provoked someone... or some *thing*... in that house; Gabriel for obvious reasons, and you, I, and now even Bill, for befriending him." He blew out smoke. "We know how Tillinghast feels about him, which makes Gabriel the most likely target and Tillinghast the prime suspect. ...But I don't think the man is *psychotic.* To throw a crowbar from four stories high! He's surely rational enough to know that if one of us had been killed or hurt... hurt more than Gabriel was... the police would investigate."

Angela looked thoughtful. "He could claim it had been accidental; he was up there inspecting the windows for leaks, making sure Elwood was doing his job, and the bar slipped out. At worst he'd be charged with criminal neglect for not taking reasonable precautions for the safety of anyone below. But he could afford an expensive lawyer... 'a very tragic accident, ladies and gentlemen of the jury, but hasn't this poor man suffered enough with this horrible thing on his conscience?'"

"He might lose his job at least," said Jerry. "For tarnishing the school's reputation, not to mention Miss Morrison's name."

"Possibly," said Angela. "Through probably a small risk for someone well-connected. But we're past happenstance and coincidence now to full-on enemy action; though we've yet to eliminate the impossible." She exorcized another ghost and counted on her fingers. "We know Tillinghast has the motive. And he has the means. And he has free run of the house, which gives him opportunity."

"But he said Elwood has the only keys to the upper floor."

"Perhaps establishing alibi, and before the fact. And there must be duplicate keys."

163

Jerry stopped for a red light as they reached flatter urban terrain. "And even if Elwood has them, possibly in the basement, Tillinghast could access them, or have other duplicates made."

Angela nodded. "But, taking Tillinghast out of the picture; assuming he isn't hateful enough... or crazy enough... to do such a thing, just like spilling that bottle of ink, we can't be *absolutely* sure Elwood didn't drop that bar and simply won't admit it. He would have had time to get downstairs before you ran into the house, then claim he'd been in the basement when I came in a few minutes later." She paused and cocked her head. "Is that why you asked if he'd used the lift, which might have been faster than the stairs?"

"I didn't think of that," said Jerry. "But *someone* used it recently to go beyond the second floor. The third floor hall is covered with dust except for a trail down the middle, but there were also footprints to the elevator."

The light turned green and Jerry drove on. "Of course there would have been some disturbance when the lift was installed, but that was over three years ago and those prints are fresh." He flicked ashes out the window. "Regarding our improbable suspect, and granting her not impossible..."

"Still," said Angela, "despite that baleful portrait, I get the feeling she must have liked kids... and possibly still does."

"I got that impression, too," said Jerry. "Though in her day children were 'seen and not heard'... rather like decorations."

"Like all those young stone fauns and cherubs populating her grounds."

Jerry smiled. "Let's not grant her Medusa powers beyond the realm of common ghosts. ...But, if we *do* grant her the power to slip a crowbar out of a window, why would it be unreasonable to assume she could also guide its fall? Not to actually harm Gabriel but, like disabling the elevator and possibly defacing his Art, to tell him he isn't wanted here... to get his black ass out of her house."

Angela smiled. "That's calling a spade a spade. Maybe I'm a little wack, because that actually seems to make sense."

Jerry laughed. "As you said, neither of us is completely sane by this society's standards." Then he looked at his watch. "I suppose there's a certain irony that our near-death experience will make me late for an undertaker. Though I guess he's used to waiting; customers being inevitable in his line of business."

Angela consulted her watch, an inexpensive digital. "You could still make it on time if you didn't take me to BART. Keep your appointment and drop me off after."

"You'd want to go to a funeral parlor?"

"I'm going to one eventually so I might as well know what to expect."

Jerry touched Angela's hand. "I'd be grateful for your company. It's a lonely feeling doing... these things."

Angela took his hand in hers. "I can imagine it is, and I dread the day when I'll have to do it for my mom and dad."

"Hopefully not alone," said Jerry.

# Chapter Twenty-two

Angela smiled. "That's what I call a cherub!"

It seemed somehow appropriate that Serenity Funeral Ser-vices reposed in a grand Victorian house. Though half the size of Miss Morrison's, it was three stories tall plus an octagon tower, and stood amongst many old-growth trees which had probably watched it being built and far exceeded the height of its spire. Some of the trees were eucalyptus imported from Australia during the mid 1800s, as people had once been imported -- and whether or not they'd wanted to be -- to serve a "superior race." But they, like those people, were strong and resilient, not only surviving on meager resources but rooting deep and multiplying, competing for and eventually winning, an unassailable place in this land.

The house stood near the foot of a slope where, above the breeze-ruffled treetops, were seen the grounds of a cemetery... in which Jerry's mother's grave waited.

Though having a small graveled parking lot beside its high veranda, the house's front yard still looked residential with a lush green lawn and bright beds of flowers... Elwood could have done no better. Also in many hues was the house, resplendent with delicate gingerbread: most modern people were unaware that paint in many vibrant colors had just become available during the Victorian age and had been applied with vigor... sometimes too much so. But in this case it was tasteful to Jerry's artistic eye... though to someone determined that death must be drab it might have seemed inappropriate.

Also in Victorian style were a sparkling fountain and garden Art, the latter mostly fauns and cherubs, most looking over a century old,

166

weathered, and furry with moss. The exception stood near the front staircase on a pedestal not unlike a tombstone -- though maybe that impression was only in the beholder's eye -- and it was The Cherub, remarkably fat, who served as the... company logo?

Surely they wouldn't have called it their mascot.

Seen in life, so to speak, as Jerry parked the Gremlin, it was all the more astonishing for the loving attention to detail, though its race was rather ambiguous, and even more so in dove-gray marble. Its bushy mop of wild curls was shared by children all over the world, and its spherical cheeks engulfed its snub nose above expressive rosebud lips seemingly parted in wonderment at the infinite vastness of the sky, toward which a chubby hand was spread atop a rolly upraised arm.

Jerry hurried to open Angela's door, but she was out and inspecting the sculpture before he could arrive. "Oh, sorry," she said, as he joined her. "I'm not used to that sort of thing."

He caught himself before asking, why not? Instead he said, watching her eyes, like onyx in the clear sunlight, admiring the fat child of stone, "This is the one I want for my mother. May I have your artist's opinion?"

Angela smiled. "He looks very full of life; though it's hard to tell if he's waving goodbye to a heaven-bound soul, or waiting to catch a falling star. And the workmanship is magnificent." She touched an opulent cheek and stroked a substantial shoulder." I guess I should feel grateful that he only seems to do graveyard art."

"You do disdain political-correctness."

"Oh, he's a he," said Angela.

Jerry regarded the cherub's chest orbs, which even in stone looked like bobby balloons that might fly away hissing if poked with a pin, then patted the figure's massive belly, almost expecting it to ripple like Gabriel's would have done. "You'd have to raise this considerable curtain to be sure of that."

"The *artist*, Jerry. I'll bet you a Quarter-Pounder he's male."

"A double with cheese... though I'm sure I'll lose."

"I'm sure you can do the same with paintings."

"Most of the time, though it's hard to explain." Then, like a shadow crossing the sun, Jerry remembered why they were here. Angela must have sensed it, because she took his hand.

Jerry sighed, scenting the living sweetness of flowers along with the musk of eucalyptus, hearing the musical play of the fountain, which seemed to invite him to tarry a while in leaf-dappled shade amongst cherubs and fauns, while feeling as he had last night that he was sealing his mother's fate. Then, Angela's hand still in his, they climbed the steps and crossed the veranda.

The double doors were mahogany and set with beveled glass panes. There was a bronze lion knocker on each, reminding him of *Christmas Carol*, but he paused feeling slightly uncertain as to whether it was proper to knock. No doubt the house was a residence for the undertaker and family, but it was also a business, as understated by a small bronze plaque. He glanced to Angela, who nodded, then grasped a brass doorknob and opened a door.

The foyer was large, almost a parlor, and cool in contrast to the warm afternoon, its plaster walls of mustard-gold above wainscotting of tongue-and-groove oak and not as somber as he'd expected. Like the Morrison house, there was still a gas light on the high, vaulted ceiling, and brass electric scones on the walls with small, clear, candle-shaped bulbs, though these were brighter and no shadows lurked. He supposed it was normal to wonder, in light of his recent experience, if the gas lamp was still operational. The floor was also of oak with a square of rose-patterned carpet. There were plush antique chairs and a love-seat, and claw-footed tables with magazines -- *Sunset* and *Smithsonian* -- and though he hadn't considered it, also some child-ren's publications, including one devoted to skateboards. The tables were equipped with ashtrays, spotless though obviously meant to be used, and there were two free-standing types. He had almost expected formaldehyde to be ghosting about in the air, but except for spirits of lemony polish, fine old wood and furniture, and that 1970s shade of tobacco, the atmosphere was otherwise neutral.

A quartet of paintings adorned the walls, three the kind of soft landscapes popular in the Victorian Age, of golden summer afternoons in uninhabited countrysides, their distant features ethereally hazy, mountains rendered in mauve and blue; though the fourth was clearly recent, though done in the same archaic style, of a rather remarkably fat-tummied faun playing pipes to a trio of chub-padded cherubs, one of whom was African, and another Asian, lounging in a leafy glade and drowsily attentive... or maybe the tune was a lullaby. Perhaps, like the youthful magazines, it was there to comfort children during their introduction to Death.

"Good afternoon."

Jerry and Angela turned from the painting as an ebony man in an ebony suit appeared in a doorway across the room -- a man in black indeed -- and Jerry was jarred for a moment. Though he'd told himself it shouldn't matter while doing his mournful homework, due to the tasteful advertisement as well as the upward-inclining location, he'd assumed this would be...

Well... calling a spade a spade... a white business.

While his mother had never been prejudiced in regard to race or size, inviting the fat Cub Scout to lunch in a time when people of his persuasion were as alien to her neighborhood as newly-landed Little Grays; and she'd certainly taken to Gabriel from the moment she'd seen Jerry's drawing -- which now, thanks to Harriet Cole, hung framed in her room beside Trevor -- Jerry pictured again what he knew, or thought he knew, of the "laying out" process.

Absurdly, he looked at the man's midnight hands. Then he glanced to Angela, who didn't seem surprised... though why did he think she might be?

The man was around Jerry's age, with a build that Jerry thought sturdy despite all the hate blogs and TV commercials ranting that anyone not a cadaver with skin stretched over impending bones – Amanda Teabrook came to mind -- was "morbidly obese." But the man looked full of life to Jerry, who, in spite of the stereotype, had been expecting a skeletal ghoul... and of course a pale one.

"Mr. and Mrs. Mathers?"

He hadn't expected that, either. "Colleague" seemed pretentiously formal, so Jerry took Angela's hand and said, "A good friend, Angela Davis."

"Angela, please," said Angela as Jerry relinquished her hand, which the man took for a moment.

"Nice to meet you, Angela. Mr. Mathers."

"Jerry," said Jerry.

"Jacob," said the man, shaking Jerry's hand, his grip dry and firm, his palm, perhaps appropriately, soft, which Jerry, thinking again of his mother, found relievedly reassuring. He wondered what might come next: he assumed he'd made it clear in his email that his mother hadn't yet met the Reaper -- *so sorry for your impending loss?* -- but Jacob made an inviting gesture:

"If you'd care to step into my office."

Jerry took Angela's hand again.

# Chapter Twenty-three

"How do you feel?" Angela asked, as about thirty minutes later, after an ushering out by Jacob who'd gently closed the door behind them, they stood on Serenity's back porch.

The final arrangements had been made, papers signed, the coffin ordered -- except for consulting the artist about a cherub tombstone -- and a parlor, though of course not the grandest, which would have been a needless expense (as his mother would certainly say) had been selected by Jerry. There had been several options within his budget, all with quaint Victorian names, but the one he'd finally chosen was appropriately called The Cherub Room, both for a painting of rolly children lounging around an amphora of wine from which they had obviously imbibed, as well as aloft in burnished bronze on a functional gas chandelier, their little wings spread and soft tummies swinging like pendulous pouches as they soared. He'd also chosen a classic hearse from options in a brochure; this an ebony Hudson of 1950s vintage. He supposed, as his mother had said about coffins, a hearse should look like a hearse.

"I suppose the way I should feel," he replied. "My shoulders at least relieved of some weight by a pleasant, efficient professional, and one I'm inclined to trust." He paused at the head of a six-foot staircase that led to a graveled and brick-bordered path across a rear yard as lush as the front and even more populated with Art, again mostly cherubs and juvenile fauns. "Though..."

Feeling somewhere between shamed and silly, he explained how he'd felt the night before when sending his dealing-with-death email and then a half an hour ago when resolving to enter this house.

171

"Sounds natural to me," said Angela, as Jerry naturally took her hand and they descended the steps. "I suppose, in modern terms, one could say it's part of the closure process."

"In modern terms," Jerry mused as, following Jacob's directions -- Jacob would have escorted them, but a young black couple in obvious mourning were waiting in the foyer -- they walked toward one of several buildings at the foot of the wooded slope, above which lay the cemetery. "Modern terms are so one-size-fits-all, and sound inhumanely unempathic. They imply that all of human experience... every feeling, every emotion, everything that makes us alive, has been autopsied from a corpse after the soul has departed... stripped to the bone and pickled in jars... and cold, clinical definitions assigned to every dead part of the whole."

He paused to look up at the clear blue sky. "And if one won't accept those definitions, or questions if the living whole might have been *more* than simply the sum of its purely physical parts and was therefore above our earthly conceit that pretends an understanding of what is still beyond our grasp, it's crassly dismissed as denial."

He looked back at the stately old house with all its intricate adornments, none necessary to being a house in the clinical sense of the word, but making it its *own* house and like no other in the world. "Even with all their prudish reserve and prim professed morality, Victorians granted not only a soul, but a soul unique to each human being, believing we weren't cookie-cutter creations stamped out on some god's assembly-line. Or nature's robotic Babbage engines stoked by biological steam and pre-programmed to perform our functions, assuring survival of species."

Angela smiled. "That sounds very Bohemian."

They passed another youthful faun lounging in a leafy bower and resembling Parker Foxworthy to a remarkable degree; and Angela asked:

"You didn't know, did you?"

"...That this was a black-owned funeral parlor? No. But I'm glad I've entrusted my mother to Jacob, and I'm sure she'll approve when she meets him."

"You're not going to tell her?"

"I'm sure it won't matter." Jerry laughed. "And she did say to surprise her."

He looked ahead to one of the buildings toward which they'd been directed, shaded by towering eucalyptus. It had once been the stable; and any Victorian family possessed of such a magnificent home would have had many horses to draw their coaches. And they must have had several of those, judging from a carriage house that rivaled the stable in size. Its six double doors were all closed, but Jerry assumed it now housed the hearses and funeral cars. There was also a grounds-keeper's cottage, as well as a "garden shed," the latter looking more homey than much of the low-income housing in Oakland's flatland neighborhoods.

The big twin doors of the stable stood open. From within came the ring of steel upon stone, a sound faintly heard when they'd left the house but which had grown louder and more distinct above the play of another fountain and bird song amongst the whispering trees as they approached the building; which, though only housing for horses, was adorned with delicate gingerbread and boasted an octagon cupola.

Jerry supposed it would have been crass to have called it a tombstone factory, especially in light of the fine artwork that stood in tree-latticed sunlight on either side of the doorway; though some of the pieces -- which ranged from the stereotypical slabs and simple crosses that first-graders drew in anticipation of Halloween, to several exquisitely-rendered angels -- were bound with industrial strapping to wooden cargo pallets.

And there was a little forklift with bulldozer tracks instead of wheels, of obvious antiquity, though gleaming with marigold paint, its name, TERRATAC, highlighted in black; along with an elderly Mack flatbed truck of possibly 1930s vintage, though either lovingly maintained or meticulously restored, its boxy cab of emerald-green, its flowing fenders glossy black, its prominent headlamps gleaming chrome, with a grouping of contemplative cherubs roped to its varnished wooden back. Script font letters in gold on its doors discretely displayed the company name.

An alluvial fan of stone chips in various shades of marble and granite spread from the building's doorway and paved the earth in front. The scene, though not quite Victorian due to the "modern" machinery, was still early 20th century, and Jerry was jarred back to the future when, about to enter, Angela's hand still in his, there burst forth the staccato clatter of -- Jerry assumed -- a pneumatic jackhammer.

Angela also seemed startled as if she had also been yanked from the past, but then she smiled and almost shouted above the cacophonous din, "That's not cheating. I use one for roughing-out." She added as the rattling ceased, "As I'm sure Michelangelo would have done if they'd been available."

Jerry smiled, too, his ears still ringing. "I don't grind my own pigments."

Though bare bulbs burned amongst spider-webbed rafters, the building's interior seemed dark at first compared to the sunlight outside, and it took a moment for Jerry's eyes to adjust to the dusky shadows. There was also a feathery mist in the air, which gave the lights haloes and softened details. Though the "tombstone factory" image persisted, he substituted "studio," and imagined that Angela's West Oakland loft may have looked something like this... though not having an earthen floor and probably far less populated with work that commercially had to be done.

And of course not graveyard art.

Those pale stone shapes were the first discerned as his eyes slowly accustomed themselves to the relative dimness and drifting mist; and like the pieces waiting outside to be transported to -- installment? -- ranged from simple round-topped slabs to figures of angels and cherubs so real they might have capered in welcome or bowed in benediction. There were also several youthful fauns playing pipes atop monuments already carved with names and dates. Most of these were charmingly chubby, a trait, which if not preferred by the artist, was still an attractive attribute he rendered very well; and all, to Jerry's experienced eye, had either been sculpted from breathing life or, in light of their destiny, perhaps from family photographs.

Last to appear, and naturally so, and maybe explaining his inclination, was an equally chubby young black man, or perhaps a midteen boy, shirtless in jeans and gleaming with sweat as if someone had polished a midnight, though dusted with pale chips of marble and poised with a brutal-looking jack-hammer, obviously roughing-out the base of an otherwise mostly completed faun who appeared to be newly into his teens and who, at least above the waist, resembled Bill Malone, though his face was undoubtedly African.

The artist at most was seventeen, Jerry guessed as his eyes fully adapted, which seemed almost miraculous in light of his masterful skills. His chest was boyishly-breasted and his belly far overhung his jeans, his navel overlapped by rolls which gave him a Gabrielish "second smile;" and though despite an overhead hoist with dangling chains that ran on a rail, as well as the antique forklift outside, he probably had to do much heavy lifting, his musculature was plumply concealed.

Unlike Michelangelo -- the jack-hammer notwithstanding -- who had almost lost an eye to his Art, he wore a pair of steam-punkish goggles, which left a cartoonish raccoon-mask above the pale dust on his cherubic cheeks as, seeing Jerry and Angela, he lay down his hammer and pushed them up on a "newsboy cap" as tweedly archaic as Elwood's atop a bush of stone-floured curls. Though obviously an accomplished artist, and one -- Jerry couldn't help thinking -- whose work should be gracing galleries instead of consigned to cemeteries, the visual impression he gave was of a young construction worker, and Jerry found himself surprised by a gentle voice and a cultured greet-ing:

"Good afternoon Miss Davis. Mr. Mathers. I'm Matthew."

Jerry noticed a phone in a black leather sheath clipped to Matthew's low-clinging jeans, so Jacob must have informed him that – clients -- were on their way. As they had done with Jacob, Angela and Jerry dispensed with formal appellations.

The jack-hammer *steamed* as it lay on the ground: apparently it was powered by steam, and a thick rubber hose snaked away in the dust to a small antique-looking boiler; and there was a pile of coal, which explained the softly drifting mist and tropically humid heat.

Matthew didn't offer a hand, naturally dusted with his Art, which

175

had also drawn a bit of blood -- though Jerry wouldn't have minded -- but waved toward an ancient refrigerator that stood near a battered old desk in what must have been a former stall, though atop the desk was a new PC with a large flat screen. "Would you care for a beverage? Coke? I also have water and juices."

Angela glanced at Jerry and smiled. "Would you happen to have any beer?"

"Would Bohemia serve?"

"Nicely, thank you," said Jerry.

Matthew was probably accustomed to meeting sorrowful people and matching their mournful *mien* -- albeit despite his appearance, which literally radiated life in every sense of the word -- but maybe Jacob had told him that these potential patrons didn't require the wearing of weeds. He led them to the stall, its walls and manger worn shiny and smooth from the occupancy of equines past whose aromatic spirits still lingered, and drawing a handkerchief from a pocket, dusted the seats of two wooden chairs before opening the refrigerator and taking out three amber bottles. There were glasses in the manger, upside-down for obvious reasons, but Jerry said, "That's all right" when Matthew looked a question.

Matthew distributed refreshment, then sat down at the desk. Jerry noticed a cherub ashtray, and Matthew, maybe noting he'd noticed, offered a pack of American Spirits, somehow not surprisingly blue.

Angela gestured around at the Art after accepting a cigarette, which Matthew lit with a wooden match and did the same for Jerry, and after taking a sip from her bottle, said, "You do magnificent work."

Matthew lit his cigarette and exhaled a ghost. "Thank you." He smiled. "It pays the bills."

Jerry said, trying to sound unpretentious... what else could he say: We feel you? "We understand. Angela is also a sculptor, and I paint."

"You're *that* Jerry Mathers?" asked Matthew.

Jerry laughed. "Most people who say it that way are referring to The Beaver." *Though he's DECADES older than me.*

"No offense meant."

"None taken."

Matthew took a sip from his bottle, though probably more accustomed to chug... as Jerry and Trevor had done in their youth. "I've seen your work in galleries. Your portraiture is masterful, sir. Also, of course, your seascapes."

"Thank you, sir," Jerry returned. "Though it's still the latter that mostly pay bills." He glanced at Matthew's computer screen, which displayed a green three-dimensional grid of the young black faun he'd created. Jerry knew of the "blocking-out" process from back in his Art studies days, though then it had been done on paper as Michelangelo had worked... though, as with the efficient jackhammer, he'd have probably used a computer today.

"Especially these days," he added. "When people look at digital pictures and think they're seeing life. ...Of course I wasn't implying..."

Matthew nodded. "I know what you mean, the soul isn't there." He tapped the keyboard, rotating the figure, which might originally have been of the shirtless boy on a couch or chair but which now floated in starless space. "One could program a robotic arm to chisel this picture perfectly... from the waist up, anyway. Though furry legs and hooves could also be easily programmed. But you'd still end up with a physical image and not a portrait of *him*." He studied the boy for a moment. "That might be good enough for some people. In fact it's often what they want... to be remembered for how they looked."

"Or the look they created," said Jerry. "The physical image they forced on themselves... painted on, cut into their flesh, suffered, sweated and dieted for, became obsessive-compulsive for, invented new guilt and conceptions of sin, and denied the pleasures of life to display." He thought of Gabriel and added, "Their self-created illusion of self."

"Most artfully put," said Matthew.

Angela laughed. "All to end up as 'perfect' corpses."

"The healthy dead," said Matthew. Then he met Jerry's eyes. "Your time will come... though that probably wasn't the right way to put it."

Jerry smiled. "I took it how it was meant, sir, and thank you again."

The boiler hissed out a pale cloud of steam -- a safety valve, Jerry presumed, since the hammer wasn't in use -- softy misting the air again.

Matthew turned to Angela. "I know your name, too, and your works are beautiful portraits in stone."

"Thank you," Angela replied. "I'm also hoping my time will come, though for the present I pay a few bills."

Jerry had another thought and turned to Matthew again. "Did you do the cherub fountain at Elysian Nursing Home?"

"Juvenilia," said Matthew. "Also a bench, and too overly-crafted: too much blood and sweat invested, literally and figuratively, for commercial work."

*How juvenile could they have been?* Jerry thought. "But both superb," he said. "My mother thinks so, too."

"Thank you both," said Matthew, then took on a graver expression, though his face was more suited to smile. "Jacob explained your..."

Jerry's smile was a bit forced, but though the circumstances were sad, he hated to throw a pall on the moment. "Please don't say, 'impending need.'"

"I was, and I'm sorry," said Matthew. "One does have to play a role at times."

"All of us do," said Jerry. "On many levels for many reasons, and not the least to pay our bills. But... as I suppose I should say... shall we get down to business?"

Matthew exhaled another ghost, which melded with the drifting steam, then steepled his chubby, stone-scarred fingers. "Jacob mentioned a cherub."

"That's what my mother wants," said Jerry. "And not a sad one. 'No little boy crying alone,' as she put it."

Matthew looked relieved. "That... I think unfortunately... is the most requested theme. Though cherubs were never created to cry. They're a celebration of life, as well as whatever lies beyond."

Jerry's smile came naturally now. "I'm inclined to agree, and my mother shares that conviction."

Matthew flicked his ashes into the cherub's offered bowl and took another sip of beer. "What do you have in mind?"

"Something like your company... figure. Very much like him, I hope... the boy in front of the house."

Matthew seemed intrigued. "He's also juvenilia. But I've never had a request for him." He patted his belly, making it ripple. "No doubt for obvious reasons these days."

Angela asked, "Of course you wouldn't sell him."

Matthew sounded teenage now. "Nah, he's part of the family."

"Perhaps a copy?" asked Jerry. "You will do copies of pieces?"

Matthew's smile turned a bit wry. "'All children are artists. The problem is how to remain an artist once you grow up.'"

"Pablo Picasso," said Angela.

"And paying bills is part of that problem, so, yes, I could copy him."

Jerry said, "I'd imagine finding another model might be difficult these days."

"Sadly true," said Matthew. "And more difficult, a happy one to bare his soul in stone... fat kids being today's new niggers and persecuted mercilessly as if they have no right to be happy."

He didn't apologize, and Jerry was grateful for that. Angela simply nodded.

Matthew freed another ghost. "You'd want him life-size?"

Jerry smiled. "And every ounce as full of life."

# Chapter Twenty-four

"**D**id that faun look familiar?" Angela asked, as Jerry guided the Gremlin around a curve on the tree-shaded road, passing a jogger who didn't look happy -- though he'd never seen a jogger who did -- and down a grade through a ferny canyon.

"Parker Foxworthy?"

Angela smiled. "I noticed him; but I meant the one Matthew was finishing from the model on his computer."

"Now that you mention it, yes," said Jerry. "At least above the waist, and definitely his face. A boy like Gabriel's sleeping prince but awake and smiling. ...I wonder if those were his parents waiting when Jacob showed us out?"

"I'm sure they're in good hands with Jacob no matter who they are. As well as their son, if they are his parents." Angela smiled again. "Not to mention Matthew's hands. He's certainly a Master."

"I wonder who's the mechanical Master?"

Angela looked a question, and Jerry went on, "Someone at Serenity is, judging from that antique truck and the pictures of their classic hearses. Even the forklift looked restored."

"I noticed that, too," said Angela. "And it is an art form."

Jerry paused at a stop sign about two miles from the Rockridge BART station. "I hope Matthew can clone the soul, at least metaphorically speaking, when he copies the cherub. Or maybe find another model with a soul unique to himself."

Angela looked thoughtful. "You wouldn't mind a black one?"

"Being white, I never thought of that, but I wouldn't mind at all. Nor, I'm sure, would my mother." Jerry smiled. "Cherubs must come in all colors like that picture in Serenity's foyer."

He told her about the Cub Scout as they rolled down rural Broadway, passing Lake Temescal, where a multi-racial group of boys, shirtless, in their early teens, one black boy defiantly fat — as it seemed these days -- were skateboarding in the parking lot. "I'm sure Matthew will do beautiful work no matter who the model is, but..." He sighed. "With so many other pieces waiting, he can't even start in less than a month, with another month for completion, and I wanted it to be there for her."

Angela touched his hand on the wheel. "You said the doctor didn't know."

Jerry thought morbidly of money, and of his seemingly cruel speculations of how long his mother might live. ...What if she departed in mind but lingered on for months in body? He supposed, against her wishes, he could mortgage the house. ...But, what if it came to the absolute worst and he had to either bankrupt himself or pull the proverbial "plug?" But, burying those thoughts, he smiled. "That's true."

Angela shook her head as if sensing those shadows in Jerry's mind. "What a fucked-up culture we live in! Where our elders become liabilities, only expensive burdens to bear instead of treasured assets. ...And don't say, 'if you'd only been better.' None of this is your fault."

"I know, and thank you," said Jerry. "But sometimes I can't help thinking it is." He hesitated a moment after stopping at the BART station. "Would you like to meet her? I know she'd love meeting you."

Angela smiled again. "I'd like that very much."

181

# Chapter Twenty-five

Gabriel laughed in the clear morning light. "Sorry, Mr. Mathers, but duh."

They were at the foot of Morrison's staircase, a few other students already ascending -- including Parker Foxworthy, who'd given Jerry a friendly smile with no innuendoes attached -- though there were still about fifteen minutes before the Regulators chimed.

Angela would have also been here, ostensibly for substantiation that Jerry wasn't as mad as a hatter, but had called his house as he'd been leaving to say there had been a delay on BART. Of course he'd offered to pick her up, but she'd said he wouldn't have time; and because of the crowbar "accident" he should be there to meet Gabriel. He'd thought, absurdly, of hard-hats when passing a construction site, but though he'd been watching the third floor windows, all were closed this morning. The tower curtains *might* have moved but he couldn't be sure.

Now he regarded the laughing boy, who undulated all over with mirth, as the huge black Packard, murmuring softly, rolled away up the street. He'd been prepared for different reactions, including being dismissed as mad, but amusement hadn't been one of them. Feeling foolish, he asked, "You *knew* the house was haunted?"

Gabriel smiled. "I know a ghost when I feel one; and we should probably get inside in case of flying objects. The elevator would be faster if you'd like to chat in your office."

"You're not afraid of it?" asked Jerry.

"We're not expected to use it."

The cage descended obediently when Jerry pushed the button, and Gabriel backed through its doorway. Jerry squeezed himself in,

182

closed the grille and pushed the 2 button. As on that rainy morning, the machinery seemed to strain a bit, but the cage ascended smoothly, passing Miss Morrison's vigilant eyes... though they seemed to look normally watchful today instead of malignly focused on him.

Gabriel noted Jerry's finger hovering on EMERGENCY STOP. "You'd have to be a real good mechanic to disable the safety brake, so it's highly unlikely we're going to fall. And though Elisha Graves Otis... no relation of which I'm aware... invented the elevator in 1852, I doubt if Miss Morrison knew much about them. Ghosts are souls still here on earth: call it an oxymoron, but they don't have knowledge beyond the grave. And sometimes they don't even know they're dead."

"Like in *The Others?*" asked Jerry.

"Exactly."

The lift stopped on the second floor and Gabriel tractored out, the planking creaking beneath his treads. Jerry followed him up the hall, which was filling with students heading for classes, and asked while unlocking his office door. "You think it's Miss Morrison's ghost?"

Several kids gave him curious looks, but Gabriel only shrugged and said, "She seems the most probable spirit, especially since her bones are still here, but we won't know until we meet her."

Jerry let Gabriel enter first and closed the door behind them. "You seem to know a lot about ghosts. Is your house haunted?"

"Our spirits are just passing through," said Gabriel, with enigmatic casualness. "Most are harmless, and/or confused about where to go from here."

Jerry accepted that from someone who seemingly knew such things since Gabriel's mind seemed as vast as his body, though wondered, *what about those who aren't?* He glanced at the clock, and Gabriel smiled. "Expecting Miss Davis?"

"How did you know?"

"Backup in case I thought you were nuts." Gabriel opened one of his packs and drew out a McDonald's bag. "I got you a breakfast sandwich and coffee... both of you. Figured you'd be waiting for me."

Jerry sat down in the visitor's chair and gratefully opened the bag, his stomach growling eagerly at the tempting aromas of sausage and cheese. "How long have you known this house was haunted?"

Gabriel fired an American Spirit. "There's a difference between a haunted house... some houses haunt themselves... and a house that's being haunted. But I knew there was a ghost in here when I first set foot through the door... figuratively speaking."

"And you knew... she... didn't want you here?"

Gabriel looked thoughtful. "I knew someone didn't."

There was a knock on the door. "Come in," Jerry called.

Of course he'd hoped for Angela, but it was Amanda Teabrook, who looked more cadaverous than ever. "Mr. Mathers?"

"Yes?" said Jerry, trying not to sound annoyed at the interruption.

"I wanted to tell you I'm trying hard..." Amanda saw Gabriel and finished, "You know? What we talked about?"

Before Jerry could think of an answer -- at least a politically-correct one -- Gabriel spun his chair around. "Nobody wants to draw you 'cause you're too fucking skinny! But you don't have to worry about it, because if you don't start eating *today* you'll be dead tomorrow!"

Amanda's bony jaw dropped. For a moment she seemed about to scream -- perhaps yet another deluded assertion of being morbidly obese -- but burst into tears and slammed the door.

Jerry was horrified, but Gabriel turned back around and shrugged. "Somebody had to tell her the truth, and... pardon me, sir... you weren't going to."

"...Do you think it will work?"

"That's entirely up to her. She has to draw herself from life and really see what's there." Gabriel smiled wryly. "And what isn't."

"Don't you think you went too far?"

Another shrug. "People don't always get a god-slap, so sometimes you have to give them a bitch-slap. When you see the skull beneath the face... and not just physically like hers... the Reaper isn't far away."

Jerry wondered what would happen if Tillinghast heard of this? It could be construed as bullying, and students had been expelled for that... which would be a convenient excuse.

Gabriel exhaled a ghost. "I assume you and Miss Davis are concerned for my safety?"

Jerry took a bite of his sandwich. "I'd think that would be obvious after what happened yesterday. But we'd already planned to warn you that something nasty was in this house."

Gabriel smiled. "Thanks, but what about your safety?"

Jerry glanced at the gas light. "We've also considered that. As well as Bill Malone's." He took a sip of coffee. "We think Elwood is on your side, and, for whatever it's worth, he said you're safe in regard to the house... in the physical sense, I assume."

"But obviously not on the sidewalk outside."

"What happened yesterday seems to prove that."

"Which means it's beyond his vigilance, or maybe his control."

"...I hadn't thought of it that way, but I suppose it's true." The Regulators began to chime. "Damn!" said Jerry and bolted the last of his sandwich.

Gabriel snuffed his cigarette. "Life goes on."

Jerry started for the door, but paused with a hand on the knob. "Be careful, Gabe. Don't go anywhere alone in this house."

Gabriel Caterpillared out when Jerry opened the door. "You be careful, too, Mr. Mathers. And, of course, Miss Davis. I'll watch out for Bill." He paused in the hall to point to the ceiling. "Don't go up there without me."

Jerry also raised his eyes. "The third floor? What makes you think I would?"

A mischievous smile. "Ghosts can be very persuasive."

# Chapter Twenty-six

"Jerry."

Jerry looked up from his office desk where he'd been grading the morning's artwork -- one of the girls had been the model, and most of the kids were improving, actually starting to draw from life instead of only interpreting it -- as Tillinghast steamed in from the hall. The Regulators had chimed, tolling the knell of another school day, and the house had emptied of students and staff, becoming broodingly silent again. Two days of sun had loosened the windows, and Jerry had opened them. He hadn't seen Elwood in all that time and wondered if that was intentional: was Elwood ashamed of what had happened with the flying crowbar, an accident... like spilling the ink? Or, he simply might have been busy keeping the ancient house alive.

Gabriel and Bill had lunched at McDonalds, Jerry and Angela escorting them down the staircase to the street, watching the boys on the sidewalk while also scanning the windows above, several of which were open today, though none on the topmost floor. The tower curtains *may* have moved, though whether by an observer's hand or simply from a lofty breeze couldn't be discerned. After dining in the back yard -- another magnificent Morrison meal of broiled lamb chops with mint sauce -- in company with the tumescent faun silently playing his pipes, they had gone back to the street and waited until the boys returned, again keeping watch on the windows.

Gabriel had winked at them while tractoring up the staircase, Bill riding the rear of his mighty machine, and Bill had bestowed a princely smile, though seemingly not in conspiracy, so maybe

186

Gabriel hadn't told him of any possible danger; and Jerry supposed, based upon Gabriel's knowledge of ghosts, he hadn't thought it necessary. Or maybe just not yet. Nevertheless, after school, Angela and Jerry had escorted the boys again to see them safely into their cars... Bill's the Corbitt garbage packer, presumably driven by his father, and which, though absolutely spotless – one could have probably dined in back -- seemed a sort of bitch-slap to all the ostentatious rides.

Now, Jerry studied Tillinghast's face, but he looked more perplexed than anything else.

"Do you know anything of Amanda Teabrook?"

*That she might be dead tomorrow with malnutrition the autopsied cause?* But Jerry said in a neutral tone, "She wasn't in my class today."

"She asked me leave to go home this morning. Said she wasn't feeling well. She certainly didn't *look* well, but also seemed very upset... close to hysterics, in my opinion."

*Perhaps an attack of brain fever at hearing the politically-incorrect truth?* "I'm sorry to hear that," said Jerry. She apparently hadn't reported being 'bullied' about her size... or rather the lack of same. It also seemed from Tillinghast's manner he hadn't heard of the flying crowbar. "I hope she's better soon," Jerry added.

"As do I," said Tillinghast. "Her family is quite influential and her presence very much honors this school." He extracted his watch, and Jerry realized now -- and wondered why he hadn't before -- it was only a pompous performance, because he could have looked at the clock like any common person. "Will you be working late?"

"A few more drawings to grade," said Jerry, wondering why he'd been asked. Did Tillinghast want him out of the house? Or to know if he'd be here a while, his presence possibly inconvenient if some sort of scheme was afoot? ...Or was he being paranoid?

"May I...?" said Tillinghast.

"Of course."

Tillinghast encroached on the desk and scanned a few of the pictures. "May I see Gabriel's interpretation?"

Jerry presented the work, which was not an interpretation, and which of course he'd graded A.

"The boy does have talent," Tillinghast grudged. "Attractive girl... clearly good breeding." The latter statement may have been stressed.

"Have there been any more parental complaints?"

Tillinghast frowned. "One this morning, as I warned there would be, concerning Crystal Sterling's... work. I smoothed those feathers... but carefully, Jerry, as we discussed. ...A pleasant evening, Jerry." Tillinghast came about and navigated out the door.

Jerry put Gabriel's drawing into his portfolio. He'd called Harriet after lunch, but she'd said his mother was not at her best; and though Angela wanted to meet her, the time apparently wasn't right. He'd offered Angela a ride to BART, but she'd said she had some shopping to do, which included another block of marble for a project "recently inspired," and apparently inspiring enough to warrant the price of a taxi. Jerry had planned to work on the seascape as soon as he got home – it had to be finished soon -- with maybe a break for a drive-through dinner, though he couldn't afford it. But there had to be a few pleasures in life...

He raised his eyes to the gas light.

...or what was the point of living?

About thirty minutes later he added a note of praise to the last of the morning's drawings... Raymond Blakemore's, a surprising B. Raymond had obviously worked very hard to render this female figure, perhaps to convince everyone he liked girls... and/or perhaps himself

The house's silence was total now, not even the creak of a settling joist. Presumably, Tillinghast had left. Jerry wondered where Elwood might be. Then he took one of his last Marlboros out of the pack in the drawer and put it in his shirt pocket for later. Tillinghast's expensive cigar was also in the drawer. He regarded it for a moment as if it was a mummified phallus, then rose and threw it out a window. He draped his coat over a shoulder and picked up his portfolio. Out in the hall he listened again, but only silence ruled. Then he locked his office door and headed for the staircase, but paused at the elevator, its indicator pointing to 3. Of course he remembered Gabriel's warning: *Don't go up there without me.*

Had Gabriel been teasing... just being a boy of thirteen? His assumption that Jerry might go up there seemed a little unsettling, though that Jerry shouldn't without him childishly challenged his manhood. But, assuming they ever would – though Jerry couldn't fathom why -- it might be wise to check out the floor, which he'd noted yesterday, besides being almost buried in dust, had also been sagging in places.

Would Elwood give him a tour despite the third floor being forbidden? Surely Elwood owed him for not reporting the "accident."

He pushed the button and the cage descended, its motor hum and clacking cables echoing through the silent house, but Jerry went down the staircase, glancing at Miss Morrison, who only seemed to regard him with her usual doubtful expression, and called to the empty first floor hall, "Elwood?"

He waited a minute and called again, but there was no reply. Of course Elwood might have been out, possibly digging up Period parts to keep the ancient house alive, or maybe tending the grounds. Jerry crossed the foyer and opened the brass-plaqued CUSTODIAN door to the basement stairway, of which he'd only gotten glimpses during the past fifteen years.

Apparently, like the upper story, and being only a common region, the basement hadn't been wired, and the stairs were only dimly lit by a single gas globe near a closed door at the bottom. This portal, though plain by Victorian standards, was nevertheless of mahogany and clearly very substantial, so Jerry's knock was mostly absorbed. He knocked again, harder, abusing his knuckles, and called Elwood's name but without result.

He dithered a moment in the wavering glow cast by the faintly whispering flame, then tried the doorknob and found it unlocked. He half expected a hair-raising creak like the *Tales From The Crypt* introduction, but of course Elwood kept the hinges oiled. The basement was, not surprisingly, huge and forested with massive timbers to carry the mammoth mansion's weight, its nethermost regions in absolute blackness, making it seem all the more vast like pictures of ancient catacombs, though, as far as Jerry could see, without any piles of skulls and bones. From what little he could discern in the pale glow of another gas fixture, the walls were rusty-reddish brick and only a part of the floor concrete -- this an area near the door -- the rest of grayish hard-packed earth, which probably not unnaturally suggested a graveyard scent. Also not unnatural were the ghostly shrouds of spider webs eerily swaying in distant perspectives that dwindled into darkness.

A hulking iron monster occupied part of the paved area, surmounted with pipes like Medusa's hair, with a toothy grille and pressure gauge eyes, the latter seeming to study him. Though there was a coal bin, the furnace had been converted to gas. A huge arcane electrical panel with many glass fuses and copper knife switches like something out of Frankenstein's lab, was mounted on the wall near the door in a maze of tube-and-post wiring of the fabric-covered type. No doubt Elwood could have tapped in to provide himself with electric light, but maybe he liked the soft glow of gas?

Also upon the concrete floor was what looked like a Victorian stage play set, circa 1890... Sherlock and Watson would have felt right at home. There was a brass bed, neatly made, surrounded by fine antique furniture -- a dresser, chairs, a bedside table, an *armoire* and a claw-footed desk -- arranged on a square of rose-patterned carpet. There was also a glass-fronted bookcase filled with expensive-looking volumes bound in buckram or quality leather, and possibly first-editions of 19th century literature. Even if Elwood preferred antique light -- there was an Argand lamp on the desk and another on the bedside table -- he might still have tapped electricity for a TV or radio, but nothing amongst his possessions seemed to date much beyond 1900.

Of course, there were radios and TVs in many of the classrooms and the teachers' lounge, which he could have used after school hours. And, assuming he wanted to, could go online from many computers.

Jerry noticed framed photographs on the dresser top. All were time-faded black-and-whites of the type once known as Cabinets, and may have been of Elwood's grandfather, and maybe his father as a young boy -- the latter shirtless in "dungarees," his tummy proudly prominent in the sway-backed stance of many young kids, and standing with a shovel in hand. There was also one of Miss Morrison upon a stone bench in the mansion's back yard overlooked by a fat young faun, a plump arm fondly around the boy and most uncharacteristically smiling, but he didn't want to invade Elwood's space by taking a closer look. He had no right to be here, and was about to leave, when he saw a wooden key board mounted on one of the mammoth timbers.

Most of the keys were skeleton types -- through the proper term was bitt key -- and were probably duplicates of those on Elwood's ring, arranged on hooks below hand-lettered tags that indicated what doors they opened... including "Third Floor" and "Tower."

And, ominously, "Crypt."

But there were also a few modern keys, one labeled "Gas Main Valve," another "Electric Meter Box," and another "Elevator"... the latter presumably fitting the lock on the third floor grille.

This confirmed that Tillinghast -- or actually anyone -- could gain access to these keys and have other duplicates made.

Jerry hesitated... this could cost him his job. A job he desperately needed right now.

But that crowbar could have cost Gabriel's life, and the next "accident" *could* be deadly.

He raised his eyes... there *was* something up there, he was sure, besides "only shadows and dust."

He hesitated a moment, then took the grille and tower keys.

# Chapter Twenty-seven

In many ghost and horror films there came the almost inevitable scene in which someone incredibly stupid, more often than not a dim-witted teen, against all reason and sane common sense, went down to the basement alone.

Or, up to lofty places where grinning evil lurked.

Jerry wondered if he was playing that role as, after ascending back to the foyer, he pushed the elevator button. The machinery hummed, the cables thrummed, and the cage descended for him. The keys felt strangely cold in his hand, though he found his palms were sweating as he entered and pushed the button for 3.

Miss Morrison watched him rise away with a seemingly enigmatic smile not unlike the Mona Lisa's that hinted of secrets beyond mortal grasp. Being no longer a dim-witted teen -- and *perhaps* not a stupid adult -- he had second-thoughts on the second floor and almost pushed the button to stop. On a purely earthly level, he was maybe foolishly risking his job by defying Tillinghast's edict, and that alone should have been enough to make him go back and return the keys. On a supernatural level, he was ignoring a warning from someone he should probably trust.

But he didn't push the button, and the cage came to rest in gloomy half-light. The *hollow* sensation engulfed him again as, clutching the grille like a prisoner, he scanned the shadow-shrouded hall. The floor indeed was sagging in places, probably from dry-rot, which, he'd read, was a kind of fungus that fed on the bones of old houses.

The strange illusion of *distance* returned as he looked toward the tower staircase, and again he told himself the safe and sanest thing to do was put those keys back and go home. He rationalized, for all he knew, Tillinghast might not have left and would have heard the elevator -- which Elwood purportedly didn't use -- and might come to investigate. Perhaps, as Angela had said, he was snooping in teachers' offices, presumably for justification should any dismissals be required; so shouldn't Jerry be *sure* he was gone before justifying his own dismissal?

He pushed the 2 button.

Nothing happened!

As on that night at five-years-old -- as on that night in recent past -- he almost screamed for help! He stabbed the button repeatedly, sweat breaking cold on his body, but the machinery didn't respond... and now he really *was* a prisoner locked in a brass-bound casket!

Fighting electric jolts of panic, he grasped at straws of reason... perhaps a fuse had blown? But the little light bulb in its own cage was on. Maybe a separate circuit? He pushed the 1 and G buttons, but again without result. A skeleton finger ran down his spine as he thought of the oncoming night. To be trapped up here in darkness with... *her!*

Below EMERGENCY STOP was a button labeled ALARM. Almost, he pushed it, and almost he was terrified lest it wouldn't work.

But then *some* reason returned. He wasn't a scared little boy! Though, like a child, he searched for excuses for being caught doing something naughty: he'd come up here to... search the old records. ...A former student had called him.

Like a child he embellished his lie: the student had asked for his juvenile works, which hadn't been in Jerry's closet, so Jerry had assumed...

That might save his job.

Once more he almost pushed ALARM.

...But *was* he really trapped? Trying to still his trembling hands, he took the modern key and fitted it into the grille's padlock... which fell instantly open. Leaving his coat and portfolio, he cautiously stepped into the hall, the floorboards creaking underfoot even beneath his negligible weight. Keeping to the well-worn trail, he went to the stairway door, which of course was dead-bolt locked and needed its own key to open. Still, he was no longer helpless; he could call for help from any window, and even if -- she -- jammed them, could always break the glass.

He turned toward the tower end of the hall, lit by several shafts of sunlight, dimming to yellow as evening approached, through randomly open west-facing doors, and again there was that illusion of *distance*. Keeping again to the trail, the floorboards crying with every step, he went to the first open door and peered in.

The room was small and bare as bones, the sunlight subdued through the one window's curtains of yellowed old lace. There was only a single gas light globe on a wall thickly shrouded in spider webs. Dust swirled around as he crossed to the window and puffed from the drapes when he parted them. The latch mechanism was rusty, but finally yielded to his efforts and he was able to raise the sash; though, as Elwood had said, the cords had apparently rotted away and it wouldn't stay up by itself. Bracing his back against the sash, hands on the sill, he leaned out and looked down.

There was his car on the street below partly obscured by the oaks. There was a click and clatter of wheels, and a swag-bellied boy of maybe thirteen, shirtless in butt-baring oversize jeans, his hair in a Mohawk of black and bleached blond, and toting a hefty McDonalds bag, rolled past the front stairs on a skateboard. He suddenly tailed to a stop and picked something up from the sidewalk... Tillinghast's twenty-dollar cigar.

"Cool!" he exclaimed, expertly biting off the tip, then producing a plastic lighter and firing the big fat cigar like a latter-day Little Rascal, then rolling away puffing smoke.

A middle-aged woman was walking a dog; one of those designer dogs like a cross between a dust-bunny and rodent... "rat-dogs," Trevor had called them. As if to prove something -- that he wasn't looking out from within another dimension or time and might not be visible in the present? -- he called an absurd-sounding, "Good afternoon."

The woman seemed slightly startled, scanned around at her level, then looked up at him. Her smile was a little uncertain, but then she returned the archaic greeting.

194

Jerry let the window down and locked the reluctant latch. No doubt he could have prevailed on the woman to summon help with her phone -- of course he could! -- which he found childishly reassuring. Provoking more harmless dust-bunny ghosts, he returned to the shadowy hall.

Again, the silence was eerily *hollow*, and again there was that impression of distance as he started for the tower staircase, but he felt no sense of impending threat or tingle on the back of his neck as if he was being followed... by a yellowed skeleton in a shroud? Still, he looked back to be sure.

The next door was closed, but the floor showed signs of this room being entered. The hinges shrieked when he opened the door, in proper ghostly movie fashion, but the space was occupied by dusty wooden file cabinets of the early twentieth-century type, no doubt containing the old school records. Jerry considered examining them, if only to -- absurdly -- ascertain there *had* been other Directors prior to Tillinghast, but didn't want to take the time. Tillinghast indeed might have left, but Elwood, if he had gone out, or was working in the back yard -- perhaps even dutifully dusting the crypt -- could be returning any time and might notice the missing keys. He did owe Jerry, at least technically, but this felt like betrayal.

Jerry closed the door and went on, the light growing dimmer and yellowing more as the sun descended across the Bay in San Francisco's famous fog. He peered into other rooms as he passed, each one small, dusty and empty, lath showing like bones where plaster had fallen from slowly crumbling ceilings and walls. He assumed all the furniture had been sold or auctioned long ago and Elwood's father -- or grandfather -- had been given a few of the finer pieces in gratitude for continued service. Or maybe they had been willed to him, including those surely valuable books? He probably had a pension, as well as full health coverage, and, assuming those things in the basement were his, his declining years would be comfortable, and his future a lot more secure than Jerry's.

Despite the persisting illusion of distance, as if the hallway were telescoping or, like the speed of light in theory, the tower staircase could be approached but never actually attained, it seemed to take no longer than it actually should have to reach the stairs.

Though the trail continued up the steps and the banister rail was free of dust as if often gripped by a living hand, Tillinghast had not been lying about the stairway's condition: the treads were sagging ominously, and though Elwood wasn't weighty, he was certainly risking life or limb every time he went up there. Also as Tillinghast had said, the stairwell indeed was "dangerously dark," the narrow steps spiraling away into absolute blackness.

Jerry studied the rotten treads in the slowly fading daylight. Did he dare? ...And why did he want to? If he had to call for help, it would be wise to do it soon while people were still on the sunlit street.

He looked down the hall to the elevator and somehow knew it would work again. It was if he'd been drawn to this point -- *ghosts can be very persuasive* -- but left here to make his own decision of whether or not to...

Go up there.

He hadn't needed Gabriel to get this far without meeting a ghost, but *should* he have him to go any farther?

But, even if Gabriel had been with him, the boy couldn't possibly get up those stairs; too narrow for his mechanical steed even if they could bear the weight; and how could he climb without it?

He noticed a wall-mounted gas light a few feet up the stairwell. There was probably another at the top... but his lighter was back in his coat. Then he remembered his keychain light and drew it from a pocket. The tiny bluish bulb was sufficient, and warily, testing each creaky tread, one hand on the uncertain banister, he cautiously climbed to the upper landing.

A golden pin-point of daylight showed through the tower door's keyhole. The brass doorknob, like the banister rail, had been recently grasped and was free of dust. It seemed strange that this door would be locked... but why did he assume it was locked? He reached for the knob, but hesitated, then crouched to put an eye to the keyhole.

An elderly woman's voice commanded, "Young man, come here."

# Chapter Twenty-eight

He'd always thought it was just an expression used in Victorian horror tales, but hair *could* actually stand on end! Just as one *could* freeze in terror!

Both states may have lasted for seconds -- or minutes -- as Jerry remained in a crouch at the door seemingly unable to move, his eye not quite to the keyhole. Of course he'd seen countless movies, usually with Trevor during his youth, about haunted houses and ghostly encounters. And he'd watched many TV shows, some purporting to be on the real... but none of those disembodied voices had ever sounded *this* real!

"Dawdling doesn't become you," admonished the voice beyond the door. "Nor does peeking at keyholes... childish, as I'm sure you agree." The tone altered to mild impatience. "I distinctly said, young man, come here." There was a pause and a chuckle... which didn't sound the least bit malign. "Are you frightened of me?"

Suddenly feeling more foolish than scared, which seemed to free his frozen spine, Jerry stood up and faced the door. ...How could that possibly be a ghost?

Still, he remembered a Lovecraft story of – things -- in old houses locked in rooms and enticing fools to let them out by sounding harmlessly benign. Though still feeling foolish, he asked, "Are you locked in?"

"What a silly idea! Come here, young man. And please wipe the dust from your boots."

It was the last that convinced him there was nothing to fear. Of all the things a ghost might say, that seemed the most improbable. Nor, he found, was the door locked.

197

For a moment his eyes were dazzled after the stairwell's darkness by evening sunlight through ivory lace curtains, then gradually his vision returned and he found himself in a circular room perhaps twenty feet in diameter and not unlike a lighthouse except for the curtained windows.

And the lavish furnishings.

Like Elwood's incongruous abode in the vast and nighted basement, this lofty, spotless, sunlit place was like a stage set from the 1890s -- or perhaps a tiny bit of the past somehow transported into the present -- and Jerry, stepping through the doorway, obediently pausing to wipe his "boots" on a rectangle of coconut matting guarding a rose-patterned carpet, felt a slight *wavering* sensation like pushing through an ethereal curtain.

Victorian rooms had been fussy and cluttered, and this one seemed all the more so, maybe because it had been condensed from all the lavish furnishings that once had filled the mammoth house... condensed into a "bedsit" as if for some grand old gentlewoman who'd fallen upon hard times.

Indeed there was bed, of brass, which may have been "modest" during her time, perhaps in one of the "lesser" bedrooms -- perhaps even once in Jerry's office -- but took up a fourth of this small space and was neatly made with a silk counterpane and a folded, embroidered quilt at the foot. In addition to several small, ornate tables, all topped with polished Argand lamps, and many nineteenth-century treasures -- delicate vases and *objets d'art*, chubby young fauns and fat-padded cherubs -- there was a massive writing desk with pens, ink bottle, and fresh green blotter. There was also a glass-fronted bookcase, an apparent twin to Elwood's, and every bit as impressively stocked with obvious fine and no doubt first-editions. Atop it was an Ormolu clock depicting another rolly-fat cherub holding the mechanism aloft, and its time agreed with Jerry's watch... although, he couldn't help thinking, there was no way to tell what year.

There was a washstand with pitcher and basin beneath a rose Victorian mirror; and behind a Japanese screen were facilities for "nature's calls." He also noted a silver tray on one of the claw-footed tables, and the scent of today's Morrison lunch wafted from under its cover.

These things, like the order to wipe his boots, dispelled most doubt in Jerry's mind that whoever was here in this place of the past still breathed the air of the present. As well as the scent of tobacco smoke. Also, as he'd reasoned before, why would a ghost need to part curtains?

Still, a new shiver ran down his spine as, after perusing the room, which he'd done for only seconds at most, he saw the figure in the chair.

Maybe not unnaturally, scenes from *Psycho* flashed through his mind: it was a wooden rocking chair, and the figure sat turned away from him facing the western-most window, which also overlooked the street and in which he'd seen the curtains move. The drapes were presently drawn, and the shape was only a back-lit shadow. Like Vera Miles in the fruit cellar, all Jerry could see was gray hair in a bun above the top of dress-clad shoulders. The obvious dread wormed into his brain of what he *might* see should that chair turn around!

Yet, those shoulders seemed reassuringly plump.

He darted another glance at the bed, but there was no impress of a figure lying motionless in death. Still, thoughts began shooting around in his skull like flying insects trapped in a jar: as he'd discussed with Angela, he might grant -- however improbable -- it *was* biologically possible that Elwood, despite his relatively youthful, or maybe preserved, appearance, might have arrived on earth as an infant before Miss Morrison gave up her ghost... say, in 1900. And, granting that much, he might even grant him another five years... he'd read of a man in Tibet who'd supposedly lived to 130. So, and however improbable, it was not beyond the bounds of reason that Elwood *might* have been the boy in that photograph with Miss Morrison.

But, according to her obituary, *she* had been 97... when she had died in 1901!

*Her bones are still here,* Gabriel had said.

But, were they in that vine-covered crypt?

Again, only seconds had passed... Jerry was sure of that, even if

199

time had been warped in this place. Then the figure moved... not much, not turning around, but only raising a white-gloved hand in what may have been a gesture of welcome.

"I believe, Mr. Mathers, you wished to see me?"

# Chapter Twenty-nine

Jerry found himself in the Gremlin parked in his driveway in darkness. From under the hood came ticking and clicks of the engine cooling down. ...Had he fallen asleep? He switched on the dome light and looked at his watch, recalling that during his boyhood it had been an automotive joke that dome lights never worked. The time was a little past eight. Then he felt a stab of fear... he had no memory of driving home! ...In fact, he had no clear recollection, only jumbled images like kaleidoscopic scenes from a dream, of *anything* that had happened since he'd seated himself in a plush velvet chair and accepted a fine Durham cigarette from...

*Miss Minerva Morrison!*

He wasn't sure what scared him most... whether he actually had, or whether he only imagined he had.

But maybe the second alternative was the most terrifying... that would mean he was losing his mind!

At the least it might mean that the strain and foreboding of his mother's impending death -- as he'd considered the other day -- had made him have black spell.

And, if he had, when had it begun? When he'd taken those keys from the basement?

He felt around in his pockets but didn't find the purloined keys. Which meant he'd either put them back...

Or never taken them at all?

And if he hadn't taken them, which would mean he hadn't gone *up there* -- as Gabriel had warned him not -- what had he been doing since he'd left his office?

Then, perhaps even more frightening, a third possibility came to mind... was *this* what she could to him to make him bow to her will?

He suddenly felt *very* scared. ...Also very, very alone.

*Who you gonna call?*

He had the school psychiatrist's number, but wished he had Gabriel's.

He heard the old-fashioned bell of the telephone in the kitchen. He scrambled out of the car, dashed up the back steps and unlocked the door. It wasn't until he grabbed the receiver that another chilling thought came to mind... this might be the call he'd been dreading.

His voice caught in his throat, but he managed to quaver, "H... hello?"

"Jerry? ...Are you all right?"

Relief washed warmly over him, melting some of the ice from his spine.

"Angela! ...Yes. ...No! ...I don't know."

Concern came into Angela's voice: "Jerry, what is it? You sound horrible."

Jerry managed the ghost of a chuckle. "I'm sure I do."

"Jerry, what happened? ...Is it your mother?"

"No. ...At least I don't think so. ...I mean I don't know. ...What happened, I mean... Or if anything did."

"Jerry, slow down... take a deep breath... maybe a drink."

Jerry tried to force a laugh. "At least I have a cigarette... Oh my god!"

"Jerry!"

For a moment Jerry could only stare at what he'd pulled from his pocket... not his common Marlboro, but an expensive Durham!

"Jerry!"

Then another voice spoke in the background: "Better let me talk to him." And it was Gabriel on the line, sounding impish, or simply thirteen:

"Told you not to go up there without me."

# Chapter Thirty

It was not a nice neighborhood by anyone's definition. Though, as Angela had said, gentrification was creeping in -- perhaps like a cancer benign to the rich but malign to those not immune with money -- it hadn't yet penetrated this far into a former industrial district near the West Oakland waterfront. The last Starbucks had been many blocks back, like a fort at the edge of a dark frontier, and lights were few and far between on a cracked and pot-holed concrete street with rusty railroad tracks down the middle. The buildings were mostly empty warehouses made obsolete by containerized cargo, and long-dead manufactories killed by American corporate greed since things could be made in other countries by paying steam-age wages, with broken windows and boarded-up doorways; though Jerry had noticed a LOFTS FOR RENT banner flapping half-torn on one derelict shortly after passing the Starbucks; which, although it was just nine o'clock, had been closing for the night, its staff of Caucasian twenty-some-things seemingly fearing a zombie attack... assuming Jerry could trust his impressions.

That was scary, too, because Art was based on impressions, and clearly *she* could distort them.

Since then he'd seen only seen one living person -- at least he assumed it wasn't a zombie -- a ragged man pushing a shopping cart loaded with junk and aluminum cans. Perhaps the new American Gothic?

Gabriel had offered to send his car, presumably driven by James, but though Jerry's reason -- to put it mildly -- was tottering on the brink of collapse and he felt like the figure in The Scream, he'd retained enough perceived manhood to make the journey on his own; and despite his fear and confusion wondered why Gabriel, especially at night, would be at Angela's loft.

Avoiding a battered Dumpster, which stood in the middle of the street as if to display its own feral art, he saw the great Packard on the next corner parked at the crumbling iron-shod curb in front of another ancient warehouse; this building like most of its centuried peers of the unreinforced masonry type so vulnerable to earthquakes, though it seemed to have survived fairly well and showed no signs of a retrofit. But, despite being four stories tall, there were no lights in its skull-eye windows except for three on the topmost floor.

James, perhaps not unnaturally, considering the neighborhood, sat in the car with the dome light on and seemed to be reading a leather-bound book, which might have been a Bible… or maybe the *Necronomicon*. He smiled and nodded to Jerry as, after parking the Gremlin in the limousine's aura of shadow, Jerry crossed the trash-littered sidewalk to confront an immense iron door, which Angela had said would be open. Presumably she had meant unlocked, as it was, he found, after trying the latch. After a glance back at James, who probably hadn't been informed that Jerry might be haunted, he entered a vast and echoing cavern filled with shadows and dust. There was only a single small bulb overhead, and a rusty door with a grimy window stood open to what had probably been some sort of receiving office, though now as devoid of furnishings as the servants' rooms in Miss Morrison's house.

But he didn't want to think about that!

Angela had instructed him in the use of the freight elevator, one of those primitive platform lifts with heavy slatted wooden gates, which could have accommodated the Gremlin. Its posted capacity was 3 TONS, sufficient for Gabriel anyway, but the memories -- or at least what he *thought* were memories -- of whatever he'd done that afternoon made him uneasy about elevators; and though the stairwell was forbiddingly black, and therefore also *déjà vu*, he took out his flashlight and started to climb.

The ghostly blue glow of the LED was sufficient to make the ascent past dust-shrouded concrete landings where iron doors marked 2 then 3 guarded presumably nothing. Since he'd been expected to use the lift, which was probably noisy, he arrived unannounced on the topmost floor.

As when stepping into that tower room -- again assuming he actually had -- his eyes were dazzled at first after the stairwell's Stygian gloom. This was also *déjà vu*, though there was no wavering sensation as if passing through some ethereal curtain, and much of that been-here-before illusion was due to his preconception of what a stone-carver's loft would be like. And no doubt further influenced by Matthew's graveyard Art studio.

The space was vast, the entire fourth floor, of scarred and unpainted concrete, with ranks of pillars supporting the roof, but only a portion was lighted by three big unfrosted bulbs in rusty shades like Chinese hats, the rest, like the Morrison basement, dwindling away into midnight shadow, which further enhanced its enormity. Another unsettling reminder was a neat "bedsit" on a square of old carpet, though its furnishings -- an iron-framed bed, a kitchen table with trio of chairs, a chest of drawers and a steel locker, the latter presumably Angela's closet -- were only junk-shop modern.

Then he saw The Cherub!

Considering what he'd been through today -- *whatever* that had been -- for a moment he doubted his eyes. Then he saw it was Gabriel almost glowing like polished onyx under one of the brilliant overhead lights. The boy was naked... or assumably so, since frontally viewed and vertical, standing atop a block of gray marble, his vast belly reached his dimpled knees, its huge scalloped "smile" now a wide-open laugh. He was posed like the Serenity boy, an arm upraised and a chubby hand open as if in release or catch something.

Jerry flinched for a moment as the stuttering blast of a small jackhammer -- this one obviously pneumatic since there was no swirling steam -- shattered the urban silence. He shifted his eyes from Gabriel to see Angela in jeans and "'beater" roughing out Gabriel's rolly shape in another block of dove-gray marble... a shape that would certainly be life-size and was therefore remarkable in girth.

Maybe not surprisingly it was Gabriel who first spotted Jerry, though Jerry, in light of the day's events, could have believed the boy had sensed him. Gabriel grinned and waved, giving Jerry the impression -- though not in the least unsettling -- The Cherub had come to life. Angela turned around, about to wield her hammer again, but raised the goggles that guarded her glasses. Her smile was warm and welcoming, but her eyes seemed to search his state of mind... which he could easily understand since he didn't know, himself.

Since Gabriel had known he'd gone "up there" -- never mind for the moment how -- there had seemed no reason to try to explain anything on the phone.

Angela lay down her hammer and came quickly over to grasp Jerry's hands, her own floured with silvery dust that somehow suggested powdered star stuff. "Are you all right?"

"He probably doesn't think so," said Gabriel, now with hands on hips, or rather the rolls overlapping them, leaning far backward to balance his belly and peering between the balloons of his breasts.

"I don't," said Jerry, almost clinging to Angela's hands.

Gabriel said, "I prescribe a beer. And there's some pizza left... hope you like ground beef and sausage."

"...I do," said Jerry. "But I don't think I could."

"Life goes on. ...If the lady and gentleman wouldn't mind...?"

Assisting Gabriel down from the block required more than a little exertion -- Jerry wondered how he'd gotten up there -- they taking his arms over their shoulders and easing his undulant mass to the floor. His Caterpillar machine stood nearby but, wobbling, quivering, jiggling all over, every cubic in motion, a virtual earthquake in ebony blubber, his belly plunging with every step as if determined to touch-tag the floor, he waddled slowly to Angela's table, not so much actually walking as heaving his bulk from side to side and shuffling like an enormous penguin. Finally completing his ponderous journey, he carefully settled his mammoth bottom, which looked like two midnight moons colliding, onto an apprehensive chair.

On the table were two Domino's boxes and twin empty bottles of Bohemia beer. Angela motioned for Jerry to sit, and went to an elderly fridge, while Gabriel opened a pizza box containing a third of a jumbo size and offered it to Jerry... who discovered he was actually hungry. Gabriel snagged a slice for himself and chomped a huge crescent with startling teeth, saying matter-of-factly around it, "You should have listened to me, Mr. Mathers."

As when he'd awakened in the Gremlin and during most of the drive to West Oakland, Jerry had struggled to remember whatever had happened since leaving his office. But again there was just a kaleidoscope of wavering, watery, uncertain scenes like blurred random clips from a movie.

Gabriel devoured more pizza. "You *did* go up there, Mr. Mathers. That, at least, was no illusion."

Angela returned with three bottles and popped their caps with an old "church key" and Jerry took a grateful gulp. "Thanks, I needed that."

Another infusion of beer seemed to help, melting some of the mist from his mind, and for an instant he saw something clearly. He turned to Gabriel, who'd finished his slice and was starting another. "She couldn't *possibly* still be alive!"

Angela had seated herself, and her mouth fell open. "Miss Morrison?"

"Maybe some fluke of nature," said Jerry, a third swallow giving more clarity. "Or truly higher evolution. ...Haven't there always been rumors... stories since the dawn of time... of incredibly long-lived people? And, if she *is* still alive, she wouldn't want the world to know. She wouldn't have any rights... humanity wouldn't let her have rights. She would be hated, envied and feared. Some would call her a miracle, others a blasphemy. Science... or the government in the guise of science... would lock her up to be studied." He stopped. "I'm babbling, aren't I?"

Gabriel chugged a third of his bottle and unabashedly blasted a burp. "She told you that, though it's probably true."

"...Maybe she did." Jerry drank again, then asked, "Why does it seem more possible to believe she's long-dead and a ghost than...?

"Because," said Angela. "Unless you believe in *The House And The Brain*, nobody lives to..." She seemed to do some mental math. "...two-hundred-and-ten! ...Which is just an estimate assuming she was 'only 97' when her corpse was consigned to that crypt."

Jerry spread his hands. "Okay, it's *very* improbable. But is it completely impossible? ...Why would a ghost need a washstand? Or sanitary facilities? Or, for that matter, a bed? ...And there was a silver tray, so someone... I'd guess Elwood... obviously brings her meals. ...And..." He reached in a pocket. "I've never heard of a ghost who smokes."

Gabriel held out a cherubic hand, and Jerry gave him the Durham. The boy examined it for a moment, passed it under his snubby nose, then returned it to Jerry. "A bit too aged for my taste. ...May I?" he asked Angela.

Angela passed out American Spirits, lighting them all with her Bic. "Some unknown descendant," she said, "who apparently wants to live like a hermit... or would that be hermitess?"

Gabriel exhaled a ghost and turned again to Jerry. "Looks just like her portrait, doesn't she?"

Jerry searched the mist once more. "...Yes."

Angela smiled. "Then she certainly seems to have aged well, since I'd guess she was in her late seventies whenever it was painted."

Gabriel looked amused; and Angela suggested, "Maybe an illegitimate daughter? In those days that would have been kept a secret. ...No, even a daughter couldn't live that long."

Jerry drew deep on his cigarette. "So, we're back to the possible improbable."

Gabriel gulped more beer and smiled. "You'll probably remember more when you stop trying to. It's like trying to recall a dream, and you'll probably never remember it all." Then he looked impish. "Did she say anything about me?"

"...I believe we discussed you at some length. ...And..." Jerry added with some surprise, "in a not unfavorable light."

Seemingly despite herself, Angela asked, "Could she... I mean whoever it was... have thrown that crowbar yesterday?"

"Possibly," said Gabriel, downing the last of the pizza, though his tone sounded enigmatic.

Jerry flicked his ashes into a Heinold's ashtray, then studied his hand, which was no longer shaking.

"That's my man," said Angela.

Jerry's laugh was natural, and Angela raised an eyebrow.

"Something just came to me," said Jerry. "I'm sitting here in a sculptor's loft... or would that be sculptress... having beer and pizza with not only a beautiful artist but also her handsome model. And I thought I wasn't Bohemian."

He decided he must be returning to normal -- or at least what passed for him -- because he found himself admiring Angela's lush-breasted full-bodied figure so well displayed in the tight-clinging "'beater," the snowy white cotton an artful contrast to the dusky ebony of her skin. Then he looked at the block of marble. "You two are creating the cherub."

Angela said, "It was supposed to be a surprise, however sad the circumstances. I spoke with Matthew this afternoon... because you wanted it there for your mother and maybe there wouldn't be time."

"Thank you both," said Jerry. "But, the materials... and your time..."

"We know what an artist's time is worth," Angela replied. "At least to most of the world. And Matthew furnished the stone for free. If you approve of the finished work, pay Matthew his commission. I may even do future pieces for him to pay my earthly bills."

Gabriel laughed. "She enticed me with pizza and beer, corrupting my youthful innocence."

Angela glanced at her watch. "Speaking of which, it's almost ten. Maybe you should be getting home."

"I usually work late, myself." Gabriel turned to Jerry. "I did another drawing last night."

"I'd love to see it," said Jerry.

"It's in one of my packs." Gabriel drank the last of his beer and blasted another burp. "Perhaps we may return to our Art? Our often painful labors of love."

Angela nodded. "And just as often unrequited."

"May I draw you?" asked Jerry. "I have a painting in mind, but..."

Gabriel laughed again. "You were scared to ask me to pose."

"I'm sure we all know why."

Gabriel shrugged. "We live in a culture of witch-burning warlocks who try to hide their own sins in the smoke." He rose with effort to his feet, his rolls and orbs and cascade of belly obeying the law of gravity and rearranging themselves. The puzzle of how he'd mounted the block was solved by an aged TowMotor forklift. Then, provided with pencil and pad from Gabriel's ample stock of supplies, Jerry drew up one of the chairs in the clear cone of overhead light as Gabriel reassumed his pose and Angela took up her hammer.

"I have him on my computer," Angela said before starting work. "Like Matthew has his faun. But drawing from life is always best."

"It is," agreed Jerry, plying the pencil, which seemed to create of its own accord as it always did when truly inspired. And, despite what he'd been through today, his impressions felt pure and undistorted. He thought several times of the irony... that here in this place of dust and decay, surrounded by darkness and desolation where lonely people defeated by life wandered past below in the night, higher things could still be inspired and beauty could be created.

They worked until nearly midnight when Jerry, coming down from the high of doing what he wanted to do -- what he still believed he should be doing -- realized that Gabriel, though determinedly holding his pose, was tiring from the effort of keeping all his weight on his feet. Angela also ceased her work, and again they assisted him down from the block. After they'd helped him don his jeans, which barely covered half his bottom and puddled over his big chubby feet, Gabriel mounted his mighty machine and they took the elevator, rumbling and creaking down to the street, where enormous James stood by the Packard having a conversation with an apparently homeless man -- or maybe a friendly zombie -- while smoking, probably James', cigarettes. After passing the man a twenty, James helped Gabriel vertical and opened the car's rear passenger door, then loaded the boy's machine in the trunk, which was mostly a matter of folding its back and letting it climb in by itself. Gabriel loaded himself in the car, studied Jerry a moment -- Jerry holding Angela's hand -- and said, "You shouldn't be alone tonight."

Jerry, caught up in his inspired work and, if thinking at all of the future, of only the portrait he wanted to paint, either from his drawing tonight or hopefully from life, had not considered that. A shadow crossed the light in his mind as he thought of his mother's empty house and those long, lonely hours ahead before dawn.

Angela seemed to sense his thoughts because she pressed his hand. "He's right, Jerry. Please stay here."

Gabriel wouldn't have winked, however impish he sometimes seemed, but bestowed them both a benevolent smile as James settled into the driver's seat. The car gave a deep muffled cough, like a sleepy lion clearing his throat, then majestically murmured away, exhaust pipe trailing a ghost of steam in the salt-scented breeze off the Bay. Jerry glanced at the Gremlin, now alone and vulnerable to things that might go boost in the night.

Angela smiled. "We'll bring it up in the elevator to keep the forklift company."

# Chapter Thirty-one

"**M**r. Mathers?"

There were still about fifteen minutes before his class began, and Jerry, at his office desk, the windows open to a warm sunny morning, was studying Gabriel's latest work, yet another masterful drawing, this of an elderly black man asleep. While Gabriel had unquestionably proven he could reveal his subjects' souls, his vision seemed all the more divine when their earthly shapes were slumbering. The Victorians had believed that faces, especially in repose, did reveal a person's true self, and Jerry's thoughts had drifted back to when he'd awakened in Angela's bed to find her asleep beside him. Had this been a modern American story, they would have made passionate love last night before falling asleep in each other's arms, but though he was sure they could have, they were no longer young adolescents desperately wanting everything NOW; and holding each other and kissing, and simply not being alone anymore, had been all they'd needed there in the dark... though he couldn't speak for the forklift and Gremlin.

And, there was a new road ahead, and they now had the wisdom of years to choose if they wanted to take it together.

After a working-person's breakfast of sausage, eggs and hash-brown potatoes artfully cooked by Angela upon an ancient iron gas ring, they'd arrived at the mansion around eight o'clock. The tower curtains *might* have moved, and Jerry supposed he should have felt scared, or at least apprehensive, to enter the house -- or should they have waited for Gabriel? -- but Miss Morrison's portrait only looked normally watchful and there was no aura of hovering malice.

Some of the other staff were upstairs, their voices and footfalls

212

reassuring, and the scent of Elwood's unearthly coffee ghosted temptingly through the halls. Jerry could have believed he belonged here... or maybe convinced himself he did. Of course not the road he would have chosen fifteen years ago -- a sensible, safe and easy route a now middle-aged man *should* probably take -- and like a defiant adolescent he was only making life hard for himself by pursuing a painfully thorn-ridden path through a tangled wood to an uncertain end. But Angela didn't seem tempted, her manner showing the resignation of one who had to do a job to keep her artful dreams alive, as she'd kissed Jerry's cheek in the second floor hall then vanished into the labyrinth.

Amanda Teabrook stood in the doorway as Jerry looked up from Gabriel's drawing, still a skeleton clothed in skin but now with a faint spirit of rose in her formerly sallow cadaverous cheeks. She smiled timidly but announced with vigor, "I had a *big* breakfast at McDonalds!" like a child who'd just discovered ice cream. She turned to someone in the hall. "And we're going to have *lunch!*"

Walter Wadsworth Wainwright III, his zebra-striped belly on partial display in another proudly outgrown shirt, appeared beside her and took her hand.

An odd pair of strange ones, thought Jerry. ...Or simply a duo of young teenage souls trying to find their way to the light in a world where too many still dwelt in the dark and feared any form of enlightenment lest it show something ugly, shriveled and dead.

"I think I can model," Amanda added. "If anyone wanted me to. ...But maybe in a week or so?"

"Of course," said Jerry, smiling. "And, though I know it's hard, especially at your age, never, never feel compelled to be an illusion for anyone else."

"I think I know what you mean," said Amanda. "Thank you, Mr. Mathers." She smiled, still holding Walter's hand. "I already said thanks to Gabriel. He saved my life... I mean seriously!"

"I'll model today if you want," offered Walter.

Jerry smiled again. "Thank you, Mr. Wainwright. You'll be a very handsome subject."

"He is," said Amanda, and kissed Walter's cheek.

213

Jerry glanced up at the gas light as the kids walked away down the hall. "I took the one less traveled by. And that has made all the difference."

# Chapter Thirty-two

"**L**et me do the talking," said Gabriel, regarding the ominous tower staircase with a confidence either bolstered by wisdom or simply the reckless defiance of youth. "If things start getting serious."

"What do you mean?" asked Jerry.

"Trust me, you'll know."

It seemed funny that Jerry had wondered who might be grinding pigments for whom, but he'd never dreamed he might be a student in the art of "settling" ghosts. And Angela might have felt the same as she stood beside him.

Assuming, of course, the elderly woman Jerry had met, plump though she was and looking quite lively, her mind, from the flashes Jerry recalled, still nimble with perceptive wit, who'd exiled herself to that lofty tower amid a place of shadows and dust – perhaps like old Miss Havisham wounded by an ancient wrong and left forever handicapped – did not still breathe the air of earth.

They had made their plan over lunch at McDonalds – or rather Jerry and Angela had listened to Gabriel's instructions -- and had gathered in Jerry's office before the end of sixth period.

After the knell of another school day, Jerry had locked his door and they had waited quietly, Gabriel in his mighty machine, Angela in the velvet chair, and Jerry standing at a window watching the students descend the front stairs... Amanda and Walter again hand-in-hand and strolling to McDonalds. He'd tensed for a moment as Raymond Blakemore, who'd obviously been stalking Parker, seemed on the verge of attacking the boy. But, after reaching the foot of the stairs, Raymond had stopped, seeming undecided, as Parker also

215

walked toward McDees. Raymond had gazed after him, though Jerry couldn't read his expression, then had turned in the other direction with fists that may have been clenched in rage.

The staff had left during the next thirty minutes, someone using the elevator, and silence had once more shrouded the house. Jerry had turned to Gabriel, who'd been regarding his mother's portrait as if seeing the loving soul within. The boy had raised a palm and touched a finger to his lips... then weighty footsteps had trooped down the hall. A moment later the doorknob had rattled as someone tried the lock. No doubt it had been Tillinghast, and of course he would have a pass key, an actual skeleton key in the literal sense of the term; and Jerry had readied an explanation -- a consultation with Gabriel and Angela -- in case Tillinghast invaded, but then the steps had continued on and another doorknob was molested. Though he'd never paid any attention, Jerry assumed that Tillinghast probably made an inspection after the end of every school day, even if not always to snoop. Likewise, he'd never given much thought to where Tillinghast might have kept his car. There was a narrow driveway, mostly concealed by trees, that led through stately wrought-iron gates upward along one side of the house to a stable-like structure behind the crypt; this building presumably off-limits and segregated from the back yard by a seven-foot evergreen hedge. It would be in Tillinghast's nature to park his car back there instead of out on the common street.

Jerry's Regulator had devoured another thirty minutes, biting off seconds with toothy ticks, as silence settled ever deeper into the mansion's brooding old bones. Though because of the ivy and trees he couldn't see the driveway, Jerry assumed Tillinghast had left. He hadn't seen Elwood all day, though he probably spent much of the daylight hours tending the mansion's grounds. Jerry had glanced at Gabriel, who'd nodded and powered up. Then Jerry had asked, "Anyone like a drink?"

Gabriel had replied, "We need all our wits about us now, but a drink may be needed later." He'd added in his impish way, "Possibly lots of them."

Hoping Elwood *was* outside because Gabriel wasn't equipped

for stealth, Jerry had unlocked his door and scanned the dim-lit hall to find it apparently lifeless. Then Gabriel had tractored out, followed by Angela, they waiting at the elevator while Jerry had gone downstairs to again -- he couldn't help feeling -- violate Elwood's home.

Miss Morrison had watched with her seemingly vigilant eyes though otherwise appearing neutral as if implying *it's your funeral*, as Jerry opened the CUSTODIAN door and descended the gas-lit steps. He assumed he'd returned the keys yesterday in whatever spell or trance he'd been in, and since there had been no repercussion, either from Elwood or Tillinghast, also assumed whatever he'd done while up in tower hadn't been discovered. And, it seemed he'd been correct because, after a tentative knock, he found the basement door unlocked. It was *déjà vu* once more to see the Victorian "bedsit" amid the cavernous shadows, and again he'd wanted to look at the pictures, those time-faded black-and-white images of what could only have been Elwood's father, *not* Elwood himself as a boy -- especially the one of the boy and Miss Morrison sitting intimately -- but there wasn't time.

The keys *were* back on the board, and he'd taken the one for the elevator. And though the tower hadn't been locked -- unless, as Gabriel had cryptically said, he'd only believed it hadn't been -- had also taken its key.

He'd mentioned the elevator failing yesterday afternoon, but Gabriel hadn't seemed concerned; and even with all of them aboard the cage had risen smoothly into this place of shadows and dust. Jerry had warned Gabriel about the uncertain state of the floor, and the boy had left his machine at the lift, his vast belly pouring out of his shirt and every inch of him in motion as he'd penguined up the twilight hall to the creaks and cries of ancient wood, Jerry and Angela helping by supporting him under his arms as if frog-marching a mammoth cherub far too fat to fly.

Unlike his impressions of yesterday, Jerry saw no telescoping illusion; nor did the silence seem hollow today, though Gabriel's steam locomotive puffing, and even the bright boyish scent of his sweat, soon soaking his shirt from the exertion, seemed to enliven the lifeless air.

Arriving at last at the tower staircase, where Angela pulled up Gabriel's jeans, which had all but abandoned his bottom, Jerry had lighted the lower gas globe, and Gabriel's midnight moon of face glistened in the wavering glow, while his cave of a navel leaked glittering drops, bombing dust on the floor like little atomic explosions. Jerry had peered into darkness where the sagging steps spiraled away. "I thought you couldn't climb stairs?"

"Never said I couldn't," Gabriel had panted. "It's just not one of my favorite things."

"But *those* stairs!" Angela had said, regarding them almost in horror.

Again the boy's smile had been cryptic. "I'm sure they'll accept me on the way up."

Jerry had thought of *The House Of Usher*. "What do you mean?"

"Depends on what happens up there. You don't have to come with me." Despite his puffing, Gabriel laughed. "I ain't afraid of no ghosts."

"Don't be silly," Jerry and Angela said together.

"Then, for obvious reasons, stay off the stairs till I get to the top."

Now, after pausing to regain his breath, Gabriel started to climb; this a slow and ponderous process, one hand on the banister, the other braced against the wall, while somehow hoisting his wobbly weight one laborious step at a time, the whole structure creaking and groaning as if about to collapse any moment. A logical thought came to Jerry's mind, but before he could voice it Gabriel puffed, "Of course she knows we're here."

It seemed to take an eternity, though by Jerry's watch it was less than five minutes after Gabriel vanished in darkness, his panting echoing down above the cries of tortured timber, until his voice, an exhausted gasp, came from the black void above, "Okay."

Jerry called, "There's another gas light near the door."

"Yeah, but I can't reach it."

Jerry and Angela quickly ascended, there seeming no reason for caution since Gabriel had proven the stairs, and joined the boy moments later, Jerry lighting the landing's globe as Angela tugged

Gabriel's jeans part way over his bottom again. Miss Morrison -- or whoever it was – hadn't seemed to be hearing-impaired during yesterday's interview, and Jerry found himself surprised, considering all the noise they had made, that she hadn't already invited them in.

"I suppose," said Angela, "it would be polite to knock?"

Gabriel gave her a smile, his teeth flashing bright in the dimness. "She would expect that courtesy."

Angela did so with proper restraint, but there was no reply from beyond.

"Maybe she's taking a nap?" said Jerry, absurdly in a whisper.

Angela smiled wryly. "I imagine at her age she'd take quite a few."

After a decent interval, which Gabriel used to recover his breath, his life-scent strongly overcoming those of dust and slow decay, Jerry, almost feeling foolish, gently called, "Miss Morrison?"

But again only silence responded except for the ghostly whisper of gas.

Jerry looked Gabriel a question and received a nod. He grasped the doorknob and said, "It's locked."

Gabriel nodded again. "As I'm sure it was locked yesterday."

"What are you saying?" Angela asked.

Gabriel only gestured, and Jerry took the key from a pocket. The mechanism turned easily, obviously kept well-oiled, and after a glance at Gabriel, who merely looked attentive, slowly, almost warily, Jerry opened the door.

The *déjà vu* was no surprise as he blinked in late afternoon sunlight filtering in through lace-curtained windows, and again it took a moment for his eyes to adjust. The room was just as he recalled, a cluttered though spotless Victorian scene, every fussy thing in its place, with an abundance of cherubs and fauns, the Ormolu clock ticking softly; and the time it showed agreed with his watch. There was the same scent of fine tobacco... and there before the west-facing window, a shadow back-lit by the lowering sun, was the neat bun of silver-gray hair and the plump outline of dress-clad shoulders.

Then she spoke, and moved. ...Though only raising a white-gloved hand briefly from the arm of the chair:

"Good evening, Master Graves. I've been looking forward to

219

meeting you."

# Chapter Thirty-three

"Also good evening to you, Miss Davis. And, of course, Mr. Mathers. Please come in and be seated. You will, I am sure, forgive me for not rising to greet you." There was the ghost of chuckle. "Age does grant a few privileges."

Jerry glanced at his companions, mostly to assure himself they were also hearing and seeing this. Angela seemed more curious than showing any other emotion, while Gabriel may have looked... sad? He nodded to Jerry, then waddled in and carefully settled his undulant bulk onto the strongest-looking chair. Jerry and Angela seated themselves, and again the white-gloved hand lifted briefly.

"I believe, Mr. Mathers, you know where the cigarettes are kept?"

Jerry again glanced at Gabriel and received another nod. Taking a sliver box from a table, he opened its cover and offered it, Angela and Gabriel taking Durhams, which Jerry lit with a strike-lighter, including one for himself. Then, as he had yesterday -- he was sure -- started to rise for his hostess.

"No thank you, Mr. Mathers. I'll simply sit and enjoy the view. At my age one never knows if each sunset may be one's last."

Angela spoke, "Does one ever know at any age?"

"Very true, my dear. And the world would be a far better place if everyone lived by that maxim. And, speaking of a better world, I'm very pleased, Master Graves, by your presence in my school."

Gabriel said, "Thank you, ma'am," but Angela blurted, "You're pleased?"

"Indeed I am, my dear. Just as I'm pleased you're teaching here, though I cannot fathom the subject, being somewhat remiss in keeping up with current times. ...You seem surprised." There came a sigh.

221

"It was always my intention this school be open to *all* children... those, of course, who met its standards."

"Rather wealthy standards, if you'll forgive my saying so."

"But, my dear, would you not agree that learning how to acquire wealth... by diligent and honest means... is one proof of intellect?"

"I will concede that," said Angela. "Provided opportunities are truly equal for all."

"And I will concede that an artist should be judged by their Art instead of monetary standards, and that their work is just as important as any other form of labor, be it mental or physical, to any society worthy of name. But the standards of the school I intended did not specify a color of skin or racial ancestry."

"I am surprised," said Angela.

"That you are, though I understand why, deeply saddens me. But after..." There followed a hesitation, perhaps a lapse of memory. "...I retired, so to speak, my power became very limited, and *he* defied my declaration that my school be open to all."

Jerry asked, "'He' being Crawford Tillinghast?"

For a moment the air seemed to crackle as if with an angry electric discharge. "Detestable man! Despicable man! If only I still had power...!"

"But there have been other Directors?" asked Jerry.

"Of course, it *has* been a long time. ...So long I cannot remember the years. But every one of his odious class, believing themselves 'superior' while embodying only the absolute *worst* of what it means to be human."

Then the air seemed to soften, and the light took a golden tone... or perhaps just the gold of approaching sunset.

"But now this wonderful boy has come!"

Jerry seemed to feel a smile, and considered that in Victorian times "wonderful" had meant full of wonders.

Gabriel smiled, though sadly. "Thank you, Miss Morrison. I'm sorry you had to wait so long."

Jerry didn't know what to feel: unlike yesterday's vague memories, everything now was lucid and clear. He'd *almost* been sure on hazy reflection that whoever he'd spoken with here did indeed still

222

live and breathe; and later last night in Angela's loft he'd almost accepted the explanation of some unknown descendant who, for whatever reasons, had chosen this lofty obscurity. But Gabriel speaking her name seemed to confirm the impossible.

The impossible spoke again: "If I may presume your thoughts, Mr. Mathers, I have indeed outlived my time... what some might term my 'proper time'... and have many past regrets. But the one most painful to me is realizing all the years I wasted before I actually learned how to live. In that respect I was fortunate to find, at last, a teacher."

The gloved hand lifted again and gestured toward the bed as if to indicate something. "There is a very true proverb of 'better late than never.'"

Glancing again at Gabriel, whose sad expression hadn't changed, Jerry rose and maneuvered his way through the Victorian clutter. Upon a little bedside table was another faded photograph in a gilded frame. Apparently it had been taken in the secluded back yard. There again was the round-tummied boy portrayed in Elwood's pictures, but now he was dressed like a young gentleman in collar, suit and tie, even a watch chain crossing his vest, and standing between Miss Morrison and a handsome ebony man of possibly late middle-age, both of whom had their hands on his shoulders and the clear light of love in their eyes.

Angela had joined him, though Gabriel remained in his chair. Finally Jerry murmured, "That was another kind of love that dared not speak its name."

There was a sigh of sadness. "In a time I had hoped to outlive."

Gabriel glanced at the picture. "The man is Elwood's grandfather."

Again a sigh, but not of sadness. "And who, as are you, dear boy, was like a prince in a fairytale come to awaken a sleeping princess... if I may indulge my silly conceit. His name was Edmond."

"But, the boy..." said Angela, turning to the figure facing the slowly setting sun. "Please forgive me, Miss Morrison, I don't mean to seem indelicate, but he can't be over thirteen in this picture."

"I understand, my dear. Would he have been my son by blood, I still could not have loved him more. ...Alas in that, love came too late."

Another voice spoke: "Edmond's wife... she was housemaid here... died of a fever... an epidemic... a year after Ethan... my father, was born. Ethan is the boy in that picture, and he was thirteen then."

Elwood stood in the doorway, bearing a covered silver tray, a mix of expressions crossing his face like sunlight and shadows through leaves in a breeze. "And she did love him like he was her own." Then his eyes went to the window. "Grandmother?"

Once more the gloved hand lifted. "It's all right, Elwood, I've wanted to meet them, and Gabriel most of all."

Elwood started to enter, but Gabriel rose laboriously and stayed him with his mass. "It's time she rested, Mr. Clay, and in your heart you know it."

Elwood hesitated, but Gabriel made his way to the window, the light dimming now as sunset neared. He took the white-gloved hand in his of chubby midnight, then leaned to kiss the figure's cheek. "Thank you, Miss Morrison."

Elwood suddenly tensed. "No!"

But Gabriel went on, "All your work here is done... and it was very *good* work... and the light you see is a new sunrise. Go to it now and find a new day."

"No!" cried Elwood again. Dropping the tray, he started forward, but acting on instinct Jerry restrained him. Then Angela came to take Elwood's arm, also gently holding him back.

Gabriel sighed. "I'm sorry, Mr. Clay, but I guess I have to do this."

Jerry suddenly knew what was coming, unlike when he'd first seen it as a child on a ghost-haunted black-and-white TV, and almost closed his eyes as Gabriel turned the chair around.

224

# Chapter Thirty-four

"You saw her... that way... all the time?" asked Jerry, laying down his palette and brush. "Or should I say, as she really was?"

Gabriel looked mischievous, an impish and almost impossibly fat ebony cherub upon a tombstone. "I couldn't see any more than you until I went to her chair." He smiled at Angela, who'd lain down her hammer and chisel. "In fact I saw even less, because her shoulders were *far* from plump, and only you two saw her lift a hand."

Angela, always practical, asked, "Then how do you know she did?"

"From the way you both responded. Just as I knew Mr. Mathers saw her as she looked in her portrait when he first went up there... as she believed herself to be."

"But, you heard her speak," said Jerry.

"Of course, because she *was* there... just not in the way you saw her." Gabriel smiled again. "Would you care to take a break, and perhaps order a pizza?"

"Of course," said Jerry. "It must be tiring holding that pose."

Gabriel laughed as Jerry and Angela came to help him down by taking him under the arms and easing his bulk to the floor. "Labors of love are often painful."

It was two evenings after the "settlement" and they were in Angela's loft. Jerry had started his portrait as he'd wanted to paint Gabriel, and Angela was well into her sculpture of Gabriel-as-cherub. After school that afternoon, Jerry had taken them all in the Gremlin -- Gabriel filling the rear seat and the car well aware of his weight – for a visit to his mother, who'd been delighted to meet not only "the

225

charming boy" but also, she'd said with a wink, "Jerry's artistic associate." Just as they'd been leaving, she'd called Jerry close and whispered, "Better late than never."

Now, Jerry asked, as Gabriel waddled to a chair at the table, "She didn't know she was dead?"

"As is sometimes the case with ghosts," said Gabriel, sitting carefully down. "Though in her case she was haunting her corpse... to put it indelicately... rather than the house."

"She certainly did it well," said Angela, going to the fridge for beer. "Convincing Edmond she hadn't died... calling to him from the crypt, I suppose, as if a 'mistake' had been made. Then all those years with Ethan their son, and then all those after with Elwood."

"Also convincing herself," said Gabriel, accepting a bottle from Angela. "Going through all the motions of living... as many do who actually breathe. She also believed she was eating, sleeping, smoking, and answering nature's calls. She'd created her own self-illusion of self... or rather her self-earthbound spirit had... and because she believed, others did, too."

"But, what of the food?" asked Angela.

"I thought I just explained that... the trays went back to the kitchen untouched, but those who carried them believed."

"Because she believed," said Jerry.

"You win a celestial cigar." Gabriel smiled. "Sometimes it's hard to tell in life what's only an illusion of living." Then his round face saddened. "But she did it out of love, love she had found so late in life she couldn't bear to let it go. She knew, of course, when Edmond passed. Also when his son, Ethan, died... who she did love just as much as if he'd been her own by blood."

"As," said Angela, seating herself, "she loved Elwood, her grandson."

Jerry, also sitting, said, "As much as they loved her. To the point of never questioning how she could still be alive. ...But, what about the 'sightings' describing bones and a shroud?"

Gabriel drank and boyishly burped. "As you've noticed in drawing from life, most people see what they expect... again, their self-created illusions... just as you saw her as her portrait. As for others, assuming they really saw anything except maybe shadows and tricks of light, they expected a scary-looking ghost to be haunting a spooky old house."

Jerry nodded. "If she had been haunting the house I'm sure Tillinghast wouldn't still be around."

Angela took out her phone, the number of Domino's Pizza naturally in memory. After placing an order, she said, "Knowing her as we do now... or should I say having known her... we know she couldn't have thrown that crowbar, and wouldn't have even if she could."

Gabriel fired an American Spirit. "I'd think it would be obvious who did."

"Occam's Razor," said Angela.

Gabriel nodded. "To Tillinghast's self-created illusion he was defending his 'higher race' from contamination. He knew Elwood would open some windows on the third floor after the rain, and probably knew he would use the crowbar. Maybe he only wanted to scare me to get my black ass out of 'his' school, but even assuming deadly intent, could claim it had been accidental."

"Or, he might have blamed Elwood," said Jerry, "for leaving it in a window."

Angela sighed. "'Nothing in the world is more dangerous than sincere ignorance and conscientious stupidity.'"

Gabriel nodded again. "Doctor Martin Luther King Junior."

"I'd say except hate," said Jerry. "...So, Tillinghast also spilled the ink, no doubt in rage that a little nigger could create such beauty."

Angela and Gabriel applauded.

Jerry bowed and went on, "And tampered with the elevator assuming Gabriel needed it, hoping for a legal excuse to deny his rights and make him leave."

"Which might have succeeded," said Gabriel, after another gulp of beer, "since that form of discrimination is both allowed and sanctioned by law."

"Sadly true," said Jerry. "But all those other 'hauntings' were only my stress and fatigue?"

"Or coincidences. But your instincts were right, Mr. Mathers... instincts usually are... there *was* something evil haunting that house, but it was still alive."

"More's the pity," said Angela. "And more that it still is."

"But?" asked Jerry. "What about when the elevator wouldn't take me back down?"

"Happenstance?" said Angela. "Or another coincidence?"

Gabriel smiled his cryptic smile. "The most probable explanation."

"...She wanted to meet me," said Jerry. "So she 'persuaded' me up there."

"Because she approved of you, Mr. Mathers, and obviously also you, Miss Davis."

Angela smiled. "We're equals here, Gabe."

"And we have a future," said Jerry. "Though I'm not sure how to get there from here. We laid Miss Morrison's bones to their rightful rest in the crypt, where everyone but Elwood always thought they were. Her soul, I assume, has gone to the light?"

"That you can believe," said Gabriel.

"And Elwood is retiring," said Jerry. "There's nothing for him in that house anymore; and besides his pension, Miss Morrision's will provided for Edmond and all his descendants, which leaves Elwood pretty well off. But..." he glanced at Angela. "We still need our jobs for this year."

Gabriel said, "And your students still need you. Though I have a feeling you'll both be recognized soon."

"Thank you, and likewise I'm sure," said Angela.

"But," said Jerry. "Tillinghast is still Director, and we can't *prove* he did anything, so aren't we all still in danger?"

Gabriel smiled. "We know where his skeletons live."

# Chapter Thirty-five

"Mr. Mathers?"

This *déjà vu* was familiar, the Regulators tolling the knell of yet another Morrison day as Jerry looked up from his office desk, though surprised to see Raymond Blakemore standing in the doorway.

It was late October but Indian Summer, and the afternoon was sunny and warm, the breeze through Jerry's open windows bearing the dry grass and turning-leaves scents that heralded an Oakland Autumn. It seemed fitting his mother's funeral would be in this last blush of a year.

The pumpkin harvest had been so abundant -- perhaps because the Brown family kids had tended them so well -- that Jerry had requested one to carve his annual jack-o-lantern to place on his porch for Halloween; and, as his mother had always done, had bought a cornucopia of treats most desired by normal kids – full-sized candy bars -- as he and Trevor had once lusted for.

Tillinghast, of course, had blustered -- in Victorian terms going apoplectic -- when Angela, Jerry and Gabriel had opened the door of his closet unsheeting a nasty skeleton, thundering, "how did they DARE!" And even so far forgetting himself as to bellow, "YOU HAVE NO PROOF!"

To which Gabriel had serenely replied that only a ghost of proof would be needed to float about on the Internet and haunt Tillinghast for the rest of his days… so the question became, did *Tillinghast* dare?

Tillinghast had blanched -- as white as the proverbial sheet -- and a "settlement" had been performed.

"Yes, Mr. Blakemore?" said Jerry now, thinking, *life indeed goes on.*

"Um, remember you said we could draw at home?"

"Of course," said Jerry. "Please come in."

He indicated the chair as Raymond, holding a sheet of paper, actual quality drawing paper, entered without his usual swag. Reaching the desk he remained on his feet, though obviously not in defiance, and offered the paper to Jerry.

"I did this last night. ...Um... maybe it's not very good?"

The skills did need improvement -- though that's what Jerry was here to teach -- but the soul of Parker Foxworthy within his softly androgynous body, bare in apparently only jeans, and not without a glimmer of good, had seemingly been drawn from life.

"That's from his Facebook page," said Raymond. "Hope that's not cheating?"

"One must roll with the changes." Jerry studied the Art again, then took a pencil and graded it A.

"Thanks, Mr. Mathers," said Raymond, a blush of rose on his cheeks as Jerry returned the work. "Um... you think he'll like it?"

Another dangerous moment... as so many were with fragile young souls. "You realize, Mr. Blakemore..."

"Ray... please, sir."

"Ray. That one can never *make* anyone like them... much less make anyone love them... but they can, and very easily, make anybody hate them."

Raymond seemed to work that out. "Yeah, guess I do."

"I'm sure Parker will like your work." Jerry held the boy's eyes. "Beyond that, Ray, all you can do is offer yourself as you truly are, neither as an illusion for others, nor a self-created illusion, and accept for whatever reasons... and *often* through no fault of your own... that some will like you, a few may love you, but others simply won't."

"I think I get it. Thanks, Mr. Mathers. ...Did you like my drawing of Gabriel?"

"Very good, and also an A, though we'll have to work on those skills a bit more."

"Thanks again, Mr. Mathers." Raymond looked at his drawing, then seemed to set his jaw in resolve as he left the room.

Gabriel had been the model today by a unanimous vote of the class, though of course a few of those votes hadn't been cast out of friendship, nor for artful study, or even for egalitarian reasons: the girl with the triple-X crucifix fanatically wanted to illustrate one of the seven deadly sins, while another had hoped to humiliate Gabe, ostensibly into losing weight to conform to her culturally-brain-washed illusion of how everyone had to look. The Disruptor had hoped for amusement in the form of a fattie freak show; and Walter -- who was still ballooning – lusted after an idol to worship; while one or two of the other students had probably only wanted to see if Gabriel was brave enough to bare himself to the world.

Still, and regardless of motive, all had found him an intriguing study; and whether or not interpreting him to fit their own illusions, all had worked hard creating Art, and most had raised their grade levels, if not their degree of enlightenment.

Perhaps another few turns of the Wheel?

Jerry studied Crystal's rendition, which hadn't required any randy enhancement -- Gabriel's soul was impish enough -- then put the Artwork into his desk, no longer fearing an "accident" from either a living or spectral hand. Then he rose and went to a window, watching the students descend the stairs.

Amanda, no longer a starving stick-figure but actually starting to have a figure, was hand-in-hand with Walter, whose interest in her, though presumably noble -- at least for a boy of thirteen -- may have included a hopeful illusion. Of course they headed for McDonalds.

Parker, again being trailed by Raymond -- though now Jerry knew Raymond's honest intent and understood why, a month ago, Raymond had clenched his helpless fists and turned away before daring to speak -- paused at the foot of the stairs to hoist his slipping jeans a bit. Raymond came timidly to him, offered a very vulnerable smile, then his drawing of Parker to Parker. Jerry recalled many images, some classic paintings, others cartoons, of a bashful boy presenting flowers -- though invariably to a girl -- and Parker looked wary at first, but then scanned his image and smiled in return. Then Raymond gestured toward McDonalds and the boys walked away together.

Jerry thought of Trevor and of that possible road not taken. Or would it have simply been a detour, or perhaps a scenic route, through territory left unexplored by less adventurous travelers?

Today he found he had no regrets.

"Hi."

"Hi." Jerry smiled as Angela entered. She had changed after class from her working clothes into a modest black dress, as Jerry had changed to his seldom-worn suit. Gabriel was also attending, though meeting them at Serenity.

# Chapter Thirty-six

Trevor looked very prosperous in the Victorian sense, the chubbiness of his childhood having expanded far beyond Jerry's while likewise subtracting some years from his past. He'd also prospered materially from opening The Book Of The Dead, as evidenced by a new Suburban, metallic green and four-wheel-drive -- he took his family camping and fishing -- which rivaled the size of both Gabriel's Packard and the hefty Hudson hearse parked in front of Serenity... this Brobdingnagian trinity dwarfing the Lilliputian Gremlin as Jerry parked between them.

Trevor's somber charcoal suit had likely been purchased for this occasion: his wife -- of possibly Dutch descent and looking equally prosperous -- was also formally clad in dark dress; though their sons, who'd been admiring The Cherub, wore new jeans and button-front shirts, the latter somewhat sweaty from the two-hour drive on this warm Autumn day, enhancing the opulent orbs of their chests; and, in cartoonishly fat-kid style, their pendulous bellies had all escaped, presenting a trio of "Gabriel smiles" as Trevor called them to be introduced.

Jerry had been a little surprised when Trevor had asked to bring them. For a moment he'd flashed on his own memory of first attending a funeral, but Trevor had asked about pall-bearers. Jacob, of course, had discussed this with Jerry, and Angela had volunteered, as had Harriet Cole, but of his mother's still-living friends -- only two attending -- both were elderly women barely able to bear themselves. Jacob could have provided mutes, and Jerry had thought of Matthew, but now there would be Trevor and sons.

The oldest of these, Jerry, thirteen, with a bushy mop of golden

233

hair all but hiding indigo eyes, the honor roll student in steel spectacles -- these days called "Harry Potter glasses" -- like a rolly and rosy-cheeked Hummel, now manfully shook his namesake's hand before taking Angela's with a bow. The middle boy, Dale, twelve-years-old and sporting a spiky brown Mohawk, the metal bass-player and proportionally fattest, was next to be introduced. Then Mikey, the artist, eleven, his coppery hair in a '70s style like a triple-X Danny Bonaduce.

All the boys, Jerry noted, who stood like a trio of fellowship Hobbits amid this flowery, leaf-dappled setting of sunlit trees and shady bowers, the fountain playing its liquid music, the air sweetly scented with herbal life and earthy eucalyptus -- not to mention their own aromas of subtle pubescence and strong adolescence -- had a healthy bronze skin tone, which also included their lolling bellies, revealing they went shirtless a lot, which indicated self-esteem and perhaps a feral faun-like defiance in a culture controlled by conformity and cowed by the contagion of fear.

Jerry and Trevor had hugged as fondly as when they'd been thirteen, and Trevor had whispered, "It's about time," obviously meaning Angela.

Jerry had murmured in reply, "Better late than never."

Now, Jacob emerged from the stately house and invited all for sustenance, the service set for five o'clock with about twenty minutes remaining. The boys, of course, were eager – life, after all, did go on, and one of its purest pleasures was food -- but Jerry hung back as the group walked away, ostensibly to study The Cherub but really to delay, if only another few minutes, the confirmation of life's conclusion in its physical form. Angela nodded when he pressed her hand, and followed the others up the path.

"Gabriel," he murmured, regarding the smiling boy of stone in his pose of release or anticipation. He'd completed Gabriel's portrait last week in not surprising harmony with Angela's masterful sculpture; and Jerry's agent had called it superb, undoubtedly his best work to date, and -- maybe tactfully -- "defiant." But the whole, she had said, the sum of its parts -- a cherub gazing toward heaven at night in a star-lit cemetery -- was hauntingly inspiring. And that enigmatic smile hinting of knowledge beyond mortal grasp...

Jerry had interrupted to say, with an enigmatic smile of his own, that children were closer to the source, having newly arrived from the light and fully-equipped to love everyone... until that love was beaten, coerced, starved, brainwashed and/or scared out of them. But perhaps this child watching souls ascend toward a light their earthly remains had forgotten, had never been so corrupted?

"Good selling point," the agent had said, although raising an eyebrow when Jerry had set an appropriate price that only patrons doubly blessed with a genuinely divine love of Art, as well as the earthly means to indulge it, would be willing to pay.

Or, he'd added thoughtfully, he might donate it to a children's center where Angela volunteered.

At least, his agent had replied -- accustomed to artists' insanity -- in light of the oncoming Holiday Season, Jerry's seascape would surely sell.

"It is Gabriel," said a voice.

Jerry turned to see James -- immaculately black-suited as always -- which of course wasn't surprising since he'd chauffeured Gabriel here in the immaculate Packard... Jerry assuming Jacob had invited Gabriel inside, probably for sustenance. But James, with a white linen handkerchief, was flicking specks of dust here and there off the gleaming ebony hearse.

It had never occurred to Jerry to ask about Gabriel's guardian or how he could afford the price of Gabriel's private education, but now it all made sense... the Packard was a *funeral* car, part of Serenity's classic fleet, and *James* was the mechanical Master who restored and cared for them, including, of course, the tombstone truck and the antique forklift. Also, obviously, the driver of the hearse today.

James offered American Spirits. "Gabriel modeling for Matthew."

"Of course," said Jerry, accepting a light from James' classic Ronson. "I'm surprised I missed the resemblance, facially, anyway."

"Matthew intended that," said James. "Serenity is here for all."

"As in, 'everyone is a friend in our house?'"

"As Gabriel puts it," said James.

Jerry studied the huge black man. "I have a feeling we've met before... before Gabriel, I mean... though I can't remember where or when."

James smiled. "I also had that impression of you and it took me a while to figure it out. ...I still have the drawing you did of me, framed on my wall. It meant a lot then and still does. You made me proud to be me. Going into your neighborhood then was a pretty scary experience, until your mother invited me in and you asked if you could draw my picture."

"...Oh," said Jerry, and reached in a pocket. "I still have the knife."

"Everyone is connected," said James, "from somewhere and some time. It's too bad so few understand that."

"Are you related to Jacob?"

"My older brother, and Matthew's the baby."

"If you don't mind my asking..."

"How was I blessed with Gabriel?" James raised his eyes above the trees to the cemetery on the hillside. "I found him up there one morning thirteen years ago when I was installing a stone. He wasn't much more than a few hours old, and someone had either left him for dead or figured he wouldn't last very long. They'd left him in the arms of an angel... a stone angel, of course. I guess there was some kind of logic in that."

"Maybe there was," said Jerry. "And he came into life among ghosts."

"Who persuaded me to find him." James opened the hearse's driver door and took out a page of old newspaper he'd used to guard the carpet. He was about to crumple it when Jerry saw a photo.

"May I?"

James handed Jerry the page... and there was the face of Matthew's faun. ...Not only the handsome young faun, but also Gabriel's African prince. Jerry checked the date. "This is the boy who was killed last month by a BART cop."

James nodded sadly. "Who claimed the boy had been going for a gun when all he had was a phone." He studied Jerry's expression. "I

236

presume a logical progression of thought?"

"Maybe a dawning light," said Jerry.

James made an inviting gesture, and Jerry followed him into the house, where he ushered Jerry along a hall to the doorway of the Cherub Room. There were still a few minutes before the service, and all was quiet within. After glancing at James, who nodded, Jerry looked inside.

The cherub chandelier had been lit, filling the room with a soft golden glow, while candles held by other bronze children haloed the coffin surrounded by flowers. The gentle light warmed his mother's face; she looked serene, and merely asleep, all her work done and resting in peace.

And perhaps it *was* only a well-earned rest amongst cherubs and fauns in some leafy bower; merely a nap by the wayside along a great eternal road.

And there beside her was Gabriel quietly drawing from life.

# The End

# About The Author

Jess Mowry was born in 1960 near Starkville, Mississippi. When he was only a few months old his father took him to live in Oakland, California. Mowry's father was a voracious reader who introduced his son to books at a very early age. Jess attended a public school, but despite his love of reading, dropped out at age thirteen, part way through the eighth grade and worked with his father in the scrap-iron business. In his late teens, Jess moved to Arizona to work as a truck driver and heavy equipment operator. He also lived and worked in Alaska as an engineer aboard a tugboat and as an aircraft mechanic on Douglas C-47 cargo planes, as well as at a children's refuge in Haiti.

Mowry has written twenty-five books and many short stories about black children and teens in a variety of genres, ranging from inner-city settings to the forests of Haiti, the wilds of Alaska, the Arizona desert, the Caribbean Sea, and the African veldt. While some of his novels are set in Oakland and deal with social issues, such as poverty, violence, drugs, gangs, teenage sexuality, and school drop-outs, Mowry has also written ghost tales, as well as novels featuring Voodoo and African magic, in addition to sea stories, and compiled an anthology of Victorian ghost stories.

Jess Mowry lives in Oakland, California.

**THIS BOOK IS ALSO AVAILABLE IN A KINDLE EDITION**

238

# OTHER ANUBIS BOOKS

Song For A Summer Night

Mark Dennis

**AVAILABLE ON AMAZON**